Critical Acclaim for I

'Mary Hocking is an undisguised blessing'
– *Christopher Wordsworth, Guardian*

'Mary Hocking's wry straightforwardness makes posher novels
about marital unfaithfulness seem arch, pretentious and
overdone by comparison' – *Observer*

'Mary Hocking is a most accomplished writer and should be
more widely known than I think she is' – *Nina Bawden*

'In its formal wit, Hocking's dialogue is often reminiscent of
that of Ivy Compton-Burnett . . . Hocking tells a strong, moving
tale with unobtrusive skill' – *Francis King, Spectator*

'A splendidly sturdy novelist' – *Times Literary Supplement*

'Mary Hocking subtly charts the disintegration of family
certainties with a telling eye for detail and a gleam of humour
. . . a novelist to watch' – *Daily Telegraph*

'Mary Hocking has a mind as sharp and neat as a pair of scissors
. . . She writes dramatically about conflict, but the true conflict is
inside her characters – their dialogue with themselves, their fear
of their own passions, deceptions, violences' – *Glasgow Herald*

MARY HOCKING

was born in Acton in 1921, and educated at Haberdashers' Aske's Girls' School (of whose name she remarks that 'all those apostrophes were supposed to be good for our English grammar'). From there she went to serve in the WRNS, first in the meteorology branch and later as a coder. After the war she worked in local government as an educational administrator and, later and part-time, in a Family Clinic.

Mary Hocking's first novel, *The Winter City*, was published in 1961. Since then she has written twenty novels, many of them based on her own experience: educational administration gave her the background for *The Climbing Frame* (1972) and *The Mind has Mountains* (1976), while the Family Clinic furnished material for *March House* (1981). Her experiences during and immediately after the war contributed substantially to the Fairley family trilogy, *Good Daughters* (1981), *Indifferent Heroes* (1985) and *Welcome Strangers* (1986). *An Irrelevant Woman* (1987) was widely acclaimed, and *A Particular Place* is her most recent novel, first published in 1989.

Mary Hocking lives in Lewes, Sussex.

VIRAGO
MODERN
CLASSIC
NUMBER

352

A Particular Place

MARY HOCKING

VIRAGO

Published by VIRAGO PRESS Limited 1990
20–23 Mandela Street, Camden Town, London NW1 0HQ

First published in Great Britain by Chatto & Windus 1989
Copyright © Mary Hocking 1989

A CIP catalogue record for this book is available from the British Library

Printed in Great Britain by
Cox and Wyman Ltd, Reading, Berks

TO A. L. BARKER

1

It was a still, grey evening. The smoke from the bonfire, watered down by thin mist, exuded a sour odour. Charles Venables, standing discreetly in the shelter of the yew, thought that if flames, labouring in such an uncongenial atmosphere, could sweat, this was how they would smell. Yet how charming these unrehearsed effects were! People feeling their way between tombstones, eagerly holding candles towards the flames – here was something so small and particular it might indeed have taken place in a garden. Oh, the many gardens of myth and antiquity, where are they today? It was good that this one, at least, should be cherished.

St Hilary's had a new vicar. An Anglican friend of Charles had once said bitterly, 'The Parochial Church Council is asked for its particular requirements and proceeds to draw up a list of qualities the Archangel Gabriel would be hard pressed to meet.' Perhaps St Hilary's had been fortunate? At least the new vicar's name was Michael: Michael Hoath. He it was who was responsible for this delightful performance. The Holy Saturday Vigil of Easter Eve was an innovation at St Hilary's, something hitherto peculiar to the goings-on of the Romans further down the high street. It seemed to Charles that the congregation was happier with this sequestered event than with the more public Palm Sunday procession to which it was accustomed but not entirely reconciled. Anglicans, he had noted, didn't much care for displaying their faith unequivocally. It was all right to join the Samaritans and to campaign for Shelter – activities which now enjoyed secular blessing – but praise was a distinguishing feature and they had been uneasy as they bore their palms into the high street. A pity. He had thought it all so endearing, with the tail of the procession a verse behind the middle, who were themselves extolling 'all things bright and beautiful' while the choir sang 'the Lord God made them all'. He had great hopes of this evening.

Behind, there was a rustling in the shrubbery and turning his head he saw that he was not the only observer. Three boys were sitting athwart the wall – Puck and fellow pagans come to see who had invaded their night-time domain?

The candle flames which had been bobbing about like glow-worms all over the graveyard now began to cluster as the Vicar blessed the New Fire. Charles was unable to catch the exact words because of a minor altercation between two women standing just in front of him.

'You will have to put out your candle now, Mother.' She sounded as if she were speaking to a child whose obedience was in some doubt. 'I'm not sure you should have lit it in the first place.'

'Then why was I given it?' A reasonable question truculently put.

'I only know that you have to light it as you go into the church and you can't do that if it's already alight.'

'I shall fall.' Definitely a statement of intent.

'You can hold on to me.'

The old woman grumbled, 'We could all catch our deaths out here. Much more of this and I shall go to the Methodists.'

There was a movement away from the fire and with murmurs of 'Careful of the steps' the congregation was led towards the dark interior of the church.

Close by, with no warning stumble, someone fell. Charles Venables, stepping from his shelter, found himself a member of a concerned group. The Vicar hurried up. 'Oh dear, have we a casualty already?' Irritation only just concealed at this disaster striking before the performance had got under way.

2

'Falling over my big feet!' The woman got up too quickly for an elderly person. In the flickering light her hair was the colour of the flames. Her laughter vibrated – something not quite in control there, Charles noted, involuntarily stepping back. A man more chivalrous took her arm. 'Can't have you going head first down these steps, Norah.'

At Charles Venables's elbow a cool voice said, 'Attention seeking!' He looked round and saw Valentine Hoath, the Vicar's wife, disdainful chin tilted, revealing to perfection the long neck and dark sculptured head of Nefertiti.

'She did go down with quite a thump.'

'Good.' She passed on into the church, soberly followed by the two women who had disputed the extinguishing of the candle.

'I don't know what cause *she's* got to be falling about.' The old woman sounded aggrieved at being thus upstaged.

'Maybe she should have thought before she fell?'

Obscurely cheered, they went chuckling into the church.

Charles Venables stood to one side while the believers filed slowly past him. The last among them was the Vicar's aunt, Hester Pascoe, writer of short stories in some of which children turned the fairy stories round and the adults became lost in the wood. She loitered at the door, an ageing imp looking back to the graveyard.

The children were coming from under the trees, two full-sized goblins followed by a smaller one, then a whole tribe, perhaps a dozen in all, capering noiselessly among the tombstones.

'Children are the real fairies.'

Charles Venables was not sure whether Hester Pascoe was speaking to herself or to him. 'A nice sentiment,' he murmured: he did not much care for sentiment.

'Neither good nor bad,' she corrected him crisply. 'As natural as little animals, given to glee and malice, wonder and pure spite.'

'I think perhaps you attribute too complex a capacity for enjoyment to animals. I always think of the woodland creatures as our night-time selves to whom we allow a licence not permitted to our day-time selves. Do you envy them?'

3

'Writers aren't in need of that kind of licence. If a little wickedness is all I want I can create it without going to the woodland. It's the amorality I envy. I was a child during a period when one was required to respect one's elders. Now I find myself elderly at a time when the old are not merely ignored but seen as so much rubbish to be swept out of the way.' She turned to look at him. 'You're not coming in, surely? You belong out there with them.'

As if the reference were to a similarity which extended beyond the question of belief, he ran a hand over the fine fluff powdering his pygmy skull. 'Oh well, one likes to see how these things are done. We have little enough ritual today.' He followed her into the church, feeling annoyed with himself because he had sounded like H.M. Inspector of Schools and she was sharp enough to be amused by it.

'The light of Christ.' The Vicar's voice was strong and deep. Charles thought that with a splendid voice like that the man must have been either an actor or a priest. A certain seriousness had no doubt influenced the choice and, once made, the voice dictated Anglo-Catholicism, that last refuge of the Book of Common Prayer.

The congregation, still uncertain what was expected of it, was not so splendid in the response, 'Thanks be to God'. Charles guessed that quite a few had come with the intention of being unimpressed. The Vicar, whom he judged to be a man profoundly concerned with things which most people have learnt to disregard as they grow older, would not be pleased to think that his efforts were most appreciated by an agnostic prep school master.

The great Paschal candle carried by the Vicar, who at least knew what he was about, was surrounded by four candles representing the four apostles who, appropriately enough, seemed less certain of their place in the scheme of things. And now, the candles of the people were relit from the Christ candle to signify the giving of the immortal spark from the one eternal source. Charles nodded approval: quite powerful stuff, as all light rituals are, dealing as they do with the illumination of the unconscious. Given that interpretation, he was quite willing to enter into the spirit of the performance. He went some way with Jung – not too far, of course, bad to go too far with anything.

The choir was singing the Paschal Proclamation. On all sides candles created a flickering golden sea of light, while, in contrast, an unwavering light shone from the deep blue heart of the East window. Charles, a little uneasy at finding his eyes constantly drawn to that still light, was glad when, after the Exultet, the candles were blown out. A warm smell of melting wax mingled not unpleasantly with that of incense.

There followed rather a lot of relighting and extinguishing of candles. The candles of the people were held in little frills of paper designed to prevent the spilling of wax. Unhappily, Charles's frill was ill-made and during the next prayer he discovered a spot of wax tiresomely high up one trouser leg. He scratched at it furtively during the remainder of the service, which went on rather too long for someone who had come for an aesthetic and not a religious experience. The second reading, however, redeemed much. 'My well-beloved hath a vineyard in a very fruitful hill; and he fenced it and gathered out the stones thereof . . .' He hoped the Vicar appreciated how fortunate he was in this day and age to have a captive audience for such incomparably marvellous material! But Charles had not reckoned with the Liturgy of Baptism and he was feeling distinctly fractious when the time came for the celebration of the Eucharist. He disliked the Eucharist intensely and only his sense of propriety prevented him from walking out. He had come to watch this as though it were a piece of theatre and must not now distract those whose interest was held to the end, however unsatisfactory he himself might find the conclusion. He sat still while his mind fidgeted irritably. What is someone like Hester doing with all this mumbo-jumbo? And what about the imperious Valentine, for that matter?

It was late when at last the Vicar said, 'Go in the peace of Christ, alleluia, alleluia.'

The people said, 'Thanks be to God' and Charles joined silently in the 'alleluia, alleluia' which finally released him.

'Too long for you?' Hester asked as they walked down the path together.

'By about an hour.'

'That will teach you to go slumming.'

He did not reply and she knew he was put out. In spite of his lightness of manner, he prided himself on the sophistication of his intellect. Because he was a neighbour, and one whom she liked, she said, 'Come and be rewarded with coffee, or something stronger, if you prefer.'

The grey little town was quiet at this hour. The high street, overlit because the Borough Engineer had recently found himself with money in hand at the close of the financial year, was deserted and shadowless as a prison yard. A web of mist formed on their faces as they walked downhill towards the river. The smell from the brewery was so strong one could taste the beer. At the bottom of the high street they crossed a bridge beneath which the water moved sluggishly, dark and heavy as stout on this dull night. Beyond, a road twisted up to a terrace of houses precariously huddled above the town.

'Who was it that fell?' Charles asked as they turned in at the gate of the first house. 'She seemed familiar, but I couldn't place her.'

'Norah Kendall.'

'Ah, the nurse who married the beastly barrister?'

'Yes, more's the pity.'

'You like her?' he asked and caution was justified when she replied firmly, 'I am very fond of her.'

Hester left Charles to occupy himself while she went into the kitchen. The sitting-room was pleasant enough, orderly, uncluttered, but a trifle bare to his taste – definitely a background to living and unlikely to feature in *House and Garden*. Charles, who had been in the room many times, still found it something of a puzzle. Simplicity was no bad thing, of course, but surely in the home of a writer one looked for evidence of a cultured mind? There were reproductions on the walls along with one or two quite decent prints and a competent still life. Reproductions were an offence to Charles, who was concerned with taste rather than his own preferences. He was not, he acknowledged as he stared at a sketch of a clown torn from a magazine and pasted on the wall above the piano, very sure of his preferences and this demanded a long and agonized process of decision to ensure that his judgement was never at fault. Nothing so ephemeral as a magazine sketch would ever be given space in his sitting-room. Meticulously neat from his small head to the soles of his unexceptional suede brogues, he seemed designed to fit into his surroundings rather than to impose a personality on them. 'Ah well . . .' He sighed at the clown, reminding himself that Hester had not been to university. 'There was no money for that sort of thing in our family,' she had once said. Her father had been a chemist. Charles, who had grown up in Plymouth, did not recall him but he remembered a colleague at his school saying with affection that Hester measured her words with considerably more care than her father had made up his prescriptions. Charles, brought up in an atmosphere of lower middle-class secular puritanism, had been a little shocked.

He turned from the clown and took the opportunity, in Hester's absence, to study the book shelves. Usually he avoided the subject of literature when they were together because although he had been assured that she was quite well thought of, had indeed won literary prizes, he had never read any of her short stories. Praise did not come readily to him and she would be shrewd enough to see through any dissembling. He could imagine her saying, in the same impulsive, ill-judged way which had resulted in the presence of the clown, 'You didn't really like it, did you?' Even more than having to praise, he dreaded the demands of candour.

'Milk, sugar?' she called out.

'Both, please.'

'Damn!' she muttered, reaching for bowl and sugar bag. The awareness of the co-ordination required in assembling even a modest tray at this time of night was a sign of age. She fumbled grudgingly for biscuits, thinking how nice it would be to have the homely qualities which enable aged crones in country cottages to turn out enticing displays of home cooking for the unexpected visitor. But perhaps such people never really existed outside the realm of folksy reminiscence? In reality, there they were in the kitchen, crying into their aprons, before emerging rosy-cheeked as an Olde English apple, bearing their burden of goodies! She pushed her behind against the door and entered the sitting-room backwards, giving Charles time to return *The Country of the Pointed Firs* to the shelf.

'How is your nephew settling in here?' Charles asked. 'I thought he took the service very well.'

'Ummm.' Hester wrinkled her face into a rubbery mask.

Charles saved her the trouble of threading her doubts together. 'It must be a great change from Oxford.'

'Brimming with intellectual rivalry and strident car workers?'

That was not his picture of Oxford, judging from his pained expression. 'The West Country *is* rather a stagnant pool, dearly though I love it. I don't know much about these matters, of course, but this move can hardly have advanced his . . .' he rejected 'career' in case it should sound too worldly and substituted 'prospects'.

'Valentine found Oxford rather trying.'

He raised his eyebrows, but Hester did not elaborate. She had already said more than she had intended. She was not good at either end of the day; in the morning she was not fit to speak to anyone and at night tiredness made her too talkative.

He said, 'And there are no children?'

'Yes, there are no children.' She had no intention of talking about the removal of Valentine's womb. Charles would certainly prefer her to speak of a hysterectomy because, like many people nowadays, he was content that such subjects should be veiled in scientific mystery. And quite apart from the choice of words, the attendant neurosis was a private, family concern. Or perhaps not attendant? Her mind picked over this as if Valentine were no more than a character in a story not yet fully fleshed out.

Charles said, 'A most attractive woman.'

Hester knew instinctively that this was something he had wanted to say, a little test, like putting one's nose out of the window on an autumn morning. So, that was the way of it! Well, she would not be drawn into it. She had preoccupations enough of her own without lending a listening ear. Not that any harm would come, bearing in mind the personalities involved – Valentine untouchable and Charles with, she judged, little in the way of tactile intention.

Charles was quite satisfied, even relieved, that his remark had occasioned no comment. He felt that he had essayed something rather daring and got away with it. The coffee was quite passable but regrettably the biscuit had not come from an air-tight tin.

'When does term start?' Hester asked.

'Too soon. The Governors turned down my suggestion for early retirement. I would have thought they would have been only too pleased to embrace the opportunity to drop English as a subject altogether.'

Hester had, after all, to turn a listening ear.

Charles and Hester had long since parted company by the time the Vicar returned home. Valentine had prepared a light salad for him, feeling virtuous and wifely. His mind was still on the service.

They made an odd contrast, seated one on either side of the unlit fire in the sitting-room, trays balanced on knees. They had never, in the whole of their marriage, managed to master the problem of lighting rooms satisfactorily and now the standard lamp cast a dim light in which Valentine's dark, sculptured beauty lost its fine, sharp edge while Michael – in fact, a more benevolent figure – became a looming rough-hewn presence, the more likely of the two to be a disturber of the peace.

'Yes,' she replied to his enquiry. 'I think it went off quite well.'

'And that was all?' Michael Hoath, despite his beautiful resonant voice, had difficulty with words. This made him seem something less than quick-witted in exchanges with his wife.

Valentine, grieving for the disregarded salad, said lightly, 'No, not by any means all. I thought the choir sang better than one might have hoped; I liked the shadows on the walls; the way the candlelight flickered on the brass railings; the deep blue stillness of the East window. All the inessentials.' Although she sounded theatrical, she yet gave the impression of throwing each sentence away like a useless playing card. Life, the disdainful lips proclaimed, had dealt her an indifferent hand. 'But then it's just the same at concerts. You are moved by the music while for me the pleasure is in the intent faces of the players as they bend to their bows, or pluck their lutes, or whatever. I love the sheen of light on old wood, the women in cool dresses falling softly from the stem of the neck and the men gravely attentive in formal clothes. Why will you constantly invite rebuffs? You should know by now how superficial I am.' Fit for nothing but providing light meals which are not appreciated.

'My dear, I am so sorry. I didn't mean to upset you.'

She made a dismissive gesture with eloquent hands. 'You are so fortunate. All your notes ring true. Even your distress.' All this fuss about a few sprigs of varied greenery and a confection of yoghurt and almonds!

Hoath put the tray in the hearth and came towards her; his hands, held out as if to touch her shoulders, fell to his sides as he looked into her eyes. The large violet eyes dominated her face and it was their anxiety which gave an air of fragility to features which were so finely moulded that they would stand very well the tests of time.

'I am tired,' she said.

'Yes, I know.' He looked round the room. 'But it is all beginning to take shape now, isn't it?'

'It had an unalterable *shape* to start with.'

He turned away. 'It was you who wanted to leave Oxford.' His tone had a rougher edge, indicating limits to his patience.

It was all getting out of hand. She was a lively and thoughtless speaker, heedlessly provoking emotional scenes in which he stumbled about like a lost child. She made an attempt at propitiation. 'I hated to see you being patronised by those odious dons' wives.'

He looked at her wryly. He had a long face with a jutting chin, the kind of face which taken to absurdity results in Mr Punch or the Man in the Moon. An odd companion for a woman of antique beauty and imperial temperament.

Yet when they had cleared away the supper things and he left her to go to bed, she became, alone in the sitting-room, a more frail creature. She stood for some time by the empty hearth, studying her shadowy reflection in the oval looking glass. Her expression was one of haughty contempt, yet she seemed unable to drag herself from the mirror as though her beauty held her in thrall. Eventually, however, her eyes strayed from her own image to take in the details of the room. It was a pleasant room, generously proportioned and with those irregularities – alcoves, a good Victorian bay window – which give to a room an illusion of individuality. It was a room which waited for the occupants to make something of it. She said aloud, 'If I were to say a prayer, I suppose it should be "Help me to make some sort of a decent life for him here."'

This house had the feel of a place which has long been inhabited by people who have never regarded it as home. She was not a natural homemaker. It wasn't that she was lazy, she simply did not know how to set about bringing warmth and comfort into a chill old barn of a place. Did one tackle first the matter of temperature, would a coat of paint here and there bring about an immediate improvement, or should one concentrate on wallpaper? And why was it that in houses where no marks would be given for paintwork, wallpaper or efficient heating, one simply did not notice such deficiencies because the feeling of home was so all-embracing?

Valentine had been born during the war – that time when servants departed for factories never again to return to middle-class homes. All through her childhood their absence had occasioned more notice than their presence would ever have done. Her mother had lived in a state of perpetual mourning for lost Edies and Ethels. Her father had wisely provided himself with an Edie on the sly. Her mother had said, 'It is what men of his class do.' She had never ceased to be proud of her husband's father who had never had to work for his living even although he had not handed this bounty on to his son. Valentine and her sisters had grown up bewildered rather than unhappy.

'I shall do some gardening,' she thought as she switched off the light in the sitting-room. 'At least that will be a start.' A garden was her real home: even her mother had felt no sense of impropriety when working in the garden. But the prospect of a day's gardening failed to raise her spirits.

Whatever harm she might have done to her husband, she knew that he would sleep soundly, having long ago constructed a picture of his marriage which met some, if not all, of his needs.

Had he chanced to stay awake for any length of time, he would have occupied his mind with plans for the day ahead. He was not a man who would readily live with failure, while she tended to embrace it. Tonight she would go over in her mind all the irritations and imagined slights of the day, chief among which would be the social worker who had ignored her beauty as though it was at best irrelevant, at worst shameful, and Charles Venables whom she despised because he behaved as though her beauty was all that mattered. Men! Women! she thought as she climbed the stairs. God should have made a third species especially for me.

2

It rained unrelentingly throughout Easter week and Low Sunday lived up to its name in all respects. By the following Thursday morning, however, the rain had stopped. The sky was no longer uniformly grey and to the west dirty cotton wool clouds dispersed in a sheen of silver.

The dove-grey cat, which had arrived a month ago at the vicarage in great distress, sat on the top of the old coal bunker and brushed a neat white paw against its small pink nose. Now glossy and trusting, it performed its ablutions in leisurely manner before turning its attention to the birds, dotted like dead leaves on the branches of the apple tree. Beyond, in the lane leading past the graveyard, the bare branches of the surviving elm were knotted with rooks' nests.

In the lofty stone-flagged kitchen where the Hoaths breakfasted for warmth, Michael made notes on a pad. Valentine, after watching in silence for some minutes, said, 'It's all right for you. Your dog collar gives you a licence to meddle.'

He reached for the toast. 'If it does, I don't make full use of it. I would so much sooner people came to me.'

'They do come to you.'

'Who are *they*? Devout old ladies troubled by David Jenkins's latest indiscretion.'

'What do you expect? You don't imagine you can encroach on

secular preserves.' She poured tea for herself. 'Social Services have the monopoly here. Need and deprivation there may be, but when one attempts to do something about it – however modest – one is reminded that the caring business is a closed shop. For people who claim to be overworked, social workers are very quick to defend their preserves.'

He looked up, alerted by the sharpness of her tone. 'How selfish of me. I was so occupied with the Easter services that I completely forgot. You went to make enquiries . . .'

'In answer to my request some tousle-headed female emanated from a cloud of tobacco smoke. She covered, briefly and discouragingly, a range of auxiliary duties for which I was eminently unsuited. Then, taking advantage of her coughing fit, I told her I had thought of the Citizens' Advice Bureau.'

'But that doesn't come under Social Services.'

'They have their moles at work within the organization, though. She was able to assure me that I would have to take a course.'

'Well, then . . .'

'And, furthermore, "You will have to be able to deal with all sorts of people," she informed me, making it quite apparent from her manner that I should be unable to sustain a conversation with anyone from Ambridge, let alone Coronation Street.'

'I think it was probably a mistake to approach Social Services in the first place. Why not . . .'

'On the contrary, it saved a lot of time. It convinced me that the only way that I could ever be of service to the community would be if I were to found an Order of my own. I doubt if I have the commitment – or the stamina, come to that.'

Michael spread marmalade thickly on toast while he considered this. Something occurred to him which brightened his face. 'You didn't tell me what happened at the dramatic society meeting on Tuesday.'

'My true milieu. How right you are! They are doing *Hedda Gabler*. You can guess what part I was offered.'

'Hedda.'

'The producer was obviously panic-stricken at the beginning of the audition because one of those prima donnas which every society has as its cross regarded the part as already hers. She actually did it without the book, just to drive her stake deep into his heart. When I read he looked at me as if I was a gift not merely from the vicarage but God Himself. It was quite amusing. I said I would have to think about it, because I was too old for Hedda. She, I may say, will never see fifty again.'

'You will accept?'

'I am too old, Michael. I am forty-five.'

He looked at her unhappily, recognizing the need for reassurance but fearing it would be rejected as unacceptable no sooner than offered. He said, 'My dearest, to me you always seem as young as the day I married you.'

The wretched sincerity of the tone in which this statement was made amused her so much that her gloom was dispelled. 'Well,' she said briskly, 'better Hedda than Mary Rose. I shall certainly accept.'

As he left the vicarage Michael Hoath was comforted in the knowledge that for the next month or so Valentine would be absorbed in the production of *Hedda Gabler*. This would undoubtedly give rise to a series of crises as she found herself in conflict with the producer, out of sympathy with Ibsen, unsure of Hedda's motivation, dissatisfied with her costume, hampered by the limitations of the set and, towards the end of the rehearsal period, constantly proclaiming that she could not carry the role and should stand down. But all this had happened before and he had some understanding of that kind of instability which is a part of the creative process.

Michael shared with his wife a taste for drama; but while Valentine realized her need within the confines of a theatre, he looked to life for its fulfilment. As a result he tended to see his world as a course with obstacles set up with the express purpose of testing his spiritual prowess. Now, he paused on the vicarage lawn, tossing the car keys about in one hand, wondering what kind of a course this slate-roofed town overhung by the bluff hills would offer. It was difficult to construct an optimistic scenario.

The place to which he had come was a small market town of some ten-thousand inhabitants in which light industry had never really taken root. Once it had had a modest reputation for shoes and gloves, but fashions had changed and only one shoe firm remained in the area. The only continuing feature of its commercial success was the brewery. In the Sixties there had been hopes that the new university would be sited here, but it had gone elsewhere, although some staff used the town as a dormitory, enriching its life with occasional lectures and participating vociferously in protests about developments which would devalue their property. It was a decent enough little place in which to grow old, with good cultural facilities for those of a more contemplative cast of mind; but with little hope for those seeking employment and with nothing to offer the young except a swimming pool which had been designed to Olympic standards and built to meet the requirements of the County Council for its schools' gala. The only real excitement in recent years had been its successful fight for a by-pass. Feeling must indeed have run high in those days. Michael had met respectable elderly ladies who recalled marching up and down the high street bearing banners warning 'Jugger off!' and 'Truck off!' But all that was over. The town had won and hoteliers and shopkeepers had discovered to their cost that the one-time invaders were only too willing to avail themselves of the by-pass. All passion seemed now spent. As far as Michael could judge, there were no very interesting sins. Indifference would be the major hurdle here. It was the sort of place to which St Paul, for all his shipwrecks, would have given a wide berth.

As he stood on the vicarage lawn, breathing in the damp, lifeless air, he had a premonition that here a demand would be made of him which would be unable to answer. He looked at the garden and was not comforted. Well-stocked borders and a smooth green lawn were refreshment to the eye and solace to the soul, but an unkempt garden filled him with a sense of impotence because he did not know how to set about restoring order. Here, rampant climbers and rioting shrubs menaced him on all sides. He had no idea what should be left undisturbed and what rooted out. His one attempt at cutting back roses had drawn from Valentine the comment, 'Well, they won't trouble you again!' since when she had never let him into a garden with a pair of secateurs in his hands. He did not know the kinds of soil which different plants needed nor how often they should be fed and watered. The sheer amount of detailed knowledge required to keep oneself on even terms with growing things bewildered him. His brain became confused every time he looked at a disorderly garden. This garden was very disorderly.

He experienced a moment of panic, an impulse to run into the vicarage and tell Valentine that he could not see this through – an infantile urge, blind and unreasoning as a child's refusal to go to school. He walked slowly towards the garage, forcing his shaken mind to consider what was happening to him. He had not wanted to come here, that was undeniably true; it had meant giving up much that he enjoyed in Oxford, together with any hope of preferment. But he had thought that out and accepted it. He was unlikely to suffer anything stronger than a passing disappointment at the prospect of remaining a parish priest. Ambition had played little part in his life. His father, a solicitor in a Sussex country town, had never sought to better himself by moving to a more thriving practice. His mother, the daughter of a local chemist in the town where he now found himself, had lovingly described the unsuccessful father as 'a dear, unreliable man'. Michael's parents had not been ambitious for themselves or for their only child. Certainly, there would be no lasting bitterness eating into his soul were he to end his days as a parish priest. Indeed, there was much that could be made of the situation – better by far to grow old nose to the grindstone than overseeing the mill-race from some lofty window. But there was something else, some underlying fear which had never openly declared itself. He felt it at the pit of his stomach and knew by the weight of it that it had been growing within him for a long time. He rested two fingers between his eyes, a habit he had when he wished to calm himself. 'I have to think about this, not run away from it.' But he had a busy day ahead and must put it to one side until he had read the Office and the day was spent.

He had arranged to visit a site up in the hills where unemployed youngsters were helping to erect a log cabin in a country park. This was the kind of activity which he enjoyed and he was soon at work unloading logs. He returned to the town feeling healthier in body and renewed in spirit. It was a quarter to twelve and he had to take Mass at noon. The church, sited in the high street, had no parking space adjacent but he was fortunate in finding a space in a cul-de-sac where infilling had created four cramped town houses at the back of a builder's yard.

His churchwarden, Walter Ellery, an elderly man with the face of an ancient walrus, was already in the vestry when Michael arrived. Valentine had said that he was one of those people who seem already to belong to posterity rather than the ephemeral everyday world. Michael asked him, 'And who have we today?' It seemed that the congregation consisted, as usual, of Mrs Cummins, Mrs Challoner, Miss Addison and Mrs Flack.

Michael said wryly, 'Ah well, when two or three are gathered together in His name, all things are possible . . .' The old man smiled and Michael saw that for him this was the simple truth. He felt rebuked in the presence of such humility.

After the service he returned to the church intending to retrieve a duster which he had noticed lying to one side of the chancel steps. He was half-way down the nave before he realized that Mrs Flack was still there.

He would have said that, of the four women who had attended the service, Miss Addison was the most likely to remain so long in prayer. Mrs Flack, who was no doubt responsible for the duster, was a good church cleaner but she had given little indication that she was endowed with the equipment for prolonged meditation. He checked himself, realizing that this was how he would report the incident to Valentine, hoping to amuse her.

As he came level with Mrs Flack she turned her head and said, 'I've been waiting for a word, Vicar.'

'Yes, Mrs Flack.'

'I have been examining my soul, like you told us to the other week.'

Michael, wincing at this crude rephrasing of his attempt at spiritual guidance, bowed his head and waited for whatever revelation was to follow.

Mrs Flack raised her face, the blunt features not much softened by the muted light. 'I have decided I must speak.'

'Yes, please . . .'

'Mr Hughes played the organ last Sunday.'

'Mr Painter has 'flu,' Michael pointed out, trying to conceal his impatience at the thought of another complaint about an unfamiliar tune.

'I didn't expect that Mr Hughes would be asked to play the organ. Not after what he's done.'

'What has he done?'

'Standing by the war memorial with that petition.'

It had not occurred to Michael that anyone was capable of thinking in this way. He was tempted to tell the woman that as long as he was Vicar Ewan Hughes would be welcome to play the organ whenever he could be persuaded to do so. But as he gazed at the brown coat which gave off a damp, woolly smell and saw the now familiar crease punched in the crown of the ancient velour hat, he realized that after two months in the parish these articles were his surest means of identifying Mrs Flack. What went on beneath that ungainly bundle was a mystery to him. Yet as a priest it was a mystery which it was his duty to investigate since, as she herself had reminded him, it was not Mrs Flack's outer garments with which he should be concerned, but the state of her soul. He seated himself beside her in the pew.

'What is troubling you, Mrs Flack?'

'I lost my man in the war.'

The sharpness of grief was long past and Michael groped in vain in his rag-bag of comforts for an appropriate response. He watched the branches of a tree moving unconcernedly outside the lady chapel window. Mrs Flack went on, 'Reported missing over Germany. I waited and prayed to God to bring him back to me, but He never did. And Mr Messer that was here then said I ought to be proud because Ted had laid down his life. And I was proud. But now the young ones, they laugh about the war when they see the films on telly.' She sucked in her breath.

Michael said, 'Young people will always mock the sacrifices of the older generation, Mrs Flack. The student rebels of today will be the butts for tomorrow's wits.'

This epigrammatic reflection failed to speak to Mrs Flack's condition. 'It is not just the young ones, is it, Vicar? Their teachers encourage them. And then you have people like Mr

Hughes who doesn't care about what happens to his country and he goes on playing the organ in this church.'

'But I think Mr Hughes would say that it is because he does care about his country that he collected signatures for that petition.'

'In front of the war memorial, with all those people wearing funny clothes and carrying skulls. It upset me, Vicar. And I'm not the only one who feels it. Mrs Mallory said she was amazed to see it was that communist at the organ; she said she could hardly believe her eyes.' If Michael's memory served him aright, Mrs Mallory's eyes were so dim she could not have identified Joseph Stalin at the organ. He said, 'It is very wrong of Mrs Mallory to say that Mr Hughes is a communist just because he has certain views on nuclear disarmament.'

Mrs Flack turned her head away. 'I knew it would be no good speaking to you.'

Michael felt pity for the old woman. He could understand how shocked she had been to discover that the enemy had invaded the one place where she might reasonably have expected to find herself in the company of people who shared her values. But what could he say? He was very much of Mr Hughes's mind.

Outside, traffic snuffled, waiting while a police car, banshee siren wailing, weaved its way down the high street. Mrs Flack gathered herself for departure. 'I don't know what the world is coming to. But I'm glad I won't live to see it.'

'Perhaps I could come and talk to you sometime?' he suggested.

'It doesn't matter, Vicar. I know you're busy, settling in, altering all the services.'

'Not too many alterations, I hope, Mrs Flack?'

'Well, we've Benediction now, haven't we? But I expect I'll get used to it.' She had nerved herself to speak to him, but had anticipated defeat.

'It was very sad,' he said when he recounted the incident to Valentine when they ate their sandwich lunch. 'No one has ever regarded her opinions as of much importance and I suspect her feelings have been dismissed along with her opinions.'

'What could you have done? Even I can tell that it would be a blasphemy to reject a man who plays Bach so superlatively just because his politics offend a few people.'

'Even so, I think we should bear in mind that while we may regard vigils at war memorials as a means of protesting about the waste of life in war, to people like Mrs Flack they may seem to be the desecration of a grave.'

'You may be right. So, you stop people from using the war memorial for protest – are you then going to object to all the glorification that goes on on Armistice Day? I don't think the Rector would go along with that. I can imagine him standing there weighed down with medals.'

'Mmmh.' He rapped the table with his knuckles, contemplating the war of attrition which might lie ahead of him.

Valentine said, 'Might it be an answer to tell Mr Hughes? After all, he did complain that the death masks and skulls were more appropriate to a Hallowe'en party than a vigil. He might be able to mollify Mrs Flack.'

'How sensible.' He pushed his chair back from the table, ready for the immediate demands of the afternoon. 'By the way, Mrs Flack rather suggested I had made too many changes.'

'You have made quite a few.'

He looked surprised. In some ways he was very obstinate. If he saw things which he felt needed to be done he did not regard them as changes. Now he said, 'Oh, I don't know about that. She mentioned Benediction. If she doesn't want to come she needn't . . .'

'She thinks you are heading them all towards Rome.'

'They have had the Angelus for as long as Mrs Flack can remember. If that hasn't tipped them over to Rome, Benediction won't.'

'It's another step on the road.'

'What nonsense. Whenever anyone suggests something they don't want to do Anglicans cry "Rome!" just as Labour diehards shriek "Thatcherism".' He got up. 'I must be off . . .' He checked himself. 'I quite forgot. I parked the car in that cul-de-sac at the back of the builder's yard.'

*

The cul-de-sac was deserted, but the Vicar's approach was observed by a youth in one of the town houses. He put his head to one side and mouthed words, affecting a clownish imbecility as he pantomimed a response to clerical do-gooding. As the Vicar walked past the front door, his expression changed first to incomprehension, then to incredulous delight. He turned towards the room, clenched fist pressed, knuckles outwards, to his brow in a pose of exaggerated penitence.

After a few moments the front door of the house opened and a woman emerged. In face and figure she epitomized the plump, good-natured matron who arrives on the scene of an accident knowing exactly what has to be done. It was apparent from her conspiratorial manner, however, that on this occasion she was less sure of her role. She approached Michael Hoath with all the trepidation of a producer about to suggest yet another rerun of a badly performed scene.

'This isn't *your* car?'

'I'm afraid it is.' They stood side by side regarding the windscreen on which had been scrawled 'Balls to you – you illiterate oaf!'

The woman said, 'Oh God! I should have looked at the number plate.' Her body was convulsed by a tremor which was rigidly suppressed before it found facial expression. She gnawed her lip, round face crimson. The youth was by now hanging out of the window, hand cupped to ear.

'Why?' Michael Hoath asked.

She essayed an explanation accompanied by gestures which showed her to be no mean pantomimist. 'It's the man from the Do It Yourself Shop. You know who I mean – him with the rolling gait and roving eye. He parks outside the garage so I can't get my car out. When I put up a "no parking" notice, he wrote "Balls" on the garage door – in purple.'

'People like that are annoying.'

She nodded her head emphatically. 'They are more than annoying. I could cut off his balls and fry them for breakfast.'

'Oh dear, yes, I do see.' He was beginning to sound the more harassed of the two. The youth at the window swayed from side to side in an ecstasy of mirth. 'I don't think I can drive it home like this, do you?'

She gnawed her lip some more, then said reassuringly, 'Wait here a moment.' She went indoors where her voice could be heard saying, 'And if all you can do is make those horrible faces, just go away. GO AWAY!' She returned with a bottle of methylated spirits and a roll of kitchen paper. 'I feel so awful.'

'No, no, really . . . Here, let me . . .'

They dabbed at the windscreen, apologising to each other. Later, she asked him in for a cup of tea.

'I don't usually entertain in the kitchen,' she assured him.

The sitting-room, through which she led him, gave little evidence of facilities for entertaining. It was a sparsely furnished room in which he noted a television in one corner and a tape recorder on the one armchair. There was no bookcase and a calendar hung askew was the only wall adornment. An ironing board was set up on the rug by the fireplace and clothes, sheets and towels were strewn on every flat surface except the floor which was given over to a collection of flints and fossils.

'I insist on some sort of order,' she said. 'We keep our obsessions for our bedrooms; at least –' she kicked at a flint – 'that's the idea.'

In the kitchen a small shelf had been erected perilously close to the electric stove and glancing at its contents Michael was surprised to see, instead of the cookery books he had anticipated, volumes by Tolstoy, Willa Cather, D.H. Lawrence and Edith Wharton.

She said, 'My father was a librarian. I don't know what he'd make of things nowadays. There's nothing in our library worth reading. It's got to the stage where you have to buy books.' Michael supposed she felt a need to justify this extravagance – in his experience the books on the kitchen shelf were the very ones which most libraries did have; it was the better modern fiction which was usually in short supply.

While she was talking and making the tea, a youth appeared in the doorway. He was tall, but bent at the shoulders, and with hands that hung as if they didn't know where to put themselves. The face had the look of having just come to the surface of a pool, still blurred by water, the features contorted with the effort of holding breath. He looked from his mother to the Vicar. It was difficult to tell whether his attitude was protective of his mother or dependent upon her. Michael thought he was possibly subnormal and his heart sank – this was not an affliction with which he had ever been able to cope very well.

'He's going to be an anthropologist,' the mother said with complete lack of conviction. 'So we all have to live with Neanderthal man and such of his artefacts as Desmond can lay his hands on.'

'Palaeolithic, in fact.' The voice, although hoarse and rather strained, was unexpectedly incisive. Michael was aware of his vision making those adjustments which take place – accommodating eccentricities of appearance and behaviour – once evidence is received that a brain is well in charge. The boy's face, now focused more sharply, was seen as slablike, with long, flat bones; the eyes were heavy-lidded and the big mouth exposed the fleshy underside of the lips. It was a face both sensitive and sensual, presenting Michael not only with a personality full of contradictions, but a certain rawness which always made his old scars itch. 'Neanderthal man,' the youth was saying, 'is only one species who was around for some one-hundred thousand years. But Mother likes the word.'

'I liked William Golding's *The Inheritors*,' she said, pouring tea.

'And she liked William Golding's *The Inheritors*.' A wry grimace accompanied the dry repetition which had no need of this embroidery.

'Did you like it?' Michael asked.

Desmond sat down at the table and hoisted one foot across his thigh, picking at the sole of his shoe while he considered this. He was, in every way, centre stage. The room was not large enough to accommodate three people with comfort and Michael was wedged into the space between the sink and the refrigerator. He rested one elbow on the top of the refrigerator and tried to appear at ease. Desmond said, 'I thought the picture imagery was clever enough. But there's one moment in that book about New Mexico . . .'

'*Death Comes for the Archbishop*,' his mother said.

'. . . when this bishop gets caught in a storm in the mountains and his Indian guide takes him into a hidden cave that only the Indians are supposed to know about. And he puts his ear to a cleft in the rock and hears the roar of a great underground river no living man has ever seen. I thought that got closer to the primitive than Golding got in the whole of *The Inheritors*.' He spoke with resentment of Golding, as though he had trespassed on forbidden territory.

Michael, having failed on Golding and not having read *Death Comes for the Archbishop*, said, 'I remember enjoying those programmes – on Troy, wasn't it – with Michael Wood?'

'He was talking about civilizations.' Desmond picked him up sharply. 'It's all right, I suppose, if you like that sort of thing. Although all that throwing his arms about distracts the viewer from what he is actually saying, if anything.' At this point he hitched up one shoulder, seeming to scratch his ear against it. 'I tell you what I did enjoy, though – Peter Ackroyd referring to one of those T V gurus fumbling through the centuries like a mad bingo caller.' He clasped his hands under his knees and rocked to and fro in delight. The performance was not only embarrassingly gauche but ill-executed, and he nearly overturned the chair.

Michael got the impression that the sharpness of mind served as a blade to parry any attempt at penetration. He was not so sure that the grimaces and gestures were a conscious device. They added nothing to the effectiveness of the comments and he had an uneasy suspicion that they were involuntary.

'It must be an absorbing study, anthropology,' he said tentatively when, having righted himself, Desmond had slouched out of the room.

'For him, perhaps. But it's not much joy living with someone who doesn't seem able to take an interest in anything post stone age.'

When he returned to the vicarage in the early evening Michael re-enacted some of these exchanges for Valentine's benefit and they laughed together as they had not done for a long time.

'She was rather a jolly young woman,' he said. 'It seems her husband left her to go to Canada and she and the children were to follow. There was some sort of trouble between them and they were hoping to make a new start. Then she discovered he had settled there with someone else. The boy, Desmond, is going to university next year; so he has rather too much time on his hands. There is a girl of thirteen.' Yet he describes this woman as young, Valentine noted, and was the less amused.

He said, 'It was obviously very disturbing for the boy – the father's desertion. Apparently they were very close. She said he was such an open, trusting little boy . . .'

Valentine saw that there were tears in Michael's eyes. She sighed, 'Oh Michael, not *another* case of rejection!' He turned his head away and Valentine reflected crossly on how people do nourish the little wounds of childhood. Hester had once told her that Michael's father had been rather remote with his son so that the death of the adored mother had come as a great blow. In Valentine's opinion, adoring anyone was a mistake; it was unwise to make such a costly investment. But Michael would never understand that. She said, 'Well, I trust you are not going to involve yourself with this family.'

'I got on rather well with the woman. She said she would come to church.'

'As a penance for besmirching the car windscreen?'

'No, she said she was always meaning to come but never got round to it.'

Valentine looked at her husband speculatively. A foot shorter and I shouldn't have married him, she thought. And what a fool I should have been – he has weathered so much better than the other possibles. Her eyes followed him as he went over to the telephone pad, bending his head to read the messages she had scribbled on it. 'Why phone me because the church hall is double booked? Laura Addison is supposed to handle bookings.' She saw how wirily the fading brown hair still sprang from the crown of his head and was surprised by an itching in her fingers. She clenched her hands. Weathering suited Michael; it was quite possible that he would attract a much younger woman. Despite the son of university age, the creature could still be the right side of forty.

'We have this women's discussion group tonight,' he was saying. 'I hope you will come. You know how I value your comments.'

'My comments are invariably negative, often unkind, and they usually upset you.' She wondered whether he had invited the creature to join the group.

'Darling, anything you say is for my own good. I am eager for myself, not sufficiently aware of other people's feelings. You act as a necessary brake.'

'No, not a brake, Michael. When I told you that people don't like too many changes in the services, you didn't seem to hear, let alone change gear.'

He was no longer listening. He was making a performance of going through his pockets for some mislaid notes. 'I know I jotted a few things down on the back of something . . .'

She looked out of the window, considering the wistaria which darkened the room and reflecting that it was not unknown for a sensitive man to make a fool of himself over some rustic Marilyn or Marlene.

'I'll come and see what goes on,' she said.

When he left to read the evening Office she went into the garden. It was a bright evening and the few wraithlike flecks of cloud vanished as one looked at them like ghosts disappearing with the sunlight. The garden had been much neglected recently but some unknown incumbent, years ago, had cared for it and a few interesting shrubs had withstood subsequent deprivation. The wistaria against the side of the house needed to be cut back and along the garden walls clematis and winter jasmine fought for possession with honeysuckle. It would take time to restore order, but she had a picture in her mind of what she hoped to achieve and she was prepared to work hard.

She forgot the time and it was late when Michael returned having remained overlong in the church. Valentine was annoyed. They usually had their main meal in the evening and she disliked having to rush her preparations.

In the sitting-room of Hester Pascoe's house the tabby cat looked reproachfully at the empty grate. Hester said, 'You're not the only one to be inconvenienced. I could do without this meeting.'

The truth of it was that she could have done without her nephew. Had Michael Hoath not been the vicar there would have been no question of her giving up the precious hour which was set aside for reading through the morning's output. She had lived all her life in this town and had fought a long, dour battle to order her days to suit her needs. A single woman, working at home, she must keep a firm hand on the reins of her life. It was particularly annoying that, at a time when she was trying to come to terms with old age, her nephew, Michael, should arrive here. At a distance, she had always been sympathetic about his problems but she had not wanted him to bring them to her doorstep. 'It's for you I am doing this,' she said to the photograph of her sister which stood on the top of the piano.

When she stepped into the street she was aware of the figure she presented, small, compact, resolute, a person who seemed constantly on her way to catch a train and very sure of what she proposed to do when she reached her destination. Who could suspect the turmoil contained within this seemly structure of flesh and bone? What would they think, those friends and neighbours who admired her composure, if they became aware of the unceasing interaction between the imperious demands of the intellect, the insistent needs of the senses for small satisfactions and the longing for joys no longer appropriate which found its chief expression in dreams which troubled the waking hours?

Valentine had told her, 'You always seem a very held together sort of person.' It was as well that Valentine had no idea what it was that was being held together this evening. 'Not disappointment, mind you,' Hester said aloud as she swept past the war memorial, 'that is altogether too mild a word. Fury!' Fury at the interference with her work pattern and the denial of the pleasure which would have come later as she relaxed with a generous gin and gave herself to what distraction television offered. She guarded her time as if it were a small, beleaguered territory over which she was the despotic ruler, ready to punish any invader with the boiling oil of her disfavour.

Briskly she carried her wrath up the high street and down the path into the church hall, where it was fuelled by a woman in a sloppy cardigan who greeted her in honeyed tones, 'I didn't expect to see you here among us. How honoured we are!'

Hester, eyeing the flushed face which always had the appearance of having just received a stinging slap, reminded herself that Laura Addison should be cherished as a member of a dying species: womankind would not pass this way again. 'I'm not in the business of conferring honours,' she said.

The flush suffused ears and neck, the dry lips quivered. No snub was ever wasted on Laura Addison, yet she continued to invite rebuffs with unremitting earnestness. 'My dear, you must forgive silly people who aren't clever with words. We are just happy you could spare us the time.' A gentle, restraining hand was laid on Hester's arm. How it comes you still have two hands is beyond comprehension, Hester thought. Laura, who would undoubtedly have accompanied Daniel into the lions' den, went on, 'Perhaps you could go and talk to Shirley Treglowan? I don't think she knows many people here, which is hardly surprising, is it? Since she never comes anywhere near the church. I expect it's that Desmond of hers. She's hoping a new vicar may be able to work a miracle, poor soul.'

'You seem to know more about her soul than I do, so you had better sit beside her.'

Hester was aware that this suggestion would not find favour since it would take Laura Addison away from her self-appointed place as doormat in the House of the Lord. While they were disputing the issue, Norah Kendall seated herself beside Shirley Treglowan.

Although the meeting was not due to start for some seven minutes there were already more women present than Hester had anticipated. She knew that the group had a membership of over thirty, of whom less than ten were regular attenders. Valentine had told her that much emphasis had been placed on the low attendance. 'They meet in the vicarage, so it suits the hard core not to drum up more support. But I said that if the membership was over thirty we should aim at a regular attendance of over twenty and that was too many bodies for the vicarage sitting-room.' She had been safeguarding her privacy, but it looked as if she had made a lucky guess. There must be at least fifteen women here. The town did not afford young mothers many pretexts for leaving their husbands to look after the children on at least one evening a week. The advent of a new vicar had no doubt acted as a spur to the wilting spirit of rebellion. 'There was no need for me to have sacrificed myself,' Hester thought crossly. But since she had come it was in her nature to make the best of it.

She saw that Valentine was sitting on her own, looking so excessively detached that something must certainly have upset her. As soon as Hester sat down beside her, Valentine demanded, 'Who is that trousered female who looks like one of Robin Hood's merrier men?' She eyed Shirley disdainfully while Hester replied that she was an infant school teacher. 'I would have thought her talents lay elsewhere.' Valentine noted bold, brown eyes and a healthy gloss on the cropped chestnut hair. 'She would be quite attractive to a man, don't you think? Norah Kendall could learn something from her about making the best of herself, with that fading red hair scragged up on top of her head like a bird's nest.'

'Was I relieved to see you here, Nurse!' Shirley spoke in a whisper which carried to the back of the hall. 'I suppose I shouldn't call you Nurse, now?'

'That's all right, m'dear. I was thinking of calling on you to find out how my favourite boy is getting on.'

'It would be nice if you would. Desmond isn't anyone else's favourite boy. The things he gets up to! Last night . . .'

'Why did you come?' Hester asked Valentine. 'You don't have to join in all the activities and I shouldn't think this is your scene any more than it is mine.'

'I thought it worth demonstrating that I am the Vicar's wife and to see who is making the takeover bid in this particular parish. Any other pretensions to status I might have had were soon put down by the little lady with the saintly smile who is taking it upon herself to welcome everyone.'

Hester looked at her in surprise. Even for Valentine this was an unusually sharp rejoinder and she doubted if it had been occasioned by Laura Addison, who was scarcely worth Valentine's mettle.

Valentine made a pretence of looking around at the women who had gathered here while she listened to Norah Kendall and

Shirley Treglowan. It was clear from their conversation that their relationship was a purely professional one. Yet as the two women talked, Valentine could find nothing in Norah's attitude to which she herself, so exacting in her judgements, could have taken exception. There was not a trace of condescension, no betraying hint – that tidying up of other people's sentences – of the professional woman used to taking control of others. The pitch and timing of interest, amusement, concern could not be faulted and there was genuine humour in the quiet laughter. Valentine, who had hitherto dismissed her as a subtly attention-seeking parish worker, was forced to the conclusion that Norah Kendall was one of those limited women who, given a suitably structured environment, can function very effectively.

The room was becoming quite crowded. Laura Addison said to the Vicar, 'Of course, it is just after Easter,' as though an explanation were required for this untoward show of interest. 'A lot of people came to Mass on Easter Day whom we never see again for another year. And you did announce the change of venue, if you remember.'

'So it's all my fault?' he said cheerfully.

'Well, yes, it is.' She tittered, but he could see that she was troubled.

'If there's not enough milk and coffee I could easily go back to the vicarage . . .'

'Oh no, no! Your wife insisted that I should order another pint of milk and there is plenty of coffee. But I'm afraid I only have one pair of hands.'

'That is easily remedied. I shall ask for volunteers.' He turned away and spoke at random to two young women hovering in the doorway. 'Come in and make yourselves useful.'

Laura Addison looked around for an ally and failed to find one. The newcomers could not be expected to appreciate her peril and among the regular attenders she had no real friend. She had marked out a small terrain for herself which had not been threatened for much the same reason that Switzerland's neutrality is respected – the domain was barren and contained little to attract the attention of predators. As the Vicar shepherded the two young women into the kitchen, tears dimmed Laura's eyes.

Hester, who had watched the incident with amusement, decided that this was the moment which justified her presence. As she approached Laura she was dismayed to see how genuine was the woman's distress.

'Never, never . . .' The voice was faint and the slight frame shook as though a chance gust of wind had blown away her very substance. 'Never . . . in all my years in this church . . . have I been brushed aside like that.'

She, too, is old, Hester thought, and what little confidence she ever possessed has worn threadbare.

'Come off it, Laura!' she said. 'That was just blundering masculine insensitivity. You get in there and make sure the raw recruits know who is in charge of the cookhouse. They'll probably be very glad to see you. I've never managed to come to terms with that cantankerous old urn.'

The noise level in the room had risen considerably as diffident newcomers identified kindred spirits. Shirley Treglowan, with the advantage of ten minutes' familiarity, was playing hostess to several friends of her own age. The gas fire was now thought to be giving out too much heat and a window at the far end of the hall was opened. The Vicar was rearranging the chairs. 'I don't like to see people sitting in rows at a discussion. Can we form a circle?'

'I think there are too many people here for a circle,' one of the regular attenders said, looking accusingly at the newcomers. 'We don't want to be shouting across the room at one another, do we?'

Eventually a haphazard arrangement was arrived at which allowed no one person to occupy a prominent position. Even so, it was obvious that most of those present looked to the Vicar to take charge of the proceedings. The regular attenders expected to be led, while the newcomers were interested to see how the priest would perform when freed from the constraints of ritual.

'We usually start with a prayer,' Laura Addison whispered. On her return from the kitchen she had contrived to ease a chair to the left of the Vicar. Heads were bowed while Michael Hoath, who did not care for extempore prayer, briefly commended their proceedings to God.

The subject for discussion was the role of the Church in modern life, a weighty matter and certainly broad enough to allow the Vicar to indicate his chief concerns and make his first mistakes. He sat back in his chair, however, and waited for others to speak.

A regular attender passionately advocated the need to support overseas missions and another took up the claims of nuclear disarmament. The problems of the inner cities were mentioned briefly and the closure of the Cornish tin mines at greater length. There were critical references to the appointment of bishops in which London fared somewhat better than Durham. At this point, Laura Addison said she was sorry to see that the chalice was now wiped with a cloth and a dark, gruff little woman remarked that God was not a witch doctor, keeping the faithful pure by the exercise of magical spells. Someone else said that if, in fact, silver was a safeguard against the spread of germs, she thought this was elitist – what about churches which couldn't afford much in the way of silver? The level of interest had declined. It was apparent that there were a few present who were prepared to debate the matter of the wiping of the chalice for the remainder of the evening. The Vicar intervened.

'All these issues are important, of course, and I don't think anyone would deny that mistakes have been made in things both large and small; but we should remember that *we* are the Church – not archbishops or bishops, or priests, for that matter, but the whole Christian community. Perhaps we should talk about ourselves and what we as Christians feel is our role today.'

He had hoped that one of the younger women who had not previously attended these meetings would speak; but after a short silence, Laura Addison said, 'We should be concerned with bringing God's word to people's hearts and minds.' As they were not quite sure how this was to be accomplished – or, indeed, what exactly *was* God's word for today – her hearers were left to contemplate their inadequacy. Michael Hoath, sitting with bowed head, wondered how long a pause he should allow before he spoke again.

He was saved by Norah Kendall. '*Are* we the Church? I know this is something we are told. But, you don't think . . ?' She had the look of a person about to say something which the listener certainly does not think. Michael Hoath smiled at her encouragingly and this seemed to distract her from her purpose. 'Oh dear, perhaps I should start from somewhere else.' In spite of her hesitation she was by no means inarticulate, nor, it seemed, were her thoughts as wandering as she would have her audience think. 'Could it be that one of the reasons the Church has lost its influence is that it has left so much unsaid that needed to be said, and so had to be said by people other than Christians? Sorry about all the saids and unsaids!'

Michael Hoath said politely, 'Yes, that is undoubtedly true. The Holy Spirit will make sure that the Word is said, even if the Church fails to . . . er . . . articulate it. Had you anything specific in mind?'

She responded with a sureness which suggested that she had never lost the main thread of her argument. 'I'm back with this question of our being the Church. I was thinking about the position of women. We haven't really been encouraged to think of ourselves as part of the Church – an equal part – have we?' Laura Addison gave a little sigh, but the younger women present sat up alertly as if summoned by a bugle call. 'It's sometimes difficult for us to think about our role, when for centuries Christianity has been interpreted to women by men – even advice as to how women should dress. I know that sounds a bit trivial, but St Paul didn't think it too trivial to mention, did he? And men can't really know the intimate things – the things of the heart – so well as women themselves, can they?' She looked at Michael Hoath, at once shy and respectful, yet not without a hint of provocation.

Valentine hoped her husband recognized that familiar character, the woman who needs a male priest while having an urge to challenge his authority; but she could see that he was concerned only with the question. This was a subject on which his feelings were ambivalent; he was less than enthusiastic at the prospect of sharing his ministry with women, but he knew that intellectually he was on shaky ground. He rubbed his jaw, reflecting gloomily that it would come anyway, whatever he thought or said.

Norah Kendall took advantage of his silence to continue. 'If the Church had fulfilled its role – as it did in the emancipation of slaves – not that I'm saying women are slaves' – a little laugh here, but she had, of course, inferred it – 'but if the Church had thought about the position of women in a positive way, wouldn't it have more moral authority now?'

This received vehement support from a deep-chested young woman whose emotions had for the last few minutes laid an increasing strain on her skimpy blouse. 'Some of us think of it as being rather like a working man's club – a good bolt-hole where the women can't get at a chap! Or if you want to go up-market a bit, you can let them into the visitors' dining-room, but not a step beyond.'

'I think that is rather a superficial analogy.' Norah Kendall was quick to regain the initiative. 'But it does seem to me that the Church can't speak with real moral authority when the wisdom and experience of women is not used, is so often denied . . .'

'You are not saying that women have had no voice in the last two thousand years?' Michael asked.

'I suppose I am.' She looked not so much troubled by the statement as apologetic at having cornered him.

He paused, on the verge of mentioning St Teresa and Dame Julian, to ask himself how many others? Not enough in two thousand years to weigh against the number of clergymen in this one diocese. When in trouble, ask a practical question. He said, 'Allowing for the situation as it is at present, is there any more you feel we should be doing to improve the position of women here in this parish?'

There wasn't, of course. She had had her say, created a bit of friction, and was now in retreat from assuming responsibility for any new initiatives. But the flood gates had been opened. Michael Hoath was astonished at the eagerness of even the most modest among the younger women, those worthy by their demeanour of a part in any Jane Austen adaptation, to contribute their story of male chauvinism – indeed, not merely to contribute, but to compete. As he listened to Nancy Perrins, who sang so sweetly in the choir, giving tongue to domestic discords which surely had no place outside the home, it was as if Fanny Price had made a rude gesture at the pious Edmund. Of course, one did sometimes look for a more robust show of spirit in Fanny, but who would have wished the gentle creature to develop into a virago?

35

'As soon as I switch on the Open University, he finds something he needs me for,' she was saying. 'If they put out the programmes at two in the morning, he'd be up with toothache.'

Others took up the theme. 'He doesn't know the first thing about figures. I'm the one who keeps the accounts. But I don't get any thanks for it because he can't bear that I do anything better than him.'

'His co-ordination is poor and he can't judge distances. The plain fact is he's a bad driver.'

'Oh, he *can* do things about the house, provided everything else stops. There's got to be a breathless hush followed by a round of applause whenever he knocks a nail in the wall.'

'I can do just as I like,' Nancy Perrins came in with her clear soprano. 'Join the W.I. and the painting group, even go away for a weekend with a girl friend. Anything, so long as I don't hold opinions that are different from his.'

'The weekend is like having another child about the place, competing for attention and sulking when he doesn't get it.'

'What he really wants is for *them* to play with *him*. He's sick to death because Jamie hasn't any ball sense.'

'One evening, *one* evening in the week, and there's a fuss when I came out tonight!'

Michael was dismayed that his first discussion with this group should so soon have deteriorated into a recital of marital disharmony which might well have been the introduction to a campaign to find the most selfish husband of the year. It was a relief when Laura Addison, who had retreated to the kitchen, announced that coffee was ready – and, her tone suggested, not a moment too soon.

He said to Hester, as they stood isolated from the small groups which were continuing the discussion, 'I hope these young women aren't representative of the wives of their generation.'

'They are probably not representative in being wives,' she replied.

'I find it a little alarming.' He looked round uneasily. 'Their dislike of men . . .'

She shrugged her shoulders. 'You'll get used to it. Women have had to bear man's dislike of woman for a very long time. Particularly the dislike of priests.'

'Oh come, this issue of women priests may have led to some intemperate talk . . .'

A voice behind them said, 'I hope you don't mind all this?' Norah Kendall smiled at Michael ruefully. She seemed now to regard herself as his ally. 'Sometimes discussions here need a bit of overstatement to get them going.'

He did not appreciate this belated attempt to ingratiate herself. 'You have certainly stirred up a hornet's nest.'

'It's good for them to talk.'

'But does their talk have to be so cruel? I am sure that the husbands of these women are very fond of their wives.'

Norah Kendall laughed. 'Of course they are. But then, they have managed to isolate the virus.'

He turned away. He thought of her as a spiky, insecure woman.

The time after coffee had traditionally been used by Michael's predecessor to draw together the threads of the discourse, emphasizing the points that had emerged which he considered relevant and ignoring anything which had not pleased him. Michael merely asked, 'Are there any further points which anyone would like to raise?'

Laura Addison sighed and the deep-chested young woman, who had introduced herself to Michael during the coffee break as a divorcee, a title which she had seemed to prefer to giving her name, announced that she had something to say. Her face was heavy and rather masculine and the knowledge that she was about to give offence probably made her manner more aggressive than she intended. 'This film – *The Last Temptation of Christ*. Why should there be all this rumpus because it suggests he might have wanted a human family, like any other man? What's so wrong with him having a sex life, and a wife and children? I can't see why that has to be represented as a temptation – except that it's the way the Church sees women – a temptation ever since Eve.'

'If that is the way you see it, then I think that is a pity.' Valentine looked sharply at Michael. He sounded as personally accused as if he was in the witness box and she knew that he would not be able to handle this issue calmly. 'I think what we should be concerned with is the way we see Christ.'

'It's not only one film, is it? There was a book some time ago claiming he was Mary Magdalene's lover. What's so wrong with that? Human beings do have sex, after all.'

Laura Addison's face was scarlet. She was twisting and turning her hands in her lap. Hester, who was sitting beside her, put a gentle hand on her shoulder. Poor Laura, she thought; anyone would imagine she herself was about to be denounced for some unmentionable sin – there were probably quite a few sins still unmentionable in Laura's frightened heart.

'It's all a question of how human is human, isn't it?' the angel from the choir said. 'He was supposed to share our humanity, wasn't he?' She spoke with the prim assurance of one who has always done well in Sunday School.

'But not our sins, dear. Not our sins.' Laura tried to smile, but her lips were shaking.

'Sin?' A dozen pairs of eyes turned on Laura.

The angel from the choir piped, ' "Be fruitful and multiply and replenish the earth . . ." '

Norah Kendall said, 'God did create us male and female, after all, Laura. It can hardly be counted a sin.'

Michael saw that Laura was the only person prepared to take up this challenge. The other older members of the group had the glazed look of people nodding off in front of a television programme which is unsuitable but which they have not the energy to switch off. The fact that Laura had summoned the courage to speak was a measure of her desperation. She sat crouched in her chair, her eyes bright as those of a hunted animal. He had no choice but to intervene. He said, 'I don't think there is any question of sex being sinful.'

'Then you think this film is all right?' The divorcee was as aggrieved as a dog which has had a bone snatched from it.

'On the contrary, I think it is blasphemous.'

There was a startled silence. Direct rebuke from authority was so out of fashion that it took them some moments to accommodate themselves to what had been said.

Valentine clenched her hands. Most of the spokesmen for the Church had tiptoed gently round the central issue, tut-tutting about violence and catching at any straw in the wind; but not her husband: Michael, in all his unwisdom, was about to address himself to one of the more impenetrable mysteries of the Christian centuries. She felt her stomach muscles tighten ominously. He would make a spectacle of himself and they would laugh about it afterwards. She could not bear that he should be the subject of ridicule.

He said, 'I haven't seen the film.' At least he had this in common with most clerical commentators. 'So I'm not qualified to discuss how the theme has been handled. But it seems to me to be another instance of a particular kind of blasphemy. Which has nothing to do with sex,' he added, hastening to damp down the banked fires. 'We are told that we are created in the image of God. I'm never sure what that means, myself. But I do know that Christ was and is the human face of God. He is our model, the person towards whom we move, that within ourselves which checks and holds, which enriches and guides, prevents and inspires us in our daily lives.' The older women eased into their seats as though subconsciously aware of a change to a more acceptable programme. The younger women listened not in the silence of respect, but incredulity, their faces expressing this variously in terms of outrage, blank incomprehension and an embarrassed desire to giggle. Only Shirley Treglowan, who was eager for betterment, gave the attention she would have awarded a lecture on the lost treasures of the Incas. 'It seems to me that we have become so obsessed with ourselves, that there is a danger that we fall into a habit of making ourselves the model to which He must conform, that day by day we expect Him to grow more like us. In fact, we create Him in our own image. And that seems to me a form of blasphemy.'

Shirley said, 'But Bishop . . .'

'Oh, bishops are no more immune from blasphemy than anyone else – rather the reverse.'

39

Valentine closed her eyes. He is going to get angry about bishops now, because some of them treat Christ like a product which must somehow be made more marketable. 'Lust is your problem, sir,' he had said only yesterday, throwing down the newspaper. 'Well, we'll allow Him that, too. Homosexual? That's a possibility.' She was grateful to Norah Kendall for gently prompting, 'But if He is so far beyond us . . .'

'Is that so dreadful? Mankind would have withered away long ago were there no beyond.'

'But we were talking of loving.' Norah protested. 'At least, that's how we started . . .'

This woman is as edgy about love as Laura is about sex, Valentine thought grimly, looking at the strained face.

'If He didn't love anyone I don't see how He can be our model.' The divorcee resolutely gathered her forces.

Michael thought about this. He had a disconcerting habit when he seemed to be gaining the ascendancy of breaking off, giving the impression of losing confidence.

'Human love is so exclusive,' he said. Whereas before he had seemed authoritative, even if unrelated to his audience, he had now become one of them, as though he had stepped off some invisible platform. 'Don't you feel this? It circumscribes us, hedges us in . . .'

They looked at one another doubtfully. How could they deny this, who only a short while ago had been crying their need for time on their own, away from parents, friends, children and, in particular, their own partner? Michael went on, seeming to be working it out as he went along, 'Even couples who make very few demands on each other will insist that it is essential to have some time on their own. Excluding others is a necessary part of most human loving. Not all, of course.' He searched for an example and came up with the obvious one. 'Do you think when you look in the face of Mother Teresa that she is twisted by self-denial?'

The divorcee muttered crossly, 'I knew she was going to crop up somewhere along the line. I should hope she's past it at her age.'

Shirley Treglowan said, 'She's never had the time, has she?'

'Yes.' Michael leant forward, his hands outstretched, palms upwards, as if to receive a gift. 'Let's see if we can't go a little further. Can we add something to that?'

Shirley sat back as though afraid he might spring on her at any moment.

He said, 'Space? Neither the time nor the space. It seems to me that *that's* how it was with Jesus Christ. I don't see Him like St Paul, practising all kinds of self-denial. He was self-giving and became completely filled with the love of God. There was no space left over. He didn't need a one-to-one human love which excludes others, which *must* exclude others by its very nature. He was capable of *more* love than us, not less. He loved all human kind. As for family – he did indeed have a family. We are that family.' He stretched out his arms and they looked back at him as any family will when deeply suspicious of a display of emotion on the part of one of its members. 'Occasionally we meet people who have something of this quality, don't we? And when we try to get too close in the wrong way we are hurt because we feel there is nothing there that is special to us. We say "He – or she – is like that with everyone", as if that cancelled out any genuine loving feeling. For us to recognize love it has to come with our name on the tag. But He was love. He is love. Not the image or the emotion, the longing or the satisfaction – which doesn't last – but the very essence.'

Most of his audience had become rather glazed by this time. After a few moments one young woman who had not said anything up to now, remarked with feeling, 'I'd run from anyone like that. I'd run a mile.'

Someone at the back said, 'As for Mother Teresa, there's something a bit kinky about someone who goes round looking for the dying.'

The voices came in on all sides. 'All those charity workers, rushing off whenever there's a famine . . .'

'And the Pope talking about holy poverty. Much he knows about being poor!'

They were angry. Yet, for Michael, the very anger which

had been aroused made him aware that the Presence was here. He knew better than to intervene.

Much to Laura Addison's annoyance, there was no shortage of help in the kitchen when the meeting was over. Her protests that she could manage on her own went unheeded. Even after the gas fire had been extinguished the women remained talking as they helped to stack the chairs. They donned anoraks and wound scarves slowly.

'Got quite deep, didn't we?' Shirley Treglowan said to the divorcee. 'Will you come again?'

'Oh, I'll come again! There's a lot I didn't get to say.'

Michael noticed that Valentine was joking with the older church members. Laughter always transformed Valentine's face, making her seem young and undefended. He realized that she was doing this for him because she thought he had upset the faithful and made no converts among the newcomers. He stood at the door to bid goodnight to the women as they left and was aware how many refused to make eye contact – like people who have been hijacked.

He could feel no pride in what he had done. The thing which touched him most on this issue he had not given them. For him, Christ was that pearl of great price for which the wealthy merchant sold all that he possessed. He felt so passionately hurt by the inadequate response to this figure that he dared not speak of it. Yet it was a sense of this, of something of great and mysterious worth, which sent a few of those present out into the night unsatisfied, with a hunger they knew not for what. This was his gift, to arouse, if only in a few, that hunger – not the gift for which he craved, to give, to satisfy.

Hester was one of the last to leave. He said to her, 'I'm afraid you didn't agree with a lot of that.'

The warmth of her response surprised him. 'It doesn't matter whether I agree or not. You believe it and you said it. That's what matters.'

Valentine, seeing them standing together, noted a rare resemblance between them, something positive and fierce.

She and Michael walked down the path to the vicarage

together, not speaking. He will sleep soundly after this, she thought, while I shall have a stomach upset. It was a clear night, but raindrops glinted like beady eyes on every blade of grass.

3

On a fine spring afternoon a car travelled westward down a sunken lane, the covering branches of trees still greening. It came out on a rise with a long view of fields and in the distance a grey village huddled round a church, its decorative square tower frivolous as a Christmas cracker hat perched above the slate roofs of the houses. There was pale, unemphatic sunshine and the air smelt sharp as lemon.

The driver of the car looked out over the fields where not a man could be seen and said, 'This would be mowing time, wouldn't it – end of April, beginning of May, some time thereabouts? Lois's grandmother has pictures of these fields taken during her childhood. Men with scythes wearing waistcoats and straw hats.'

His companion said, 'Yes, country folk still haven't learnt how to dress for their roles.' Hesketh Kendall delivered this pronouncement in a hoarse voice which made its ultimate point with a rasp. 'Only the town-bred know what is the appropriate gear.'

His own clothes were immaculate, dark jacket, pin-striped trousers. A general air of good living and a hint of audacity in the eyes, however, suggested a profession which had allowed him a certain licence to express himself. The broken nose, a memento of rugger playing days, added an impression of vigour. It was a handsome face, the lines cut with a dash about the self-indulgent mouth. There was, however, a slackness in his posture which was uncharacteristic and his performance in court the day before had been lackadaisical. The driver, Jack Drury, was not so handsome but he was much younger and his lean face betrayed no sign of vitality on the wane. He said, 'It's about here that I always imagine I can smell the sea.'

'We had the old coastguard cottage, my first wife and I.'

Jack Drury glanced obliquely at his companion and thought that the man had aged ten years in the last nine months. Three parts grief, seven parts self-pity. Himself being young, he could afford to pass harsh judgements on the afflictions of others.

'Lois told me you had sold the cottage,' he said briskly.

'Caroline and I were planning to sell it anyway. It seemed wiser, with retirement in mind, to settle in town.'

'And it must be a help, being married to one of the locals.'

'Yes, if it hadn't been for that I doubt if I would have come so far from London. Not after Caroline died . . .'

Silence again. Jack looked ahead, lips firmly sealed against the expressions of sympathy so assiduously solicited. He stiffened his resistance by recalling a lunch in a Fleet Street pub some years ago when Hesketh had told him, 'I have no fear of retirement, unlike some poor devils.' The fear had been all Caroline's. Lois had said of her sudden death, 'She just ran out of life. Pumped dry servicing Hesketh's needs.' Jack, who had only been married to Lois for a year, had never met Caroline. To him, she had simply been a name which Hesketh had not found it necessary to mention with any great frequency during her lifetime. As far as he was concerned she should be allowed to rest in peace. He said, 'I seem to recall Lois saying that Norah used to live out on the edge of the moor. As a child. On a farm?'

'I believe so.' Hesketh looked out of the window, his mouth turned down.

'Will you sell the London house? Lois and I might be interested when the time comes.'

'I shall have to sell it when I retire. The distance is too great.'

And retirement not far away. Jack, not yet at the height of his powers, could not imagine that a time would ever come when he would begin to fail. He was disappointed in Hesketh Kendall.

The man had been so inspiring, never settling for the safest course, taking great risks, deliberately heading into the eye of the storm for the sheer zest of proving he was in control. Some of Hesketh's clients had had a very rough ride before he brought them safe to port. And here he was, not even beached in sight or sound of the sea.

'You can drop me here,' Hesketh said when they reached the outskirts of the town, almost as though he was ashamed of the place and could not face the prospect of travelling through it, mitigating its inadequacies.

Jack, thinking of Lois waiting at the cottage, did not protest. He said to Hesketh as he got out of the car, 'Best of luck, then.'

'With what?'

Damnation! This was what came of taking one's mind off the subject, which in this case was Hesketh Kendall, renowned for his Machiavellian courtroom cunning, who, according to Lois, had made a disastrously misjudged marriage. And he was actually staring at Jack as if demanding an explanation of an affront. His face had changed completely. The urbane, con-fident man of the world had suddenly aged and the unblinking eyes betrayed the defensive anger of the poor old codger afraid that he has inadvertently revealed some secret infirmity.

'Why, in settling somewhere so different from London, of course.' Jack managed to inject a measure of admiration into his voice. 'I'm not sure I could do it myself.'

Hesketh nodded. 'It is damned difficult. But after Caroline, it was going to be difficult anyway.'

The eyes staring at him reminded Jack of nothing so much as two fried eggs filmed with oil. He turned away from the moist self-pity. 'I'll give you a ring on Sunday evening to find out your plans for next week.'

Hesketh Kendall told friends that he and Norah had managed to buy one of the only decent houses in the town. It was an old stone building which at one time had been a Baptist chapel. The previous owners had modernized it quite sensitively but an air of austerity still hung about it, as though the sobriety of the early worshippers had become a part of the very fabric. Definitely it was not a house which welcomed flamboyance of any kind. Its most pleasant feature was the garden which ran down to the river. Norah was in the garden when Hesketh arrived. She was, he had discovered, more interested in the garden than the house and once out there she lost all sense of time. In fact, for a nurse, she seemed to have surprisingly little sense of time.

He stood looking round the sitting-room which had not taken kindly to the mixture of his and Norah's furniture and had positively annihilated the wit and gaiety of the abstract paintings which had shown to such advantage in the house in Hampstead. He gazed gloomily at a sampler worked by an aunt of Norah's who must have had a lot of time on her hands and little talent in her fingers. His nostrils quivered as he inhaled deeply. No appetizing smells from the kitchen rewarded him. He had travelled a long way from Winchester. Caroline would have prepared one of his favourite dishes which would come from the kitchen attractively presented to please the eye and tempt the palate. There would have been no hint of effort. He felt again that sense of some monstrous trick having been played on him. He had bade her good day in the morning and, it seemed from the doctor's report, she had thereafter sat down on the couch and passed peacefully beyond his reach. But he still had unfinished business to conduct with her. He crossed to the French windows almost as if he expected to find her standing in the Hampstead garden, its green lawns and hedges manicured to perfection, ready with an explanation of her behaviour.

Norah looked at him in dismay through the branches of a rambler rose which she was supporting. 'Gracious! Whatever time is it?'

'Half-past five.'

'And his lordship's carriage arrived and no one to attend him at the gate!'

Initially, it had been the quirky humour and the pleasant, twinkling smile which attracted Hesketh to Norah Nancarrow. He now found himself able to resist both.

She cleared a temporary resting place for the rose and came towards him, casting aside secateurs and wire, then tugging off her gardening gloves. They stood looking at each other awkwardly, this chance-met couple, reflecting on their respective duties. She folded her hands to her brow in the sign of peace.

'The weather brightened after lunch, m'Lud. It's been so deadly recently, I just rushed out here when the sun came out.' She seemed to have some hope of winning his favour, but no idea that an apology might be required.

He experienced the now familiar spiral of rage rising in him. Hesketh Kendall was used, on his return, to gin and vermouth in tall frosted glasses and a garden to be contemplated, not one rampant with unsolved problems. Norah was now offering tea and saffron cake. After which, he supposed, she would return to succour the rose.

'What ails the thing?' he asked.

'We had a gale last night. It needs staking back to the wall. It won't take very long.' This he recognized as a phrase used to soothe a patient enduring a painful dressing of a wound, a child set to perform an uncongenial task – it bore no relationship to Greenwich Mean Time. 'I'll just make the tea and . . .'

'I'd rather have a drink.'

'Isn't it a little early?'

'I am not an alcoholic, simply a weary traveller come from distant parts and in need of refreshment – Odysseus returned to his Penelope.'

She gave him a grateful smile and moved by her responsiveness he kissed her.

'There's trout,' she said. 'That won't take long, and I've prepared the potatoes and veg.'

But first she must attend to the rose and then she must have a bath. She was meticulous about cleanliness. Hesketh sauntered down to the river. On the day when they made an offer for the house it had been a blue enamelled border to lawn and shrubbery. He had seen rather more of it since then and most of the time it wasn't blue. Now, in the early evening, it had lost what noonday charms it possessed and a faint mist was rising from it. That mist must have hung about the house for all of its three hundred years' existence. He was chilled by the time he went indoors. He went slowly up to the main bedroom and changed into slacks and pullover. Norah was singing in the bathroom, her voice high and clear and unconcerned. He ran a hand down one wall. It felt cold but not damp. He opened a cupboard and sniffed. There was some sort of smell, but rather on the warm side, as though a dusty electric fire had been left burning. He looked thoughtfully at the bed but did not examine it. Norah was fussy about the bed, it was regularly made and remade and stripped and the mattress put out to air – whatever else was wrong with the bed, it could not be damp. He went downstairs and watched *Emmerdale Farm* on television.

At eight o'clock he went into the kitchen. 'Not long now,' Norah greeted him. Her flushed face and anxious manner betrayed the person who has extreme difficulty in co-ordinating her activities. Years ago, when he had rashly undertaken some advisory work for a local residents' association, he had been given a secretary like that. He had insisted that she be replaced.

'It's not that you are slow,' he said. 'It's that you don't programme your time.'

'I had enough of programmed time in hospital.'

She had no sense of a need to plan ahead. She opened each day like a new book, saying to herself, 'Now I wonder what this will be about.' Hesketh began his days with preconceived ideas.

He went back to the sitting-room and started to do *The Times* crossword puzzle. It was after nine when they sat down to eat.

'As a nurse,' he said, making a joke of it, 'I would have expected you to be eminently suited to run a house.'

'You should be thankful I'm not like some nurses, forever fussing about every speck of dust.'

He watched her separating flesh from bone with the competence of a surgeon. She looked untidy and defiant. She had presented herself to him at her best when he first met her. A tall woman with a good carriage, she could, with some attention paid to her hair, achieve a certain distinction, if not elegance. No woman who cared so little about clothes could ever attain elegance.

'Anyway,' she said. 'I don't think nine o'clock is all that late to eat.'

Hesketh Kendall felt that life had cheated him unforgivably. He recalled how charmingly surprised and grateful she had been to find herself singled out for the wifely part she was now so inadequately performing. He had imagined himself a magical benefactor at whose touch this not wholly ungraceful woman would blossom and flourish, showered by the gifts his wealth could afford. He had congratulated himself on not falling to the temptation, so prevalent among men of his age, to rate youth and sexual stimulation above the more enduring qualities of the good homemaker. Once more, he had anticipated, he would find himself the centre of a world of warmth and security. His daughter Samantha notwithstanding.

It was dark now and night had come up to the window. He got up to draw the blinds and noticed that the panes of glass were filmed with mist. The room looked small when he turned back to it, the low ceiling only a foot above his head. He had a moment of panic at finding himself alone here with this unlikely stranger.

'There is a letter from Samantha for me, I see,' he said when they had finished their silent meal. 'I suppose I had better find out what she wants this time. Unless you would like me to assist with this . . .' He waved his hand dismissively over the plates and dishes.

'There is rather a lot, isn't there? It would be a help.'

In the kitchen he said, 'I have been travelling all day.'

She replied cheerfully, 'Then it will do you good to stand for a bit,' and passed him a plate to wipe.

When eventually they went into the sitting-room, he with a pot of coffee, she with a mug of Bovril, it was half-past ten. 'What do you *do* all day?' The question was put more in wonder than sarcasm. There were some ways in which Norah was infinitely more mysterious than Caroline.

'Well now . . . Mrs Herbert's Jason cut his knee. Mrs Petty asked me to change her dressing. Old Mr Lock got in a panic because he had a bad night and thought he was going to die – which he might well have done, poor old thing. That more or less disposed of the morning. Then . . .'

'Who are these people?' he asked angrily. 'You speak as if I knew them.' It seemed that her life went on much as usual. She had simply made a little space in it to accommodate him.

'They are just neighbours and old patients of mine.'

'But you are not nursing any more.'

She laughed. 'Nurses are always in demand, same as handy-men.'

'You shouldn't let people presume on your good nature.'

She replied with a flash of impatience, 'People don't presume when they are sick or injured, they need help and they cry out for it. That's one of the good things about being a nurse, you are always needed.'

'I need you,' he said sulkily. 'Had that occurred to you?'

She turned her head away, suddenly a great lady – haughty expression, proud carriage of the head – and he a menial who had overreached himself. She was very unpredictable. At other times when he reproached her with neglect she would cry. He had quite expected that she would cry now and tell him how much she had longed to care for and comfort him, how it hurt her that she should fail so often. Then, because he was not a sadistic man, he would console her and encourage her by elaborating the things which she did well before trying to help her to understand her little failings. It was quite apparent, however, that she was not going to cry this time. He found it unnerving that he could never be sure of her reactions. She was as bad, if not worse, than Judge Colbert. It was as if she had the emotional equivalent of perfect pitch – when he failed to strike the right note she was immediately aware of it and ruled his submissions out of court.

'That coffee is bad for your liver,' she said, picking up the newspaper. She put up a hand and took one straggling strand of hair, winding it round a finger while she read. He could imagine her doing this when she was young and the hair, so he had been assured, a great fiery bush. Perhaps she still thought of it like this? There was a certain assurance in her attitude to her hair.

He put down the cup and stalked out of the room. Some rather ostentatious slamming and banging marked his passage from room to hall and back again. She did not raise her eyes from the paper; the strand of hair was now held between her teeth. He looked down at the envelope in his hand and said angrily, 'Damn paper knife.' There followed a further disturbance in the hall – table doors opened and shut, noisy rummaging in the cupboard under the stairs, displacement of various cleaning materials, fall of some heavy object, probably the vacuum cleaner. He was one of those men at whose touch inanimate objects take on a malign life of their own. At last he reappeared in the doorway to the sitting-room, hair ruffled and red of face, ripping the envelope with his fingers. Inevitably, he tore a piece out of the letter. So he must go to the bureau and turn over its contents, pencils, writing pads, old cheque books, keys which opened doors not yet discovered, the paper knife, of course, and, at last, sellotape. He strode to the kitchen for scissors. Finally, the letter roughly stuck together, he returned to read it.

Norah said, 'Bernard Levin is so funny. When you have finished that you must read him.'

But she watched while he read the letter, saw how his eyes jerked from one line to the next, noted the heavy breathing which betrayed constricted muscles.

'Problems?' she asked gently when he had finished.

'She has lost her job. At least, she has given in her notice. The man she worked with was an absolute swine, couldn't keep his hands off her. She says she needs to get out of London for a while. So she is coming to stay here for a few months.' He looked at her, hoping for that swift, sure touch which sweeps aside the dark curtains and lets the sunlight come flooding in to dispel the nightmare; but when she said, 'You're not going to agree?' he became angry.

'Well, she is my daughter.'

'I can't!' Her nightmare was stronger than his. She looked at him in utter dismay, her features at odds with one another, making her face ludicrous. 'I can't have her here. You must see that I can't.'

'Only for a few months.' He was blundering about in the darkness from which she had failed to rescue him. 'I think it is the least we could do. A few months . . .' He only came home at weekends so for him it would be a matter of weeks rather than months. 'Things were rather bad between us about the time of Caroline's death. I should like to heal that breach.'

'What you mean is that you want me to heal it for you, to gather all the pieces together into some kind of order.' Her face had become flushed and her voice was pitched high. 'I can't do it, Hesketh. I'm not made that way.'

'You said only half an hour ago that when people were hurt or injured they cried out for help.'

'I meant physically hurt or injured. I'm trained to deal with that. And, anyway, Samantha isn't crying out for help – not to me, anyway. She hates me. She made that quite clear when she met me.'

'That was shock. You have to make allowances for the shock.'

She pressed her knuckles against her lips. He watched her with that unblinking stare which made him look so much older. This was a situation he did not know how to handle – handling had always been Caroline's province. Some kind of peace had been preserved between him and Samantha during Caroline's lifetime.

Norah took a deep breath and spoke quietly, persuasively. 'It's all I can do to manage, you know that. There is so much to get used to . . .'

'Samantha would help about the house, I'm sure.' He had no recollection of her ever having done this, but once he had stated it he expected it to be accepted as gospel.

'She would take over, you mean? I expect she has already decided how she wants her bedroom arranged. And you and she don't get on. You would get at each other through me. I couldn't cope with that. Not now. We need time, Hesketh.' She was imploring for his help, but as it was help of a kind he was unfitted to give this made him the more angry. 'Once we have settled down together, become . . . united . . . it won't be so easy for her to come between us. Can't you understand the harm it would do to our marriage if she were to come now?'

He looked down at the letter. 'But what am I to say to her?'

'You must explain to her that we can't have her just now.' Her voice became regrettably sharp. 'There must have been times in her life when someone said "no" to Samantha.'

'We can't exclude her from our lives. She is my daughter.'

'And, in any case, why didn't she write to me if she wants to stay here? That would have been the correct thing to do.'

'I expect it seemed the natural thing to write to her father.'

'She won't accept that I am the mistress of the house. That is an indication of how she will behave if she comes here. I haven't much confidence, Hesketh. What I have she will destroy.'

He folded the letter and put it back in the envelope. 'We will discuss it later. There is no hurry. She does say she is going to have two weeks in Majorca staying at a friend's villa.' He raised a hand as she began to speak. 'We will talk about it later.'

'Hesketh, it isn't that I won't. I can't.'

'I have nothing more to say. You have upset me very much. We will talk about it later.'

He went out of the room and began his nightly routine of closing windows and locking and bolting doors. He recognized this procedure as the practical equivalent of taking arms against a sea of troubles, since it was not burglars whom he sought to keep at bay, but the river. When he had finished, he called out, 'I have put out the milk bottles, so there is no need to open the front door.' There was no reply. He glanced into the sitting-room. She still had the paper spread out on her lap, but her head hung forward and her eyes were closed. After all that had passed between them, she had actually fallen asleep.

4

'I want to do in yere,' Mrs Quince informed Charles Venables. She stood in the doorway to his study, a hand like a brick resting on the vacuum cleaner, sweating powerfully.

It was Saturday morning. She had been prevented from coming during the week by the illness of one of her grandchildren. He had not sought to identify the sufferer since this would involve a recital as laborious as the Book of Numbers. It seemed to him surprising that a woman as mighty as Mrs Quince, from whose womb had sprung such legions, should have failed to produce sons and daughters capable of ministering to their own offspring. All that he said, however, was 'Now?' in a tone of pained surprise.

'Yurs.' Mrs Quince treated him as though he was a piece of furniture which had had the temerity to speak. 'I done the rest.'

They stared at each other and Mrs Quince breathed heavily. The peace of his weekends was precious to Charles. Nevertheless, he was wretchedly at the mercy of Mrs Quince who differed from the newer breed of cleaner in that she was prepared to raise her arms above eye level and to go down on her knees to scrub. Since he dared not risk losing her services, he contented himself with saying austerely, 'I should be glad if you would not disturb the papers on my desk, Mrs Quince.'

'Yurs, Mr Venbulls.' She pushed at the swivel chair and sent it reeling against the wall; an armchair followed at a more leisurely pace. Charles Venables winced. There was something obscene about this ritual baring of the carpet which was old and needed to have its worn patches and the one bad stain decently covered. He had once suggested that it was bad for the carpet to be vacuumed so often, but it had been to no avail. He retreated to the sitting-room.

He should have brought his notes on *Anna Karenina* with him, but having failed to do so he did not like to return. The less he saw of Mrs Quince's work methods, the better. And, in any case, her animal odour had overlaid Anna's traces, and it would take time for her image to reform in his mind. He sat down and pondered why it was that beauty was so vulnerable and the brutish so enduring. But then, of course, that was to compare like with unlike. Anna would survive as long as Caliban, even if in life it was the Mrs Quinces who prevailed.

To pass the time, he played a game he had recently devised to help him get to sleep. His taste in furniture was expensive and he had no means of indulging it other than fantasy. It was pleasant to drift into slumber contemplating an exquisite walnut secretaire. Now, he amused himself by refurnishing a room. There were one or two good pieces in this sitting-room which he had inherited from his great aunt, and he would be reluctant to part with them; as the room was small, this limited the possibilities. So he addressed himself to the Georgian house belonging to the head master. Its present contents were altogether too intrusive – one had the feeling the furniture had chosen the people. In twenty minutes, he successfully refurnished the morning-room but found the result less satisfactory than he had anticipated; there was something missing which fidgeted at the edge of his mind – the pictures, perhaps? or flowers? Since this was only a game it was puzzling that this elusive lack – he was sure it was a lack and not an error of judgement – should be so disturbing.

He moved his shoulders uneasily and realized that a draught was blowing into the room from the hall. Mrs Quince must have opened the study window; she had told him more than once that the house needed a good airing. As he hurried into the hall, Mrs Quince called out, 'Some of yur papers blown out the winder.'

He was scrabbling about in the front garden when a voice certainly not Mrs Quince's said, 'Someone's masterpiece blowing on the wind.' He looked up and saw Valentine Hoath standing by the gate, a piece of paper in her hand.

Her hand was long and white, the ivory wrist so small that as he stretched out his own hand he was shocked by an impish desire to encompass it with thumb and forefinger.

'My lecture on *Anna Karenina*,' he said breathlessly.

'Really? When?'

'Next Thursday evening. In the United Reformed Church Hall. I hope you will come?'

'I don't know about that. I'm playing Hedda Gabler. Should I confuse myself by considering Anna Karenina?'

'She is the most beautiful woman in all literature,' he said, gazing at her.

'Yes, of course.' She chose to take this as a rebuke. 'And so young.'

'I would have said you were far more suited to play Anna than Hedda.'

'Oh really, Charles!' She gave a light, contemptuous laugh, yet he was sure she had never before called him Charles. 'Passionate women are quite beyond my range, let alone my comprehension.'

'It is the passion, of course, which creates her beauty. The actual description of her . . .'

They stood for some minutes one on either side of the gate in the gusty wind discussing Anna and passion.

'Interesting that the way out for both of them was death, isn't it?' Valentine said. 'Perhaps one is fortunate not to have a passionate nature. Or do you think it was the authors' way out? After all, what do you do, left with a passionate woman on your hands at the end of your major work? In real life there must be a few passionate women around who have survived into old age.'

'They usually seem to attach themselves to artists. But I think perhaps it is a mistake to regard Hedda as passionate. Is it impertinent to ask how you will play her?'

'Previous rather than impertinent. In fact, I was just going to talk to Hester about it. Hester is so frank. If she thinks I can't do it, she will say so.'

He was silent, feeling rather irritated that she should consider Hester to be an appropriate judge of such matters. In his experience, people who wrote seldom knew much about literature. The wind blew one short, dark curl across the line of her cheekbone.

'I see your azalea is out,' she said.

'Yes. We face south.'

'It's really very pleasant up here. I hadn't realized. It was January when we came and everything so very drear.'

'You would like it here,' he said, and thought in dismay – 'What an odd remark!' He was glad that she seemed not to have heard.

'I can see Hester at the window, obviously saying to herself "Why doesn't the wretched woman come in, since she has decided to spoil my morning." Do you think Hester says something cruder than "spoil"? I suspect she does. I will leave you to *Anna Karenina*.'

He bowed. 'I shall hope to see you next Thursday.'

She smiled as though it was something she just might consider and turned towards Hester's house.

How good the air was, he thought; but sharp as a blade grazing his ears. He found he was trembling slightly. He returned to the house where all was now quiet. He put the papers back in his study which smelt strongly of Mrs Quince and furniture polish. He would have to defer further work on his lecture until the afternoon by which time he might feel more composed. A cup of milky coffee awaited him in the sitting-room and he could tell from its bleary appearance that it was cold. It was unlike Mrs Quince to depart so noiselessly. He walked to the window and saw that she had taken a cup of coffee to the boy Desmond who tidied up the garden. They sat side by side on the garden bench, not communicating, like Henry Moore figures.

'I know you don't like me,' Valentine said to Hester as soon as she sat down. This was her habitual preface to confidences. Hester did not, in fact, dislike her, but had come to accept the formula as one which gave some kind of security to Valentine. So she merely said, 'Well, that is the way you like to see it.'

'I'm not very good with people, I know that.' She seemed to be picking up the threads of an interrupted conversation. 'But we have had several moves since we were married and I don't think I can be accused of creating ill-feeling in our various parishes on anything like the scale of more devoted clergy wives.'

Hester poured coffee and waited.

'What would you say if I told you I had offered to take that wretched women's group off Michael's shoulders?'

'I should be surprised.'

'Michael was more than surprised. He didn't think I could do it. I told him "It's not a question of doing anything, just listening." That, I may say, is what he feels unable to do.'

'But he always seems so good at listening.'

'Not on all occasions. He gets very upset when he sees women trying to usurp the man's role. He seems to feel they will do themselves, not men, an injury. He has never been able to talk to me about it – no doubt because it is tied up with ideas about motherhood, a role I have been unable to play.'

'Perhaps not motherhood generally, Valentine. His own mother . . .'

'Anyway, I didn't want to argue with him. I was afraid I might sound like Norah Kendall. Though I don't think I could achieve quite that mixture of provocation and servility. It comes of being a nurse, I suppose. She is so conditioned to male dominance, poor thing, and being married to that awful man has made her so scratchy. She can't make up her mind from one moment to the next what role she is playing.'

'There has always been a provocative side to Norah. There wasn't much love on that farm and I think it was her way of drawing attention to the fact that she had needs as well as the animals. But she knows she must have a discipline to live by and I suppose that explains what you call her servility.'

'She is one of those women who are arch with men.'

'She has a difficult personality; a tendency to trip people when they are not looking, then she makes up for it by a rather unconvincing show of humility.'

'Michael feels I shan't be any match for her in that group. Can you imagine it? My attempting to match myself to Norah Kendall!'

'I have to say, Valentine, that I like and respect Norah Kendall.'

Hester looked the epitome of an affronted maiden aunt. It was all Valentine could do to refrain from laughing. 'Really, Hester,' she said lightly, 'what you see in that woman is beyond my comprehension.'

'In order to get time alone to do one's work one has, as a writer, to create an image which is, I suppose, fairly formidable.' Valentine, who had come to talk about herself, was astonished that it was Hester who now seemed to be the subject of discussion. 'A lot of people find me daunting. There are times when I wish it were otherwise. Norah has never been daunted, even as a child who always came to me for Sunday lunch – she sang in the choir and it was a long way back to the farm and back again for Evensong. She allowed me my black moods and I didn't fuss about her table manners.'

'Yes, well, I can see you have known her a long time.'

'Later, she became a nurse and had to impose a discipline on a naturally unruly personality. So she, more than most, understands my problem.' This must be age catching up with Hester, Valentine thought; how else could she go on and on in this agitated way about something so peripheral as her friendship with Norah Kendall? 'Moreover, she is quite capable of holding her own with me. Over the years we have established the only really easy relationship I have here.' Hester did not add 'and you, coming so lately, are not going to threaten it,' but the sense of something under threat was conveyed to Valentine.

'Oh dear, oh dear! I can't think how we got to be so excited about this. As for the group, Norah Kendall can have the running of it and welcome. I shall sit back and observe. Their talk quite fascinated me. As a study, of course. I think it might help with Hedda.'

How I do let my feelings run away with me lately, Hester thought. And it seems all she wanted was to talk about how to play Hedda!

'Michael thinks I am eminently suited to play Hedda, did you know? A woman who commits suicide because she can find no use for herself.'

'Michael admires your acting ability and Hedda is a particularly testing role.'

'Charles Venables dismissed her – not passionate, just useless. Even dry old Charles has no use for a woman who is not passionate.'

'I shouldn't have thought he had much use for a woman outside the pages of a book.'

'But I should like to know what it is that I am being told about myself in being cast for this role.'

'For Heaven's sake, Valentine! If you had been cast for Lady Macbeth you wouldn't think people were telling you you were a potential murderess.'

'No one would cast me for The Lady. Do be sensible, Hester. I came to see you because you are always so frank. What is your view of Hedda? I see her as caught in a world where a woman had to be exceptional to break free – and she was beautiful but not exceptional. I am beautiful but I cannot use the fact that I am not exceptional as an excuse because I live in a world where women have quite a lot of freedom.'

'I must have missed something – what is it that you are supposed to be excusing?'

Valentine turned her head away, looking out of the window where the boy Desmond was now working on Hester's garden. She said, 'My marriage.'

What a sad little story it is, Hester thought, the one about the person who brought her harp to a party and no one asked her to play! Yet how preferable are harpists to people who bring their hoops and jump through them one after the other. As far as I am concerned, at any gathering of mine, harps may be brought and played but hoops must be left outside.

'All this talk of freedom,' Valentine was saying, her eyes strained as though there was something out in the garden they were unable to bring into focus. 'I don't understand it. When I married it seemed to me to provide a kind of freedom, a right to a certain separateness. But I can see that some people might think of it as a form of protection, a shelter, even.'

'We all need protection of a sort. As for separateness, my writing keeps me a little apart from people.'

'But then there isn't one particular person from whom you are not supposed to be too far apart, is there?'

'No.' A shutter came down over Hester's face.

'I have always considered that it should be possible to be both sheltered and distanced. In fact, I find excessive closeness rather abhorrent. I am all for a little distance – "For the pillars of the temple stand apart, And the oak tree and the cypress grow not in each other's shadow" and all that. When Michael asked me to marry him I made it quite clear that I must have space around me. One sees more of one's husband as a vicar's wife than is often the case in marriage – all those shared meals, for one thing. He quite understood. As you know, he fell in love with me when he saw me play Beatrice in an amateur theatre festival and I certainly thought he would make a much better Benedict than the pompous young stockbroker I had to play opposite. We married three months later, as you undoubtedly recall, since I got the distinct impression you thought it a question of marry in haste and repent at leisure. He has kept to his part of the bargain and has never expected me to become swamped by parish affairs.'

'So?'

Valentine's face assumed the haughty expression with which she contemplated the undesirable, whether in the wardrobe, cellar, or the darker recesses of her own mind. 'I wouldn't want to feel in debt, to be thought to have cheated. It was quite unsettling to listen to those young women doing their emotional accountancy, calculating the credits and debits of their sexual experience, making sure of their dues. It seemed to reduce marriage to a rather sordid little swindle.'

They were silent for a few moments, then Valentine said quietly, 'I found them very destructive – quite elemental, really.'

'Better destructive and elemental than passive, wouldn't you think?'

Valentine said, 'Yes, of course. I *am* superficial. I do know that.'

62

Hester had the feeling that this was what she had been trying to say all the time, some kind of necessary confession.

They talked of other things – the vicarage garden party, public lending right, the pleasures of a fuchsia hedge. Valentine said, looking out of the window again, 'That boy is talking to himself.'

'To the wistaria, I expect. He seems to have an affinity with growing things. I took him because I thought he needed help, but he is so good that it is I who need him now.'

'Who is he?'

'Shirley Treglowan's boy.'

Valentine looked at him with interest. Michael was calling on Shirley Treglowan this very morning to discuss this lad. She said, 'Oh, that harpy!'

'I don't think she is – not that I wouldn't welcome a harpy or two in our midst.'

'He is making faces at us.'

'I'm afraid he does that rather a lot. But I think it means something this time. I had better go and see.'

It was the kind of cue Valentine seldom missed. When she had gone Hester went out to Desmond. 'You must learn to communicate verbally,' she said. 'It will be expected of you at university.'

They discussed the staking of peonies.

'You won't be able to stop pulling those faces if you aren't careful. You ought to see someone about it.'

'I'm all right. I know a hawk from a handsaw.'

'Very clever. But look how he and his family ended up.' She pulled out a seedling foxglove. 'Would you like that, Desmond? Elsinore translated to your own home, bodies strewn about you – your mother, father, sister, perhaps?'

He looked at her, his face still for once, and she saw that he simply did not know the answer.

'The things I do, it makes me blush to think of them.' Shirley Treglowan moved a rack on which clothes were drying away from the one armchair. Michael sat down and she went into the kitchen soon returning with two cups of coffee which she carried to the door into the hall. 'Turn down that noise, Tracy,' she shouted. 'What did I buy you those earphones for?' She handed one cup to Michael Hoath. 'Where was I?'

'Blushing,' he said with a smile.

'Oh yes. It's only that I'm so hustled all the time and everything gets jumbled up and then I just jump, without looking, you know what I mean?'

'Perhaps an illustration might help.'

'I'm not a fool. It's just that there's never the time to get myself composed before things start happening. I always seem to come in half-way through – like people at the theatre who arrive late for a Pinter play. Not, of course, that it makes much difference with Pinter if you don't come in at the beginning. But usually it helps.'

Michael Hoath said, 'Yes, indeed.' Outside the branches of a lilac tree were thrashing about and the last of the blossom floated against the window pane. He had the sense of a strong wind blustering through his mind, shredding what ideas he had about this situation.

'If only I had time to compose myself.' The brown eyes looked at him, eager for understanding. He was himself a person who constantly reached out to others and he liked this eagerness in her. He inclined towards her, his free hand clenching and unclenching on his knee. He prayed that he would not fail her. 'Everything seems constantly to be falling apart around me and I like order. I make sure I have order in my classroom. I'm not one of those teachers who can't keep control. But when they are all on top of each other screeching there isn't time to sort out who did what to whom. I just plunge in and take one of them by the scruff of the neck – it always works. But it's not all that effective outside the classroom situation.'

'Has anything particular happened?' he asked, hoping to pin down one coherent statement before it billowed beyond his grasp.

Shirley thought about the scene yesterday – Desmond sitting there where the Vicar was now, listening to the transistor.

'Filth!' she had shouted and switched it off. 'I don't want to listen to any more of that filth!' She bit her lip. 'I'm not sure I can tell you about this.'

'Take your time.' He was glad of the respite.

She reviewed the scene.

'It's not filth. It's the news, Mum. It happens.'

'Now, you listen to me. Your sister came home today saying something dreadful about Pete Atwood. You know him? That fellow who's always doing things for people, mending their cars . . .'

'Yes, I know him. I could hardly help it, could I? With his mending cars in our yard and you getting mad at him.'

'Never mind that. He's unselfish. He'd do things for others while his own house fell down around him.'

'So what happened that's so awful?'

'Tracy was telling me how Kelly Parsons told her he poked about right up her stack. At least, that's what I thought she said. I couldn't move, I just stood there paralysed, wondering what I ought to do about it.'

'Her *stack*!' It was '' e first time she had had Desmond's full attention in quite a v. nile.

'It's a way, I suppose . . .'

'Kelly wouldn't use an expression like that.'

'Well, you never know. But as it turned out, he *had* been poking up a stack, trying to sweep the Parsons' chimney and he dislodged a lot of bricks that came down on his head and now he's in hospital. So I don't want to hear any more about all this business of child abuse.'

'Well done, Mum. You finally got there.'

'It just shows the way we are being conditioned to think.' But she had lost him again.

No, she couldn't tell the Vicar. But the incident was relevant to her thoughts. She said, 'Life is so awful for children nowadays. I never used to believe the things people said. I thought they had nasty minds. When the neighbours began to drop hints about Clifford – my husband – I was sorry for them, being so warped. Even when I got the phone call, I didn't take it seriously. I told him about it as soon as he came home. "I've had a phone call saying you've found yourself a fellow" and waited for him to laugh. Then he told me. He went off to Canada soon afterwards, saying we could start again there once he had found a job. I heard afterwards that his boy friend went with him.'

Michael looked at her, puzzled that a woman of such warmth and vitality, who seemed so robustly healthy, should have failed to sense some ambivalence in her husband. Had she thought of him as being like one of the more sensitive children in her class, one who needed rescuing? Was that it? Had she plunged in and picked Clifford up by the scruff to comfort and console him?

'What did it do to the children?'

'Tracy hasn't settled, but that's her age – all over the place.' She sounded as if she was talking about a jelly. 'It's not to do with her father. She behaves as if he never existed. She doesn't seem unhappy. Perhaps she has that sort of mind – with compartments where things can be locked away neatly. Or perhaps she's one of those people who can just leave things behind. She's a bit like that with her friends. If anyone lets her down, she never has any more to do with them. No one has a second chance with Tracy.'

'And Desmond?'

'Clifford was a very good father to Desmond, ever since he was tiny, bathing him, changing his nappies; when he got older he would read to him, play games, go for long walks. They were great companions. Clifford was a bit like Tracy in some ways. He could be good and kind and loving and great fun to be with – and then if it suited him, he would just walk away.

'I don't think Desmond really believed it had happened. He behaved as if it was a bad dream and we would all wake up and find Clifford still there. He talked about him as if he was on holiday – "When Dad comes back he'll fix that . . ." "I'm keeping this to show Dad when he comes back . . ." Well, Clifford had to come back to see to some legal matters and Desmond found out where he was staying and went to see him. He was so sure that once his father saw him everything would be the same as before. It would be like when he was a little boy and Clifford saw that he was hurt and hugged him.'

'What happened?'

'His father was angry. He told Desmond to get out and when Desmond tried to tell him how he felt, how we all needed him, he hit him. The Head of the school had arranged for him to see a

66

psychologist about that time and she tried to explain to Desmond that this showed that his father really cared about what he had done, that hitting out was a form of defence. I expect that's true, don't you? But I don't think Desmond really took it in. In fact, I don't know what he has taken in since; there hasn't been much in the way of what you would call meaningful communication between us.'

'Was it about that time that he became so interested in anthropology?'

'That was when it really took off; he'd always collected flints and fossils and such like.' She looked at Michael expectantly.

He said, knowing he was out of his depth, 'If the psychologist can't help him, I'm not sure what I can do.'

'It's just that when I heard you talking at that meeting about God and love, I thought you'd be the person to help Desmond.'

'I see. Yes, I see.' As he looked at her, she seemed to become disproportionately large, a creature whose expectations were beyond all reason. He thought, she is capable of the same quality of belief as the woman who knew she had only to touch the hem of His gown to be healed. He felt himself getting smaller and smaller, dissolving in his own inadequacy.

'I see. Yes, I see,' he repeated; and then, drily, 'I have talked to my wife about Desmond and she is prepared for him to come and work in the garden. I have to warn you, however, that she is herself a gardener – and you know what they say about there being no room for two gardeners. He will have to work under her instructions.'

'He won't mind that provided he likes the garden. Mr Venables and Miss Pascoe have gardens that slope upwards steeply and he loves that. Major Heneker has one of those dead level gardens where every plant knows its place and Desmond won't go near it. And he's such a kind man and might help Desmond to find a job while he's waiting to go to university. But Desmond doesn't notice people, only their gardens.'

'We'll have to see if he approves of our garden. And then, perhaps, when we get to know him better, if we get to know him better . . .'

He walked slowly when he left the house. He felt as if this woman had been raised up to confront him, not with the little flaws which are built into personality and can no more be helped than a cleft palate or a hare lip, but with a failure in the very heart of being.

His next call was on the church treasurer, Mr Pettifer. He wondered in how many other professions people were expected to swing so wildly between the profound and the trivial. Perhaps it wasn't so much a matter of profession as his own inability to stabilize his emotions.

Old Mrs Pettifer opened the front door to him. 'I come up to see if I can help,' she said aggrievedly. 'But she never wants me. Thinks I ought to stay in the granny flat and never put me nose out of it.' She left him standing in the doorway to the sitting-room. Here chairs were huddled into a stockade in the middle round which Mrs Pettifer, lean and hawk-faced, rode her vacuum cleaner, all the while whooping at Mr Pettifer, beleaguered in a large wing armchair.

'I'll take you into the parlour.' Mr Pettifer, a rotund, rosy-faced man with a perpetual rictal smile, was obviously delighted at the prospect of rescue.

'Indeed you won't!' Mrs Pettifer cried. 'I'll be doing that any minute.' She switched off the cleaner.

'I'm sorry. This is obviously a bad time to call.' Michael had heard rumours of Mrs Pettifer's cleaning activities, but had imagined that she relaxed her regime on Saturday mornings when her husband was at home.

'We'll be straight in no time,' she assured him and began to put the chairs back, fitting the legs carefully on to the appropriate dents in the carpet. Michael and Mr Pettifer shuffled awkwardly while she manoeuvred round them. She talked without stopping. 'Elsie Mannering said she never dusted until *after* she had vacuumed because it *created* dust. Can you imagine that?' She ran a duster along the top of a cabinet and walked to the window to examine it. 'That's it, then!' She turned to face them, holding the duster out for their inspection, a look of such incredulity on her face that her eyes seemed to start from their sockets. 'That's it, then! We'll have to see about that. I can't dust everything twice.'

As her husband said nothing and she obviously expected a reply, Michael said, 'I suppose perhaps when one moves furniture about it is bound . . .' He flapped his hands vaguely, feeling he was behaving like a vicar in a Ben Travers farce.

'But it is moved every day, every day of my life I move that furniture. There can't possibly be any dust in it.' She banged the back of the wing armchair and dust particles rose glittering in a shaft of sunlight which had penetrated the side of a net curtain. She turned to her husband. 'It's this old chair of yours . . .'

'If the chair goes, I go.' It was by no means clear that he was joking.

'One day . . .' Mr Pettifer said when he and Michael were at last alone. 'One day . . .' He gazed at the window as though at any moment the curtain might rise on an unfamiliar scene.

'Housework does seem to become a bit of an obsession with some women,' Michael said tentatively.

'A bit of an obsession? She starts at four o'clock in the morning.'

'Have you talked to her about it?'

'Talked? We haven't talked about anything for years.'

When Michael left, Pettifer said to him, 'If you want to discuss something with me another time, why not drop into the bank? Any time. I'm there until nine o'clock most evenings. I get home at nine-thirty and she is preparing for bed then.'

'I'm sorry.'

'Nothing to be sorry about.' Pettifer had become blandly cheerful. 'We manage, we manage very well on the whole. You just came at a bad time, Saturday morning.'

'There must have been a time when Pettifer could have said something to her,' Michael said to Valentine over lunch.

'And how do you imagine he tackled it?' She was annoyed that he had called on Shirley Treglowan. 'He wouldn't have told her directly, he would have talked about someone else's wife while all the time he was getting at her.'

'How can you possibly know that?'

'It's the way men behave. They like to think they are straightforward and women are devious. But really they are hopelessly cowardly, never daring to come to the point.'

He rubbed his hand across his forehead, feeling the beginning of a headache. 'So many problems without answers! And I'm the person who is supposed to have answers. Even the ones who have no faith think of me as a magician whose vocation it is to lay a healing finger on their pain. If I can't do that, I'm a failed priest.'

'Don't forget you have Norah Kendall coming in a few minutes.'

'I had forgotten.'

'Make it as quick as you decently can. I want to get into the garden.' She began to pile plates and dishes. 'I hope there was someone in the house when you saw Mrs Treharris or Herbert, or whatever her name is.'

'Yes, her daughter.'

'There she is now.' Valentine put down the tray and went into the hall. A minute later Michael heard her talking to Norah Kendall in the study. He carried the tray out into the kitchen.

'I could do without this,' he said when Valentine joined him. She turned away and ran water into the sink. As he looked at her averted face, the delicate curve of the brow, the secret, dusky hollow beneath the ivory cheekbone, he longed to cry out, 'Just once! Surely, just this once!' His arms ached to take this whole house in one agonized embrace, bringing wood and stone crumbling down around them.

Valentine said, 'She is waiting.'

He went into the hall and stood for a moment, hands clenched, face seamed and furrowed, while he relearnt the lesson which would never be completely accepted, that spontaneous affection cannot be provided on demand. Later in the day, when she had been through whatever mysterious – and who was not to say tormented – process which was necessary to open the bowels of her compassion, Valentine would probably give what she could of tender consolation. But never would she hold out her arms to him at the moment of his greatest need. Granted, he experienced rather too many such moments. Yes, yes, he would plead guilty to incontinence. But was he never, never to receive an immediate, unrehearsed gesture of love? He looked around him and caught sight of his face in the hall mirror, the wounded eyes quite ludicrously enlarged in the pain-puckered face. Were pain not to be ironed out before it is publicly enacted, he thought, we should be laughing our way through all the great tragedies.

He walked slowly down the corridor. The study door was open so that as he came towards the room he could see his visitor. She had automatically taken the brisk little chair with the straight back and perfunctory wooden arms which Valentine had named the stool of penitence, although few who sat there seemed to him particularly penitent. Penitence was out of fashion. Now he saw in the sloping shoulders and bowed head not contrition but the feeling of liberation experienced by the person about to lay down a burden. They come to me, he thought, sick at heart or troubled in spirit, but they don't need me and most of them don't really believe that they need God. Nowadays, they think they can heal themselves, talking their troubles through to the blissful conclusion that they are not the ones to blame, it is the fault of their parents, teachers, husband, wife. Blaming has taken the place of penitence in our enlightened society. Norah Kendall seemed to him to epitomize the irrelevance of his profession. Of course, it was a sin to think like this. He sat opposite her, aware that of the two he was the greater sinner and in no way drawn to her by this knowledge.

She raised her head and looked at him, immediately noting the lines of pain around the narrowed eyes. 'How you must curse people who come on a Saturday afternoon.' She spoke with wry concern, but the statement was too near the truth of his present condition for him to accept it with good humour.

'I am always available, I hope.' He was not given to pompous utterances and disliked himself the more.

'Of course.' Something trembled in her face which could have been laughter. She looked out of the window while she composed herself and the afternoon sun caught a glint of red in the pale hair. She was at her best now. He had noticed before that in her moments of stillness this woman had that especial gravity which one sees in the faces of people who are listening intently to music, its harmonies reflected in their ordered features. Seen in this light, she looked a woman in whom one would place trust, eminently more suited to the job of counselling than was he. It occurred to him that this was probably in her mind. She had come to talk about the ordination of women.

So sure was he of this that it was a few minutes before he realized that she was, in fact, speaking of something quite different. He was alerted to this not so much by her words as the painful embarrassment which they caused her. Valentine sometimes accused him of hearing only what he wanted to hear, but this was not true. When he was very tired his brain seemed to function intermittently, so that he missed key words in a sentence and English became like a foreign language, the gaps in the vocabulary making comprehension impossible. Now, suddenly aware of his mistake, he noted not only the embarrassment but the fluctuation in tone. Her voice was light and pleasant, but when she was agitated it took on a sharper edge and her face was distorted by the acidity of her tongue.

He said, 'Can we go back a little. Who is Samantha?'

'My stepdaughter. I explained . . .'

'Yes, yes. And your relationship with her is a difficult one?'

'Very.'

'That is predictable, isn't it? Was she close to her mother?'

'Hand in glove.' She flushed and bit her lip. 'I'm sorry about that. But I wouldn't need to talk about this if I was handling it well. And I don't blame her for being difficult. I was more than difficult when I was young. But I would have expected her to see that we can't live in the same house.' Again, the rising inflection was unpleasing.

He said with studied reasonableness, 'She is not asking to live with you, is she? Isn't it that she wants to make sure she still has a home?'

'But she doesn't still have a home! I couldn't make a home for her.'

Her jangling nerves made his head throb and his reply came rather too crisply, 'But as I understand it, you haven't yet tried.'

'I haven't made a home for my husband yet. And I am trying very hard to do that. I'm not ready to cope with Samantha.'

'One must not always wait to be ready – no task can be finished until it is begun.'

That was a definite rebuke, but a justified one, surely? He thought of Pettifer, staying at the office until nine in the evening because he could not face the misery of his home; of Shirley Treglowan, whose husband had left her for another man, and who had talked about her children with such concern without once mentioning her own pain. And here was a woman who had snatched at late happiness with little thought for the responsibilities of marriage and who was now reluctant to accept the intrusion of an unwanted daughter into her household.

'We think too much of happiness,' he said. 'And this is not what life has to offer. Those who grasp this fact come out well. Once let life become a search for small satisfactions and you will be in all sorts of trouble. The people who seem to have been singled out for tragedy – a retarded child, an invalid husband, personal incapacity – are so often the ones who find the mystery at the heart of life.'

The words came readily to him, since he so often reminded himself of their truth when he felt tempted to despair. They seemed, however, to offer little comfort to her. 'What am I to do, then?' Her voice was low and desolate. The face had lost its earlier clarity; it was as though a sculptor had changed it with a brush of the hand, drawing down the eyelids, pulling at the corners of the mouth and weakening the chin.

'I can't tell you what you should do. But it seems to me that you have taken up a position which leaves you no room for manoeuvre and that is always a mistake, isn't it?' The eyes looked out from the smudged features without a spark of intelligence, let alone understanding. He went on, giving examples as if to a child, 'You have said, "I will not have Samantha here" and you have forced your husband to insist that she comes. Wouldn't it be wiser to arrive at a more flexible arrangement – perhaps invite her for a weekend to talk about her problems?'

She shook her head jerkily, disposing of this suggestion as she might flick away a fly. 'You don't understand Samantha. She doesn't look for invitations, she regards herself as having right of entry. And once she has a foot in the door, nothing will move her until she herself decides to go. And that will be when she has caused as much mischief . . .' Her voice was spiralling shrilly.

He held up a hand. 'But you can't lock yourself up in your house as if it was a fortress, now can you, my dear?'

He saw her eyes darken and go cold when he said 'my dear' and himself regretted the words which, said without compassion, betrayed masculine impatience with a tiresome woman. His head was aching so much he could find no way of improving matters. He said, 'Will you think over what we have said during the next week and then talk to me again? As you know, I hear confessions at the church at six o'clock on Friday evenings. Why not come then?'

She said dully, 'Yes, of course.'

'And in the meantime we will both pray about this.'

Her eyes filled with tears. 'Thank you. Oh, thank you for that.'

He was disconcerted by this late show of humility and after she had gone spent some time in prayer until Valentine came to the window, arms full of hawthorn blossom. 'You are to say how beautiful it is,' she commanded gaily, 'and to assure me that it is a silly pagan superstition that it must not be brought into the house.'

5

'And so,' the voice came breathlessly to the difficult part. 'I know you'll understand if I say I can't come this week.'

Hester said, 'Bloody hell, Veronica!' She could see the whisk resting on the side of the bowl where she had set it down to answer the telephone. She could smell the lemon juice.

'I know you won't have made too many preparations as it's only me,' the voice continued, gaining strength now that the worst was past. 'I'm as disappointed as you are, but I really can't go away and leave the old aunt.'

'She's got neighbours, hasn't she? And Nurse.'

'But it's always me she wants at such times, poor old love.'

'So, you're not coming?'

'Hester, how can I? There is no one I want to see more than you at this moment, things have been pretty bleak lately and I was longing for one of our lovely long walks and a good talk in the evening and . . . But this is *duty*.' A pause, rather a long one. 'Are you still there?'

'Standing to attention.'

'I'll come next month, if that's all right with you. She'll be better by then.'

'If she hasn't broken the other one.'

'Even if she has, Nurse will have to cope.'

So why can't Nurse cope now? Hester wondered. She stood

asking the phone this question after she had put down the receiver. 'The answer,' she said aloud, 'is that I am Veronica's oldest friend, but I am not a duty – in fact, I am in the nature of a temptation. Friendship has an element of pleasure in it, so it is never wrong to put it to one side when duty calls. And quite right, too. All very proper and praiseworthy.' Yet how it stung, this assumption that one had no needs. But Veronica has others to consider, she told herself as she turned back to the kitchen, others more important than I. Tears pricked her eyes. Oh, the pain of never being at the centre of another's life! It was largely her own choice, of course, but that didn't mean she did not sometimes grieve over it, that path not taken.

'This is tosh!' she said, whisking more vigorously, the white of egg spattering the wall. When she was not writing, thoughts raced through her mind like undisciplined children who could not understand that while they might be welcomed and encouraged during one period of her day, they must behave themselves in more seemly fashion when she was not at her desk.

Later, as she came to terms with the clutter in the sink, she thought: how fast life moves! It doesn't allow us time to savour the joys of the present moment, and when we are old, we turn back, hoping to recapture the treasures we left undiscovered. And we get maudlin, unable to take small disappointments, such as the last-minute defection of a loved friend. She thought of the things she had never done – slept under canvas or gone to live on a barge. She would never do these things now. Why did they sound so much more interesting, the dramas of a vagrant life, than the long process of making a home in a particular place? It's the sending down of roots, she thought, as she put the last of the pans away, such a lengthy business it doesn't make for interesting chat. She looked round the room, rubbing her hands on her apron. I haven't slept around, either, and the man I loved I haven't seen for years and can no longer recapture my feelings for him.

She could not bring Harry's face to mind, but she saw her sister Sylvia as she had so often seen her in the past, standing across the table from her in this very room; the accomplice of childhood enterprises, the loving friend whose understanding had steered Hester through the less innocent adventures of maturity, the dear mother of Michael. It was Sylvia, not the defaulting Veronica, for whom she wept.

'It's me that should have died,' she said across the table. 'You were needed by so many people.'

No, no! She walked to the window and beat on the sill with her fists. 'We will have no self-pity.' Then she saw that there was not going to be much call for gladness, either. For here, approaching the back door with uncertain tread, was Andy Possett.

Andy Possett had a remarkably thin face with a fine, pale skin and soft pink lips and whenever she looked at him Hester was reminded of a flower pressed between the pages of a book. There was even a faint smell of squashed roses about his person. He lived in a small house for young men with psychiatric problems who had been released into the community because the regional psychiatric unit had found them too disruptive of its particular community. The home was run by a retired missionary, Mrs Hardacre, and loosely supervised by Social Services. Mrs Hardacre maintained that Andy was working through his problems. As Freud saw sexual implications in every object, so Mrs Hardacre, having wholeheartedly espoused the cause of Andy's recovery, was able to interpret even his more bizarre actions as symptomatic of progress. Recently he had appeared at St Hilary's wearing his underpants over his trousers and while most people regarded this as a deterioration in his behaviour, Mrs Hardacre would have none of such pessimism. 'People react like that because *they* have been troubled. The fact that he has decided to challenge them, to make himself noticed, is a sign of health,' she had insisted to Valentine who had duly reported the conversation to Hester. 'And, of course, the symbolism of pants over trousers is an acknowledgement on his part that the hidden depths must be brought out into the open.'

Hester was glad to see that on this occasion he had suffered a regression in so far as underclothes were concealed. He wore odd shoes, but this was understandable since Mrs Hardacre bought the odd shoes left over at jumble sales and distributed them to her charges.

Hester's friend Annie Cleaver, who was by way of being a saint and a constant source of discouragement to Hester, said that she did not mind Andy in the least and found him quite pleasant to have about the house because he did not want to talk all the time. Hester found him disturbing. She did not like situations over which she had no control. She did not object to the mentally unbalanced because they were different but because she did not know how to handle the problems which they presented. In a tight corner, Hester liked to know which way to jump.

She hoped that Desmond would not decide to put in an appearance in the garden. A constellation in which Andy was in conjunction with Desmond was one which she could only regard as ominous.

'I thought it was next week that you were coming,' she said.

He did not think this worthy of a reply. She wondered what would have happened if she had found it necessary to insist that this was not a convenient time for him to fix a shelf in the spare bedroom. When she was tired or upset her mind delighted in presenting her with a series of doom-laden scenarios.

'As it happens,' she said, leading him upstairs, 'my friend can't come this week, so it has really worked out quite well.'

He made no comment and she had not expected one. The remark was intended to discourage any further melodramatics on the part of her mind.

An hour later Charles Venables, who had just returned home from school and did not want to see another human being for a year, and certainly not within the hour, opened his front door to Hester.

'May I use your loo and then can I have a word with you?'

'Please.' He waved a hand towards the stairs and stood biting his lip, hoping Mrs Quince had put out a spare toilet roll. Even if it was not immediately required, he had pointed out more than once that it should always be reassuringly in evidence.

'I couldn't use my own,' Hester said when she joined him in the hall, 'because I can't get into it.'

'The door has jammed?'

'Andy Possett has taken possession.'

'Andy Possett,' he repeated, screwing up his eyes.

'Don't bother. If you knew him it wouldn't take a split second to bring him to mind. He does odd jobs around the town and he suffers from some kind of mental disorder which has never been specifically explained – to the layman, at least.'

'I see,' Charles said, in order to gain time. 'Mmmh. And what does he say?'

'Nothing. As far as I can tell, he isn't breathing. I have tried to get on to the home where he stays, but the telephone is off the hook – not an uncommon occurrence.'

'The doctor?' Keep calm, keep calm, Charles told himself.

'I rang my own doctor and his receptionist gave a sort of eldritch screech and conveyed the impression that at the moment he was on a trip to Outer Mongolia. I was to call back in seven years if Andy hadn't moved by then.'

Charles, fighting back rising panic, said, 'The police, then, I suppose.'

'I don't think I could do that to him. And, anyway, they know about him and I suspect they would despatch a constable to my house by way of the moor.'

Charles looked at her glassily, but she was a determined person and once her mind was set to some purpose she knew no shame. 'I'm sorry about this, Charles,' she said briskly, 'but I wondered whether you would go up my ladder and look in at the window. Just to make sure he hasn't done himself a mischief. Or . . .' since he looked as if he in his turn might suffer some kind of attack, 'would you hold the ladder for me?'

'No, no, of course you mustn't,' he said desperately. 'Oh no, no! I will, er . . . provided,' he snatched at a wisp of comfort, 'provided the ladder is long enough.'

'It's a roof ladder – the one your workmen often borrow from me.'

'It's not the sort of job for the fire brigade, I suppose?' he asked weakly when, after some trouble, they had the ladder up against the wall.

'It may well be, but not until we know what has happened to him.'

Charles had a bad head for heights and this, added to his dread of what he would find when he reached the window, made the ascent quite terrifying. Half-way up he was convinced that he was suffering a heart attack. In the hope that one fear might cancel out the other, he told himself that if this were the case he would undoubtedly fall from the ladder and be killed, or so seriously incapacitated that he would have to go into a home. He paused, resting his brow against the rung of the ladder and the first breeze of evening wafted a quite heart-rending smell of honeysuckle to his nostrils. He could see Hester below, looking impatient. At the door of a house further down the terrace a woman was shouting at the milkman, 'We *haven't had* that much wind to blow my note away. I'm not going to pay for what I didn't order.'

'Keep going. Don't look down,' Hester commanded. 'I can't have you stuck half-way up a ladder to add to everything.'

'I'm sorry,' he said faintly. 'I can't move. Not at the moment.'

He closed his eyes. Far below a brewery van was being loaded; the jarring of heavy crates sounded like distant gunfire. Charles clenched his hands on the sides of the ladder. A gate creaked and steps sounded on the path below.

'Having trouble?'

Beneath him Charles could hear Hester making explanations.

'Poor chap.' Such a nice voice, warm as hot syrup and just as soothing. 'I came to see how Desmond was getting on working for you. A good thing, wasn't it?'

'If you can do something, it may well be.' Hester sounded very cross.

'I'll bring him down and then I'll pop up and have a squint at Andy.'

Charles felt the ladder move beneath another weight, then a hand grasped his right ankle. 'I've got hold of you.' The voice was so reassuring that he was convinced against all common sense that her hand on his ankle would make him as near immortal as Achilles. 'Now, put this foot down on to this rung, slide your hands down a little, that's right. Now the other foot. Good! Keep going, easily, slowly, I've got hold of you, just keep going. Right foot now. There we ARE!'

He turned to see a robin-red face atop rounded curves of emerald and crimson. She seemed to be all the colours of the rainbow and he thought her the most radiant creature he had ever seen. It was quite some time before he realized it was only Shirley Treglowan wearing an exotic track suit that was too tight for her. He sat down on the grass and put his head in his hands. Hester leant on the ladder while Shirley went up. She did not even ask him how he felt. The milkman, recognizing a situation in which something strenuous might be demanded of him, walked briskly past.

'Well?' Hester called.

Shirley peered, tapped on the window pane, made 'Yoo-hooing' noises, then came briskly down. 'He's just standing there, right up against the door as though he had been turned to stone. It happened once in the Major's garden.'

'How long did it last that time, do you remember?'

'About three hours. The Major said he was quite resigned to having Andy as a piece of sculpture, peering at visitors through the rose bushes. I tell you what. I've got my bike. I'll go round to the home and get Mrs Hardacre to come along. I don't suppose she can bring him round, but at least she'll be here to take him home when he comes out of it.'

'Better still, I'll go in my car, if you and Charles wouldn't mind standing guard here.'

'I could go in my car,' Charles said wearily.

'You don't know Mrs Hardacre. And, anyway, you don't look fit to drive.' Hester felt she had treated him badly. 'Come into the house and I'll put out the whisky bottle and prepare a snack for you both before I go.'

Charles and Hester were so tired and confused by now that it did not occur to either of them that Shirley Treglowan could probably have unearthed Mrs Hardacre by the time Hester had produced the snack. Shirley did not repeat her offer because she was quite excited by the prospect of having a talk with Charles Venables.

'I am so looking forward to your lecture,' she told him as they consumed chicken sandwiches in Hester's sitting-room.

Her eyes shone with such eager anticipation that a man less sure of his ability might have feared to disappoint her. What misgivings Charles had, however, were concerned with the shortcomings of his audience. 'Really? I am beginning to wonder why I agreed to do it. How many people in this town will have read *Anna Karenina*?'

'Well, I have and I think it's a wonderful book. It's all gone, lost to us, isn't it? That world, I mean. People giving up everything for love.' The Russian revolution had produced the Soviet state, but it was the giving all for love which seemed to her to be the important change. He was not disposed to criticize her for this. 'You can have love whenever and wherever you want it now – and suddenly it's not around any more. There were boundaries then. Do you think you can only have love when there are boundaries? I mean, do we need forbidden territory stretching away beyond the frontier?' She asked these questions as though it really mattered that they should be answered.

It was quite apparent to Charles that here was a young woman who was thirsting for improvement. If her enthusiasm was a little raw and her questions betrayed too close an acquaintance with the cinema, she must nevertheless be dealt with kindly. Undoubtedly there was here an understanding to be awakened, a mind which might respond to proper guidance. This was more than could be said for most of the boys whom he taught. Charles was no pedant. Literature to him was a living thing and while Shirley might thirst for improvement, he yearned for evidence of sensitive appreciation.

'I think you can only have great art when there are boundaries,' he said cautiously. 'And perhaps passion needs a framework of a kind. I don't know about love.'

She looked at him sympathetically. 'I don't know about it, either,' she said sadly. It occurred to him that at this stage of her aesthetic development she was prone to the temptation to identify in too personal a way with works of art – something which he had noted tended to happen to people whose interest was not entirely cerebral. He decided that it would be wise to say something brisk and sensible about his lecture.

She was looking at him in a way that made him feel she had wrongly interpreted his silence. People rarely looked at Charles with sympathy. He did not project himself as a person in need of sympathy – self-sufficient was the way in which he saw himself. Yet now he experienced that sense of the organs of his body loosening their control that he had had as a child when his mother said to him, 'I want a word with you.' He had always felt an immediate guilt, even if he had not offended against any of her household rules. He was very suggestible. Quite suddenly, he felt himself in some obscure way to be unfortunate and in need of consolation. As he looked at Shirley Treglowan he could not think of anything brisk to say about his lecture. She had a good colour naturally and either her earlier exertions or the whisky had heightened it so that her face seemed blazingly bright and he was reminded of the sleigh ride in *War and Peace* and thought that this was how Natasha must have looked, exhilarated, rushing headlong downhill. He said, 'I haven't thanked you for so gallantly coming to my rescue.'

'Oh that, well . . .' He was pleased to note that she was not in the least brash. 'I think you were very brave even to try. I can't go in a lift. I always tell my kids – "I'll give the last drop of my blood for you, but if anything happens to you in a lift, you're on your own."'

'The last drop of my blood'. Oh dear, oh dear! She really had a long way to go.

Charles had frequently regretted the fact that nowadays it is almost impossible for two people to remain in the same room and be silent; that, in fact, to come upon a couple so engaged would be more convincing proof of intimacy than catching them in an embrace. Perhaps some such thought was in the mind of Andy Possett when he opened the sitting-room door. Certainly, he looked very stern as he gazed upon Charles and Shirley. There was now a rather alarming silence involving three people. Charles noted that he carried a tool bag from which a hammer protruded.

It was Shirley who spoke first. 'Finished for today, have you, then, Andy?' She nodded her head busily to illustrate comprehension of the situation and smiled to show that this was all as it should be.

Andy said, 'I'll see Miss Pascoe tomorrow.' He turned on his heel and walked out of the room. They watched him go slowly down the garden path, his tool kit slung over one shoulder.

Shirley said, 'Phew!'

Charles said, 'I think Hester may feel that we should have kept him here until she arrived with Mrs Hardacre.'

Hester did.

Valentine was talking to Desmond as they gardened. She talked a lot to him and always about things which interested him; the properties of the soil – what it would nourish and what it would fail to support, the remarkable adaptability shown by squirrels in their approach to the nut stocking, the intractability of snails and the industry of ants. When he made a contribution she accepted or rejected it according to its merits. The matter at issue was the garden, its flowers, its mollusc, insect and birdlife. Polite conversation had no place in their exchanges.

'Ugh!' She shook her head vigorously and the halo of gnats danced to its movement. She would stop working now, Desmond thought glumly, and sure enough she said, 'This is the time of evening when one should be indoors.'

Reluctantly he began to collect the gardening implements. She said, 'When you have cleared away would you like to look up that wild flower you were describing? I'll bring you a fruit drink in the study.' She did not ask him to be sure to wash his hands, she had already observed that he handled books with respect.

Desmond, delighted to have the freedom of the study, accelerated the cleaning-up process, rubbing away the earth from the hoe before hitching it on a hook on the wall of the shed.

'How do you find him?' Michael asked when Valentine came into the kitchen where he was pressing a lime over a jug containing a slightly bitter concoction of his own devising. It was a splendid thirst quencher and very refreshing but no one had ever asked the Hoaths for the recipe. Valentine maintained that this was due to the fact that English tastes are regrettably bland.

'He's an odd boy.' She cut another lime and handed it to him. 'But not antagonistic. I don't feel any antagonism, do you?'

'I don't feel anything at all. He is very strange.' Michael looked into the garden where Desmond was washing his hands beneath the garden tap, although he could perfectly well have come into the kitchen. His body conveyed an impression of pain, as if it had been stretched on a rack until all the suppleness had gone from the limbs. Yet, in spite of the appearance of dislocation, Michael had earlier seen him move with a kind of swooping grace, feet barely seeming to touch earth. 'I was watching you both out in the garden and I thought to myself, I have no idea what that boy sees. Of course, I don't know exactly what it is you see, but I am fairly sure it is something akin to my own vision. Whereas when I look at that blackbird perched on the wire up there, I have no idea what his view of our garden is. Or Desmond's.'

'Yes, I know what you mean.' Valentine licked the flesh of a squeezed orange. 'Like Neanderthal man, observing *homo sapiens* from a safe distance. Is it just a game he plays or is it more serious?'

Desmond, drying his hands on a piece of sacking, was well aware of his separateness but concerned only in so much as it troubled his mother. He loved his mother because he knew that his mother loved him. For her sake he had attended sessions with the educational psychologist who had gently tried to uncover the deep resentments which she felt he must be concealing. They had confronted each other across a chasm which for Desmond was quite literally there. Every time he sat down to talk to her he could see the precipice and one leg of her chair perilously close to its jagged edge. She was a plump, warm woman, not unlike his mother, and reminded him of a roly-poly pudding, oozing all the good things in which his tongue delighted, and it worried him to see her perched on the edge of oblivion – because oblivion was undoubtedly the place to which he would consign her were she to go too far; he would certainly not put out a hand to bring her to his side of the chasm. In the end she had pronounced his troubles too deep-seated for her to reach. His mother had firmly rejected the suggestion that

Desmond should see a psychiatrist. 'He will work his way out of it,' she had affirmed. And Desmond, who felt much safer on his side of the chasm, was none the less sorry because he would have liked to prove his mother wiser than the experts. But not at the price of bridge building.

He closed the shed door, took off his boots and hurried towards the house, going quietly through the open French windows and making his way to the study. It was not the dictionary of wild flowers which he took down from the shelf, but a book which he had come across a week ago. He was reading it when Michael Hoath came in with that rather awful fruit drink and a bowl of sugar – 'In case you find it a trifle bitter.' He had already contrived to upset some of the liquid and the glass was sticky. Desmond put the book carefully to one side before accepting the glass, and Michael saw the title – *The Star Thrower* by Loren Eiseley.

'An odd book, that – hardly one of the seminal works on anthropology.'

The moment the amused, dismissive words were spoken he regretted them. Desmond had not seemed to respond, yet for the first time something happened between these two. Understanding was too cerebral a word for a purely physical experience, the smarting of a wound exposed to the air. As he fingered the book Michael recalled how he had felt years ago when a master had smiled to himself when he found him reading *Look Homeward, Angel*; seeing his distress, the man had said, kindly enough, 'There's a lot to be said for exploring new continents. Have you come across Carson McCullers? Very much in command of her material, I always feel.' But it was the excess which Michael had loved in Wolfe, the passion which burst the seams of fiction.

As for the matter of being in command of material, neither the man nor the boy in this room gave the impression of having achieved harmony between mind and body. Movements were not well co-ordinated and one felt that the objects which they approached, furniture or even books, were under threat. Desmond handled glass and sugar bowl as though deliberately taking risks with them – a small exercise in the possibilities of destruction. In Michael Hoath's case, the impression was one of over-eagerness. Neither was a naturally studious person and each brought a store of unused energy into the book-lined room. Some people seem to attain early in life the air of a finished product; while others must labour unceasingly at the process of moulding and refining. One felt that, however long they might live, Michael Hoath and Desmond Treglowan would always present an appearance of incompletion, the suggestion of work still in progress.

Michael went to a shelf where the books were tightly packed. His fingers groped impatiently, scraping the knuckles before he managed to pull one volume free. 'This is Eiseley's *The Unexpected Universe*.' He pushed the book towards Desmond. 'You might like to borrow them both.'

Desmond received this olive branch with every appearance of apathy. Michael did not blame him. He said, 'I'd like them back. I do dip into them from time to time.'

'Perhaps you should write your name in them?' Desmond suggested curtly. 'In case I forget where I got them from.'

Michael refrained from saying 'I trust you' which Desmond would have found not only offensive but burdensome, spoiling his pleasure in reading because he felt himself bound by some obligation of honour. He wrote his name in both books and handed them to Desmond who departed soon afterwards.

A fine mess I made of that, Michael thought. But what could this little-known American anthropologist have to say which was relevant to Desmond? And yet he and Valentine had been fairly ruthless in turning out books before this latest move, but Eiseley's books remained. Why, he wondered? The answer came to him some time later, as is the way of answers, when he should have had his mind on other things. He found it rather disconcerting. It was for a certain rawness which he valued these books; there was too much pain in them to throw them away. One could only hope their appeal to Desmond was rather different.

Charles's lecture was to be held in the United Reformed Church Hall. The town had increasingly to cater for the needs of an ageing population which included a high proportion of retired professional people, many of whom had travelled west in search of kinder air and cheaper housing. It was these people who were behind the attempt to establish a university of the third age – a concept which greatly enhanced the attraction of courses and lectures designed for those of mature years. Shirley Treglowan and Valentine Hoath found themselves considerably younger than most of those present. Shirley approached Valentine with diffidence.

By the standards of the town, which were not demanding, Valentine Hoath looked expensive and, which was rather more offensive, elegant. Shirley thought she must spend a lot of money on clothes and appearance generally. In fact, the dark, upswept curls owed their stylishness more to the shapely head and long neck than to the attention of a hairdresser. As for the grey suit which Shirley so admired, it had been bought several years ago at one of Marks and Spencer's sales; Valentine had trimmed the skirt and pockets with turquoise braid and had lined the tie with turquoise silk. She had little dress money but a flair for transforming the mundane. It was doubtful whether the townswomen would have warmed to her had they known this, money being more acceptable than flair.

'The Vicar not coming?' Shirley asked.

'I'm afraid he doesn't have much time for reading, let alone discussing what he has read.' Valentine was aware of sounding like the worst kind of clergy wife, speaking from a higher horse than ever the husband mounted.

'Perhaps I could sit beside you, then. Would you mind? I don't know anyone here.'

Valentine, surprised but not displeased that Michael's absence should seem a bonus, moved her handbag from the adjacent seat.

'Or perhaps you were keeping a place for someone else?' Shirley hovered, unsure of herself.

'Only for Hester, who probably won't come.'

The Rector's wife moved down the row in front of them and smiled distantly at Valentine. Later she told her husband, 'I can't imagine what your flock would think if I turned up at meetings looking like a fashion model.'

'I get nervous going out where I'll meet strangers. Isn't it silly?' Shirley sat down and folded her arms round a straw bag into which she had stuffed a jersey in case the mist had come up from the river by the time the meeting was over. She rested her chin on her hands and surveyed the room like someone peeping over a protective hedge. 'I nearly turned back, but I told myself this was a good way of meeting people – not just social, learning together.'

Valentine, recognizing that nerves dictated the flow of talk, probed cautiously. 'You don't go out much? I suppose teaching is very demanding.'

'Oh, it's not that. It was Clifford going.' Shirley bounced the bag up and down on her knees. 'I was stunned. For years I couldn't seem to get myself going. I dropped out of everything.'

'He has married again?'

'It wasn't like that. It was a fellow.'

Valentine was startled. Michael had not mentioned this. There were things he kept to himself, and rightly, but as this must be common knowledge there was no point in his not telling her. Probably it had shocked him. He had deep reserves of shockability. Valentine was shocked herself. Perhaps it was Shirley's presence, ample flesh and blood overflowing the short puce tunic one could scarcely call a dress, which brought the reality home like the thrust of a knife in her own breast. The humiliation of it! And, worse than the blow to one's pride, the fragmenting of the always fragile perception of one's own personality. Most bitter of all, to be subjected to pity and the questionably motivated attempts to help one – odious phrase – talk things through. I should kill myself, she thought, that is what I should do. She felt icy calm, as though this death was actually unfolding and had a clear picture of herself on the bridge over the river; then realized it was *Rosmersholm* she had in mind. Blast Ibsen!

'I didn't guess,' Shirley was saying. 'Several of my friends told me they had always wondered. They must have thought I was an awful fool.'

'There is never a shortage of people who are wise after the event.' Valentine decided she must try to be more tolerant of this woman who did not seem so predatory now that one knew of her misfortune. 'What about the theatre club? Wouldn't that be an outlet?'

'You're playing Hedda.'

'Yes. How news does get about.'

'Rehearsals going well?'

Valentine shrugged her shoulders. 'Early days.' She was going through her bad period at the theatre. The prompt was too eager, but must be tolerated – one must never antagonize the back stage staff, the poor dears were so aware of their inferiority. The producer was a different matter and Valentine had already had to make it clear that she was unable to work with someone who mapped out every move like a drill sergeant.

Shirley said, 'I do props for some of the shows. It's the one thing I've carried on with. There's nothing like a theatre for accommodating misfits, is there?'

Valentine, to whom this idea had not presented itself, made no reply.

Shirley went on, 'I'm always making things for the kids in my class, helping with their projects. It comes in useful in the theatre, that soft of gift. I did a lot of the props for the opera company when they did *Peter Grimes* – fish and all that. Desmond and Tracy and Clifford all had parts as fisherfolk. It was such a happy time.'

It was just the kind of family activity which Michael would have relished had they had children. Momentarily, Valentine was surprised by an extraordinary blend of pain and sweetness, a brief taste of borrowed happiness.

She looked about her, irritated, not at all sure that she wanted to sit here listening to Charles Venables whittering on about Anna and passion.

Women outnumbered men, but not to a marked degree. Predictably among those present were ex-civil servants and retired teachers, but there were also several engineers, senior electricians, draughtsmen, abandoned by the firms to which they had given their lives and now, late in their day, anxious to discover the mysterious world of the imagination which had been largely hidden from them during the years when the blood flowed most strongly in their veins.

Charles did well by his audience. Something came alive in him which was allowed no outlet outside the constraints of literature. He spoke as one who has treasures to unfold and left little doubt that he loved Anna more faithfully than Vronsky. It was the only way in which Charles ever risked himself. His reward was not great. His audience was attentive and, one might have thought, sympathetic to his interpretation of the book and its major characters. Later discussion revealed a rather different state of affairs. There was not, it seemed, a great deal of sympathy for Anna and a general feeling that the book should have been about something else. The men who had come to serious literature for the first time had brought with them a requirement that it should define itself in their terms. In spite of a vague need to extend their horizons, they were not prepared to investigate a side of their personality which had never been used, but rather sought to imprison the book within their own limits. Charles was given to understand that they had expected something pretty tough-minded from a writer in the twilight period before the dawn of the great revolution. To them, Anna was an irritating irrelevance. One man asked, 'Do you think perhaps she represents the old way of life that can't survive in the climate of revolution?'

'If so, it is a very idealized way of representing life under the Czars, wouldn't you think?' Charles did not bother to conceal his impatience.

The women were more ambivalent. To Charles, Anna was true woman, but they seemed to have a different concept of womankind. Woman was emerging, what she truly was had not yet been revealed, but one thing was for sure, she wouldn't be like Anna Karenina. It wasn't just that they had little patience with a woman who placed such high value on passion as distinct from sex, some of them actually showed a tendency to defend Karenin.

'She is one of those women who want things all ways,' a retired college lecturer said tartly. 'Even when Karenin offers a divorce she won't accept it because the offer doesn't quite meet the picture of herself which she must at all times preserve.'

Another woman said, 'She must constantly see herself as noble, not beholden to others, a person who rises above the sordid.'

It seemed that Anna belonged to a kind of woman who would have no allies – her own sex turned against her now as they had then. But then she had sinned against society. What had she done, Charles wondered, to arouse such dislike in these liberated women? So close on the thought it seemed almost miraculous, he heard Valentine Hoath speak.

'Do you think it is possible that when we look at her we see something we have lost? We have become so clever, so tutored, so self-aware' – a hint of mockery in the tone suggested she might not be including herself in this examination – 'that we can't find our way back to our more unconsidered – intuitive, I suppose you might say – beginnings?'

'I don't know about that,' the college lecturer dismissed Valentine with contempt. 'I think the old Countess had the measure of her – "She must show herself something out of the way."'

Valentine had no mind to be thus dismissed. 'Or perhaps,' she said, appearing to reflect, 'it is that women secretly detest the rare ones among them who can win the adoration of men without effort – quite spontaneously.'

Charles was reminded of his occasional attendance at the golf club functions at which he had noted that women were quite indulgent of flamboyance, sexual expertise, even a little piracy, but were sour about the president's wife, a Botticelli Venus to whom all eyes were drawn. 'The silly cow doesn't know how it happens, let alone what to do about it!' As though it was like having a fortune and not investing it.

'And as for being "a person who rises above the sordid" – I think that was what you said?' Valentine turned courteously to the woman behind her. 'Do many women enter into intrigues which they can see from the beginning to be sordid, even today?'

The woman, who felt herself impaled on Valentine's lofty brows, muttered, 'I don't know that the word intrigue applies any more in that context.'

'But sordid does. Personally, I find myself totally in sympathy with Anna – in this respect, at least.'

'I can't understand her leaving her son, though,' Shirley

Treglowan said, holding the straw bag tightly to her breast. 'I can't understand any woman leaving her children.'

'It happens all the time.' The college lecturer smiled condescendingly at Shirley.

'Yes, I know all about that.' Shirley bridled. 'You see plenty of that teaching, believe me, and you see what it does to the kids. They didn't ask to be brought into the world, poor little buggers.'

Across the room Valentine smiled at Charles. A meeting of true minds, he thought. The evening had not been a total failure.

Hesketh Kendall was sitting at the back of the hall next to Hester who had come in late. Charles wondered what he had expected from the lecture. Whatever it was, his glum expression suggested he had not found it.

When the discussion was finally brought to a close and Charles had been duly thanked, coffee was served. Charles, finding himself standing beside Hesketh, said, 'I hoped you might have defended my client.'

'If I took any brief, it would be Vronsky's. I can't understand why the poor fellow should get such a bad press. After all, he gave up his career for the woman and it must have been hard for him when she started whingeing.'

Hester thought that had there been a suitable weapon to hand Charles might well have assaulted Hesketh Kendall.

Near by a man was saying, 'No one hates change more than your countryman. Khrushchev couldn't get the peasants to change any more than Levin could.'

A woman said, 'No, no, he detested women! At least he kills off Anna cleanly, but look what he did to Natasha.'

As they left the hall, Hesketh Kendall said to Charles, 'Why not a lecture on Mrs Gaskell? Now, there is a woman one can be comfortable with.'

'I can read Mrs Gaskell on my own,' Shirley Treglowan said to Charles. They seemed to have found themselves alone in the car park. The mist had not come up from the river and it was a warm, scented night. Charles, fidgeting with his car keys, supposed he would have to offer her a lift. He thought it unmannerly of Hester to have departed with such alacrity, taking Valentine with her. He had himself intended to offer Valentine a lift. 'But I need help with Tolstoy otherwise I miss so much. You wouldn't think of taking a small class? I'm sure there would be others who would be interested. We could do Dostoevsky, too.'

'Can I give you a lift?'

'I've got my bike, thanks just the same.'

He was so relieved that he said, 'Yes, I don't see why not, provided there are sufficient people who are interested. We might even take in Turgenev.'

6

'Have you come to convert me?' the old woman asked Michael Hoath.

He had come to see her because her daughter had said that her mother was dying and would like to receive a call. The old woman's head was bald and fragile as a bird's egg, the eyes receding into the sockets were no more than a glimmer at the bottom of a well. She looked as if she was indeed dying, but she gave no indication of welcoming the attentions of her parish priest. He said, 'No, Mrs Merrivale, I have come to see if there is anything you need.'

'Well, there isn't. Not from you.' She moved a claw fretfully towards the chair beside the bed. 'But you had better sit down and take the weight off your feet since you've come.'

He sat down and waited.

She had reached the stage where the burden of consideration for others could at last be shed and she took her time before she said, the phrases separated while she paused for breath, 'We have a difference of opinion on the matter of religion, Vicar, and I have the advantage of you because I am soon to discover which of us is right.'

'If you do make a discovery, I shall be the one who is right,' he pointed out.

Her hands plucked at the sheet. 'How intolerable to think that if either of us is to be in a position to say "I told you so" it must be you.' This thought exhausted her for some moments, then she went on, 'The only way religion could be made bearable would be that at the end a voice would assure me, "You were absolutely right, Gertrude Merrivale, not to ingest all that codswallop."' Even in extremity the pauses were well chosen. He recalled that she had been an actress.

He said, 'When it comes to the matter of codswallop, you may well be right.'

The lids drooped over the drowned eyes. 'Don't patronise me.'

'I am far from patronising you. I have enough troubles of my own with religion.'

'Don't unload them on me.'

'It doesn't leave us much to talk about. Would you like me to go? I don't want to tire you.'

She rolled her head to one side on the pillow; he assumed rather than saw that she was looking at him. 'You wouldn't care to give me a large overdose of those pills?'

'No.'

'I thought not. Then I think you had better go.'

When he reached the door, she said in a stronger voice, 'What would you do if you wanted a way out of all this and they wouldn't let you go?'

He thought for a moment, his hand on the door handle. Downstairs the radio was on and he could hear someone reading the shipping forecast. He came back and sat down beside her. 'I remember an old priest whom I knew years ago. He felt he had come to the natural end of his life. So he just refused food, gently and without fuss. He was very frail and ill and he went quite peacefully in a few weeks. You could refuse to drink as well, but that would be more difficult.'

'Turn my face to the wall?'

'To God.'

'You'd best be gone. I'm tired. Don't look so miserable, you've done your best.'

The daughter was waiting at the foot of the stairs.

'I'm afraid she hasn't much use for me,' he said. 'But if you want me to come again, I will, of course.'

What was I about in there? he asked himself as he went into the street. Doing unto others as I would they should do unto me when my end comes, I suppose. We should be allowed to go when Death comes for us without having the medical profession trying to intervene. But to go unbelieving?

He walked slowly down the terraced street. It was a warm early summer evening. Light sparked from the roofs of parked cars and there was a hothouse smell of geraniums. Yet he had an impression of all-pervading greyness. I can't solve these questions, he thought wearily, they are beyond me. He prayed for the old woman, a dry empty prayer from a dry empty spirit.

His childhood had been happy but since then some essential ingredient had been missing from life. He had not had much success in his ministry. Preferment did not bother him, but he cared deeply about his ministry. Now, it seemed to him that he was doomed to fail in this, the most important part of his life. The number of communicants at St Hilary's was low in comparison with his previous parish and the congregation was elderly. Recently a few younger women had started to come to church including, rather to his surprise, the divorcee who had been so articulate during his meeting with the women's group. But he felt nervous about this development, unsure what the church had to offer such women. The Parochial Church Council was dourly concerned with the maintenance of the fabric. Much could be put down to the long illness of his predecessor, but the dispirited, defeated air was reflected in the town itself. It had a quiet, rather sad aspect and it seemed to him the people had no fire in their bellies. He was by nature an ardent, hopeful man, eager for challenges, who might have done rather better in the mean streets of Brixton; but that very same nature made him dependent on the responses of others, too much in need of warmth and appreciation. The challenge of indifference – the quiet rebuff, the turning away from the outstretched hands, the sour response to the opening of the heart, ate away at the very root of his strength. And it wasn't as if he was very successful in his personal life. The treacherous little thought slipped into his tired brain before he could guard against it.

*

He was late at the church for Confession. Often no one came so it might not matter. But as he opened the porch door he saw that a woman was sitting at the back, head bowed. After the bright sunlight the church seemed very dark and moments passed before he could see clearly. Faint light shafted from the south and the lazy movement of a branch beyond the window sent green ripples across a pillar. The woman who was waiting tilted her chin as people do sometimes when they are swallowing a particularly indigestible thought. He recognized the distinctive head of Norah Kendall, the meagre knot atop the upswept hair, a style which Valentine said did not suit her because the hair was so fine and she was too old for the wispy look to be becoming. On this occasion, however, the light was kind to her, restoring the straggling pieces to something of an earlier glory. He felt guilty because he had forgotten that he had asked her to see him here, but he had had a busy day and there was nothing to justify the feeling almost akin to dread which the sight of her aroused in him. He had suggested that she should come here because he did not want her to get into the habit of calling at the vicarage. Now perhaps he must pay for this lack of charity. For some reason, he did not announce his presence in speech but sat down beside her.

She did not look at him immediately but turned her head towards the south door, looking out to the graveyard, a hand cupped lightly across her lips while she composed herself. He waited. When eventually she faced him there was no hint of the archness which made her seem a rather tricky woman.

'I couldn't do it,' she said simply. Her face – and it did indeed seem to be the whole face that was under pressure – crumpled. But she meant to control herself and did. She repeated with a dull exhaustion which shocked him, 'I couldn't do it.' She might have been given some physical trial which had left her drained and defeated.

At first he could not remember what words of his had provoked this reaction which seemed so inappropriate to anything he could have intended. She went on, 'I tried. I wrote three letters to Samantha and tore them all up. I even got as far as the pillar box with one of them. But I couldn't go through with it.' She said no more, but bowed her head and looked down at her hands in her lap, inert in failure.

In that moment he knew instinctively that there had been too much failure in this life. The signs of strain and weariness, lightly etched on the face though they might be, were unmistakable and should have told him that here was a woman living beyond her spiritual capacity, daily giving more than she could afford. Why had he not realized that for her it might be costly to lead what he, in his arrogance, dismissed as a limited spiritual life? He saw, as if it was a physical thing, the burden which this woman carried, a burden in excess of her strength which she had nevertheless borne into her forties without allowing it to break her. And the effort was not permitted to show; dignity was precariously retained and the face she turned to the world was more remarkable for good humour than martyrdom. How was it that he had not seen this? Why had he allowed his mind to concentrate on the negative aspects of an undoubtedly complex and troubled personality? Instead of offering consolation, he had lectured her and told her where her duty lay. The memory filled him with disgust and self-loathing. How could he begin to make amends? He knew only too well that once make a criticism which wounds, nothing said subsequently – more important though it may seem to the speaker – will have any effect; however positive and glowing with warm appreciation the tribute offered, to the victim it will be seen merely as the sugar coating to the bitter pill. He had found out in his own life that barbs go deeper than ever Cupid's dart.

On an impulse, he said, 'Why don't we go into the graveyard and talk about this? I may well have been the one who was wrong.'

She looked taken aback and not entirely pleased, as if he had presented her with an unmerited gift which she would not know how to use. Then she got up and walked towards the door into the graveyard and he followed. He had it in his mind that he should talk to her informally, not in his capacity as a priest. He remembered, as he stooped to cross the threshold, that moment many years ago when the family G.P. had turned away from his swivel chair and come to sit beside him to talk as a friend about his dear mother's illness.

There were bottles of coke and potato crisp packets in the grassy moat in which the church walls were now sunk. He knew that one or two people came to hear the nightingales but did not like to think that the graveyard offered other night-time attractions. He hoped this litter could be laid at the door of the choir boys.

The graveyard was not easy of access, having the church building as the northern boundary and high walls which separated it on two sides from the back premises of neighbouring shops and on the south side from the vicarage garden. As a result chance passers-by scarcely registered its existence. It was no longer used for burials and now resembled a small secluded garden with its tall trees and grassy mounds. Only a few ancient graves, the inscriptions on their headstones almost indecipherable, bespoke its province.

The trees provided a welcome shade on this warm evening. Michael Hoath and Norah Kendall sat on a bench beneath the great cedar. A low bough had recently been lopped and the smell of cedarwood brought to Michael's mind an old carved box belonging to his grandfather which had seemed to him as a child to release into the fusty suburban room the magic of some far place. The smell, or the peace of the garden, seemed to have a healing effect on Norah, for she sat with eyes half-closed, breathing more steadily. She was wearing a blue shirt and a dark blue skirt which gave the appearance of a uniform. Even now, more relaxed as she had become, there was the suggestion of a person nodding off while on duty.

'Were you nursing right up to the time of your marriage?' he asked.

She shook her head. 'I had cancer – a mole in my side. I was lucky, but it seemed to take a lot out of me at the time. I had to give up nursing. I was doing parish work when I met Hesketh.'

'You have had a lot to contend with.'

'The cancer was bad luck; but make no mistake about it, this hump on my back which I carry around,' she tapped her shoulder blade, 'that is *me*. My father was an unsuccessful farmer – he would have been unsuccessful at anything he attempted, he just happened to fail on the land. He could never see any job through. I don't think he was lazy physically, the mental energy gave out. I'm much the same. I've done better than him and my brothers because I chose an occupation where my duties were laid down very specifically and there were people around to crack the whip when my powers of application failed.'

'Your parents are still alive?'

'No. My father died of cancer. My mother died of looking after him, only she lingered a long time. I looked after her – not very praiseworthily. She adored my brothers who stayed away when she was ill. We didn't get on well and we were up to each other's tricks. Patient and uncomplaining, I was not! I suppose that was one of the reasons why I married Hesketh, to prove to myself that I could care for another person satisfactorily. He had charm and he gave the appearance of being a well-balanced person, which I needed. He had work which he seemed to relish and which – so I imagined – would prevent his leaning too heavily on me. It seemed to be one of those situations where it would be hard to fail. But I'm good at extracting failure from any situation.'

They talked about her marriage. She spoke with none of the edgy defensiveness which so often marked her manner, quietly and with a sad humour. 'Why I should think I could provide more easily for two than for one, I can't imagine.' Then, after a moment's reflection, she corrected herself. 'It isn't only that I can't cope, it's that I expected the wrong things. I thought that love would come from caring. I had missed out on the love that is supposed to hover over our cradle and still thought I might get it. It was selfish and immature and quite unrealistic, but that was what I hoped for. Unfortunately, Hesketh wants a great deal of mothering. He isn't much interested in love – or sex. That may be my fault, of course.'

They began to talk more generally about the mistakes which are made when people in their hunger for love take a wrong turning in their lives. They admitted that there was no innocent party, that choices are usually dictated by self-interest, that a burden can deliberately be placed on the one who cannot respond and was not, in any case, a party to the dream. He said,

'It is wilful flouting of what in our deepest hearts we know to be the truth.' His face became quite cavernous and his eyes had that intense eagerness which made him so vulnerable and which Valentine dreaded because it meant that he was about to offer her something precious which would inevitably turn to dross in her hands. It was that same ravaged look which presaged in the pulpit the sermon about the love of God in which he believed so passionately and to which most of his congregation were quite indifferent. On these occasions he seemed to Valentine like some carving of a gaunt, mythical creature from whose ever open jaws water gushes out, endlessly wasteful, and the congregation were like right-minded sightseers, turning away, unimpressed, thinking of important things like Peace and South Africa and whether the coach-driver would have managed to park in the shade. 'And when we flout our own truth,' he said, 'we flout God, because He is that truth. If we grow away from the love of God we grow away from our true self and we become malformed, like a tree which hasn't enough light.'

Valentine, who had come out to work in the vicarage garden, had for some minutes been conscious of people talking quietly in the graveyard. As her weeding brought her nearer to the high dividing wall, she had recognized Michael's voice although she could not hear what he was saying. The other voice was much softer but she knew that it was a woman speaking. He really should be more careful, she thought, amused rather than displeased, because she liked this carelessness in him and would not have wished him a more cautious person. She moved away to caress the cat, who was stretched out beneath the hawthorn tree.

Michael said to Norah, 'The way I look upon it is that if we insist on taking a wrong turning it doesn't mean we can simply break away and go back once the path becomes thorny, because by then we have begun to grow in that direction – and, of course, we involve others in our mistakes, drag them along with us, and we can't just walk away, abandoning them. As I see it, we have to live with our wrong turnings and make them into another, longer, more tortuous way to God. The interminable "short-cut" that adds weary time to a journey but brings one home at last.'

He was thinking of his own experience and could therefore say these things to her without any suggestion of judging her. They were in a shared situation and they were both aware of it; if what they said seemed harsh, the harshness, too, was shared.

'Yes,' she said. 'I have learnt that we have to do what we can in the particular place where we find ourselves. It's a comfort to me. I say to myself, "Here is where you are, Norah Kendall, and all that is asked is that you make your best of it." But there are times when I wish I wasn't Norah Kendall.'

'Ah yes! My dreams and hopes for Michael Hoath have heroic proportions, but the actual achievement is pitifully small.'

As they talked, acknowledging hopes bright and trite, needs urgent and unreasonable, a gentle sympathy began to temper stoicism. At some stage, without their being aware of it, their hands met and now they sat, fingers intertwined, and were silent. A weight seemed to have been lifted and Norah, closing her eyes, felt momentarily giddy with nothing against which to brace herself. The traffic in the high street was sporadic now and during the long intervals of silence there was that sense that a summer evening can give of time having run its course. It came to Michael, 'I am happy.' He turned to her and saw that she was looking at him, astonished by the same awareness. In that moment they were one person. They embraced and many years' longings were gathered into a wave of oblivious joy. After the joy came the awareness of thirst. They tumbled onto the earth and knelt there, touching and tasting with the desperate, intent application of parched travellers at a wayside spring.

As she played with the cat Valentine had been trying to identify the woman's voice. Her inability to do so was a tiresome itch – nothing more – preventing her from enjoying her time in the garden. She decided she must try to settle the matter and dismiss it from her mind. As she approached the graveyard wall she was greeted by silence. She stood, straining her ears. Movements came, but whether to her ears or her imagination she could not have said. They could have returned to the church, of course; but every nerve told her that they were there, silent on the other side of the wall. And people who do not know each other well do not spend so long either in prayer or contemplation.

Norah and Michael knelt, holding each other, quite still now. Their faces had the slightly idiotic look of people dazzled by bright light. There was a sensation that the body had been caught out with the mind away somewhere. Michael was aware of light in concentric circles whose outer circumference seemed to be extending further and further, bearing mind spinning away into some unimaginable realm from which no return could be expected.

Valentine dropped the hoe on the gravel path – and the trowel, too, for good measure. She was rewarded by a corresponding disturbance of stones and earth on the far side of the wall. Light footsteps went down the steps leading into the church. A few moments later, she saw Michael in the distance by the gate leading out of the graveyard. He will come in for supper now, she thought; but he turned away from the vicarage. Although it was a still evening he walked as if he was heading into a wind.

Much later, when he had returned and they sat at the dining table, neither looking at the other, he said, 'I must lock the church. I quite forgot about it.'

'Thieves may have taken what they want by now,' she replied. 'I thought I heard someone in the graveyard earlier this evening.'

'There was no one there when I left.' The half-truth came to his lips without apparent effort. His mind seemed to have no part in what was happening.

'Who kept you so long?' she asked, dry-mouthed.

'Norah Kendall. She has a lot of problems.'

'Norah Kendall!'

For different reasons neither could take the conversation any further.

When he left to lock up the church, she called out, 'I shan't be here when you return.'

He came back into the dining-room. She was piling crockery on a tray. 'I have to go for a fitting of my costume. Though why I am still playing this part, I can't imagine. She should have had an affair; don't you think that would have been much more sensible than killing herself?' She was speaking fast but with clarity. 'Those exchanges with Loevborg are so unlikely. They should have had an affair. I am sure *that's* what Ibsen really had in mind when he made Tesman say, "But good God. One doesn't do that sort of thing." An affair, not suicide. But I expect Ibsen was too inhibited to envisage such a scene. In those days men thought they had the monopoly in such matters.' She picked up the tray and went into the kitchen.

7

Desmond waited on the station platform. The green light showed but it had been like that for three-quarters of an hour. People were getting restive. But Desmond welcomed the downfall of timetabling as a happening to be expected, and not only where British Rail was concerned.

Tomorrow was his birthday. His mother would have bought him a more expensive gift than she could afford and she would have loaned Tracy money to 'get something special'. From his grandparents in Truro he could rely on receiving a book about one of the B.B.C.'s wild life programmes with a cheery note from his grandmother saying she had picked it up at a book sale because she realized that it was just the sort of thing he was interested in, and telling him yet again how she and Grandpa would never forget 'The Flight of the Condor'. There would be cards from some of the people for whom he did gardening and one from his only school friend, now at Durham University. Ever since his father left home his mother had worked herself and everyone else into a frenzy about his birthday. If his father had remembered to send a card it would have spoilt the whole effect. This had been going on for over six years and he considered he had been pretty tolerant of it. Now he had earned the right to choose the way he spent his birthday. He hoped his mother would not be too hurt by his absence, but he had noted she got quite a bit of mileage out of being hurt. In fact, she was creative about it. His mother put everything which came to her to good use.

'Work on the line,' a woman said resignedly.

'Points failure,' her companion countered. 'It's always points failure.'

A child in a pushchair pointed a finger at Desmond and said, 'Dada!'

'Dada's going to meet us at Exeter.' His mother sounded indifferent as though the arrival of the train and the waiting father were in the hands of capricious gods.

The tannoy made a noise like someone returned from the dead and still in a bad condition. A voice communicated a message in a language perhaps familiar to the unknown territory in which the train was in travail – Desmond visualized it stranded in one of those moonlike regions over which the condor cast its shadow.

'Whatever that may have been, it wasn't "the train now approaching platform three",' the advocate of points failure said. She and her companion walked away in the direction of the station buffet.

The child began to cry 'Dada! Dada!', eyes and mouth gaping holes of misery. Desmond was convinced that the child's father would not be waiting on the platform at Exeter. This conviction owed little to anything as insubstantial as reason, it was a flutter in the stomach as portentous as the signs on the breastbone of a goose which warn the primitive – who know about such things – of bad weather to come.

'That's not Dada.' The young woman's voice was sharp. Desmond's face as he stared at the child had something of the primitive about it. The eyes were clear as glass in the folds above the flat planes of the cheekbones, and this gave the face the look of one of those plundered antique figures from which the jewelled eyes have been removed. The young woman pushed the child further up the platform.

Desmond sat on a seat and began to reread *The Star Thrower*, which he had brought with him because at one time Eiseley had ridden the rails and Desmond thought him a good companion,

107

this man so wise to human fallacies, who knew that 'one step does not lead rationally to another.' He was particularly impressed by the idea of the trickster element in Nature which looms suddenly out of a clear sky and which has to be accepted because it leaves behind tangible evidence of its demonic presence. What he had not found before was the acknowledgement of the presence of the trickster in the life of man. It was an idea with which he felt strangely secure, not because it offered safety but because it assured him that he was not alone, that someone else had seen the demon joker looking over his shoulder, had heard the same derisive laughter amid the solemn platitudes of everyday speech. Desmond was glad that the train had not arrived. Its absence justified him.

The woman with the child walked past. Desmond pulled his Quasimodo face at the child, tongue bunched in cheek, eyes askew; the child applauded and shouted, 'Dada! Dada! Dada!'

The voice over the tannoy, now perfectly in command of itself, announced that the train would arrive in five minutes and that British Rail apologized for the inconvenience and for the fact that the dining-car had been taken off.

When the train arrived Desmond got into the guard's van where he was warmly received by a despondent Labrador. The guard, a middle-aged Asian with eyes as dark and sad as the dog's, looked Desmond up and down, from tattered pants with the regulation tear above one knee to paint-splashed vest, and came to a conclusion which caused him no joy. Desmond squatted beside the dog, careful to let it carry out its own investigations before he touched it. The guard said, 'You like dogs? You look after this one, then.' He refrained from asking Desmond whether he had a ticket, which was unusual since most Asians whom Desmond had met had been more law-abiding than the English. It seemed, however, that this man had a son who was in trouble with the police who had dealt with him very unfairly. He was disposed to be sympathetic to Desmond.

'The police don't like Pakis,' he said. 'I do not like them, either. I am Indian. But it makes no difference, they do not listen. Even when my son-in-law's grocery shop has petrol bomb thrown through the window, they do nothing.'

Desmond listened attentively to the guard's grievances while he stroked the dog's head. He felt an interest – which was as near as he ever came to sympathy – in people who are accident-prone, and the coloured community was more accident-prone than most. He could see, however, that while the guard was resigned to the precariousness of life he was by no means reconciled to it. He saw himself as a victim, not the prototype of human kind.

'I tell my MP but that man is just puffed out with promises like a hot-air balloon.'

Desmond, who found politics boring and depressing, asked when the train got into Exeter.

'What do you want to go to Exeter for?'

'There's a man I want to talk to. He is attending a conference on anthropology.' Desmond said this as nonchalantly as if he were a fellow academic and, indeed, in his own mind there was no substantial distinction between himself and Sir Arnold Bassett, merely a matter of age in which he had the advantage. 'I read about it in *The Times* in the library.' He did not add that this meeting with Sir Arnold Bassett was his birthday present to himself.

'But he will not see you, not without you having an appointment.' It might have been his mother speaking, Desmond thought. There would have been no way he could have convinced her that if only he could see Sir Arnold Bassett (and, more important, if Sir Arnold Bassett could only see him) nothing but good, in the form of interesting field work, could follow. Desmond did not expect to be liked, or loved, but he assumed an immediate awareness of his intellectual ability.

'We have corresponded,' he said. 'At least, I wrote to him. There was some rather sloppy thinking in a paper he gave on Darwin and I sent him a few notes. Unfortunately I think they may have gone astray because he didn't reply. I've brought a copy with me, just in case.'

The guard shook his grizzled head sorrowfully. 'You make that man very angry.'

'A man like that has nothing to fear from controversy.' Desmond's harsh bray of laughter betrayed anger as well as contempt and the dog's ears twitched nervously. 'It's only men with little minds who are vain.'

'No, no, the bigger the man, the bigger the appetite. You better go home, you get yourself into trouble otherwise, upsetting this man. You go home and write to him. You get out at the next stop.' He pleaded earnestly as if Desmond were his own son and the Labrador, agitated by the tone, turned his head and looked imploringly at Desmond.

The ticket inspector had reached the adjacent carriage. The guard said to Desmond, 'You go in toilet, otherwise you get me in trouble.' The Labrador put his head back and howled assent.

When the ticket inspector had passed by Desmond made his way to the rear of the train because he did not think it fair to place so heavy a burden on the guard and the dog.

At Exeter he hung about on the platform. On previous excursions he had observed that there is usually a passenger in trouble or out to make trouble at the end of a long journey. He was not disappointed this time. Soon a wiry little foreign woman set up camp at the ticket barrier, surrounded by suitcases held together by string and numerous parcels wrapped in brown paper. Desmond paused to study the method of the woman who had the staring, resentful eyes of one who is an expert at creating chaos around her.

'I can't help what they told you at Bodmin, madam,' the man at the barrier said. 'This is Exeter.'

She protested volubly and he said, 'No, no, no! The train doesn't go any further and if it did you still wouldn't get to Truro. You have come the wrong way. You understand? Wrong way!' He stabbed his finger in the general direction of right way. But, of course, she did not understand, even if she had had perfect command of English she would not have understood; incomprehension was the tripwire with which she brought authority down. Several people pushed past waving tickets in the air. 'You are blocking the exit, madam.' The foolish man toed one of the brown paper bags which turned on its side and split open. The woman fell on her knees, scrabbling in the dust and threatening litigation while the ticket collector maintained his innocence in a vigorous baritone and several passengers skidded on ripe cherries. Desmond, sorry to leave the circus behind, slipped past waving his library ticket in the air.

The woman with the pushchair was waiting blank-faced in the middle of the concourse and the child was addressing each oncoming male as Dada. Desmond went in search of tourist information.

'I want the conference centre,' he said and handed the young woman with the haughty eyebrows the pieces which he had cut out of the library's copy of *The Times*. She looked at him sceptically as if she would not let him into any building of which she had charge, but produced a map of the town and marked a building with a cross.

Desmond got a bar of chocolate from a machine and bought a banana at a stall. The conference was on from Saturday until Monday. It was now Friday evening. He was prepared to extend his birthday celebration until Monday if necessary. He would find a park in which to sleep. The life which he planned for himself would involve sleeping in places more hostile to man than a park in Exeter in June.

Hester sometimes wondered why she hadn't joined the Society of Friends. Even allowing for the fact that they were occasionally moved to speak, ministering Quakers could not possibly be as distracting as the modern child. The baby at the back of the church had been provided – to help it through the tedium of worship – with toys, all of which must surely be made of cast iron. Soft toys, no doubt, had also been lavished upon the infant, but these, it seemed, were reserved for the peace and quiet of its own home. Older children with the instincts of storm-troopers, and equipped with hobnailed boots, marched up and down the aisle. Young parents, ears attuned to such noises, appeared to have no difficulty in ignoring the racket. It was very hot and this youthful activity brought beads of perspiration to Hester's brow. She reflected gloomily on the injunction 'Suffer the little ones to come unto me', contrasting it with her own desire, growing more imperative with the years, to ensure peace, if necessary with a hatchet.

The congregation sang. The baby, incipiently musical, listened in silent wonder, but grew restive during the readings. What it really seemed to hate was the sermon during which it gave tongue while heaving about all the weights with which it had been thoughtfully provided. All this, Hester thought, and Valentine to follow! It was most unlike Valentine to invite herself for sherry on a Sunday morning. 'I simply have to see you,' she had said. 'I am sorry, but it can't wait.' Hester had looked forward to the rare treat of sitting out in her garden.

Why is it that people can't come to terms with the facts of their lives? she lamented as she waited to make her communion. All this discontent, the fretting for distant places – if only they could live in Australia, Italy, even the other side of England, they would find fulfilment. Fulfilment was there, waiting, wherever they were not. And then there was the obsession with the wrongs of distant places – Africa, South America, Soviet Russia. So much energy spent on situations which they did not fully understand and could do little to change. And so, she thought, edging forward up the aisle, the particular life they have to live in the place where they find themselves, is neglected, its joys unlooked for, its challenges not confronted, its sorrow building up through the years as steadily and stealthily as an undiagnosed disease. 'Oh God, forgive me that even here, at your altar, I am unable to compose my mind! I am so worried about what Valentine is up to now. I don't want to be involved. I am too old for all this. Please, please help me to make her see that if she wants to move yet again there is no way in which I can become involved in persuading Michael.'

Matins followed the family Eucharist so Michael would not be back at the vicarage until just before one o'clock. This would leave Valentine the best part of two hours in which to unburden herself.

'I am sorry you have to put up with me,' she said on arrival. 'If Michael's mother were alive, I could talk to her.' She looked very much offended, as though Sylvia had been guilty of a deliberate discourtesy in quitting life's party prematurely.

The invoking of Sylvia was ominous, not only because she had been much in Hester's thoughts recently, but because Valentine rarely mentioned her and when she did it was usually a danger signal. Hester had no idea why this should be so since Sylvia had died seven years before Valentine met Michael.

The sunlight glared into the room but, in the hope that Valentine might be persuaded to sit in a shady part of the garden, Hester had not drawn the curtains. Confidences in a garden would be diffused over a wider area, their concentration diminished by the threatening activities of insects, the smell of the compost heap, the blare of other people's radios and all the other distractions of a summer day. It was apparent, however, that Valentine regarded the open French window not as an invitation but an insensitivity. Hester poured sherry and prayed for the influence of her sister's more tender spirit. She could smell the meat cooking and hoped she had remembered to turn the gas down to Mark 2. She tried to visualize herself doing this and while she was thus occupied Valentine said, 'As his nearest relative I suppose you are entitled to learn, before it becomes general knowledge, that Michael is having an affair with Norah Kendall.'

Hester walked across the room, keeping a careful eye on the sherry glass which she had filled generously. When she had placed it on the table beside Valentine, she said, 'I don't think I heard you aright.'

'It's hardly something I want to repeat.' Valentine's features looked brittle as cut glass.

Hester said stupidly, warming her sherry glass in her hands as if it contained the brandy which she now wished she had offered, 'Norah Kendall! I don't believe it.'

'Not very flattering, certainly. So unlikely a love. You can imagine how I feel.'

Hester, who could not imagine it, said, to gain time, 'But he adores you. Michael has always adored you.'

'He needs someone to adore and has made do with me.' Valentine spoke in a high, clear voice which was not at all to Hester's liking.

'What nonsense!'

'Yes, really. He is the kind of man who expects to fall madly in love once in his life.' Oh yes, yes, Hester thought, seeing Michael's face sketched in her mind's eye, the ludicrously

vulnerable mouth and exposed chin, he certainly is that.
Valentine went on, as though wound up to speak at a certain
pace, 'I am not a passionate person. He made a bad mistake; but
it would be unthinkable to admit it. So he set himself to adoring
me, much as he would set out to go rock-climbing. There was
always the possibility, of course, that one day he would fall
madly in love. He hasn't closed any doors on himself.' The
words made good sense but the unvarying delivery was
unnerving.

Hester could see that if she was not careful she was going to
respond like those people who, confronted with an unpleasant
prospect, keep repeating, 'What nonsense!' in the hope that it
will see that it is not wanted and go away. She drained her glass
and fetched the decanter. 'Come on. Drink up.'

'I am in no need of stimulants, I can assure you.' But Valentine
allowed Hester to refill her glass.

'Now, tell me how you came to this surprising conclusion.'

Valentine recounted without elaboration what she had seen,
heard and not heard, in and around the graveyard. Hester did
not think there was much to it but was not as relieved as she
might have expected. The sunlight sparked from the stones on
the patio and combined with the sherry to produce spots before
her eyes. She drew the curtain across the side window. 'Aren't
you making a great deal out of very little?'

Valentine said, staring ahead, eyes unblinking, 'It's my own
fault. Of course I know that. I should have been someone's
mistress, kept in a back street.' The violet-grey eyes seemed to
consume the pale face; seeing her like this Hester could almost
believe that Marguerite Gauthier was within her range. 'I should
have been happy with a man who only came to me once a week.
I haven't the stamina to be a wife.'

'But Norah Kendall . . . No, it's not possible.'

'A woman neither young nor beautiful,' Valentine said
tonelessly. Hester wished she would begin to act a little more,
then she herself could play the role to which she was best suited,
that of the person who turns the emotional current down to an
acceptable level. She had never before realized how much she
was dependent on the emotions of others for the exercise of this

114

skill. Valentine was saying, 'It didn't matter that I couldn't love him as he needed to be loved, so long as there was no one else who could. But I feel so diminished, so humiliated. Some of those old tabbies will have the temerity to pity me.'

Hester pounced. 'Valentine, you are talking as if this affair were common knowledge. And it very soon will be if you behave like this.'

'It will very soon become known if Michael continues to be so indiscreet.' There was a tart commonsense in this rejoinder from which Hester took some comfort.

'Although it seems rather unconvincing to me, I take your word for it that there was a bit of silliness in the graveyard.' Hester put down her glass. One sherry made her feel liverish, two turned the whole world bilious. Valentine had affected jealousy before, but usually it was the possible affront to her dignity which roused her, rather than any serious prospect of infidelity. Something must have happened to put her in a state of shock. And it wasn't just shock; the eyes were not so much glazed as splintered by fear. Hester wondered if the fear had always been there, it seemed so natural a part of the face now. It gave her a queasy feeling, an awareness of fear within herself. This was Michael of whom they were speaking, her beloved sister's beloved son. Sylvia had sat in this very room speaking of her hopes for him, and of her fears, too. Hester addressed herself to the fear. 'This doesn't have to be taken too seriously, does it? Our dear Michael is easily moved and Norah is unhappy and overburdened. Give a little thought to what probably happened. At the worst, he tried to comfort her in a way that was unwise.'

'Why did he go into the graveyard with her in the first place?'

'Hardly in order to commit an indiscretion.'

'And then, afterwards, to go rushing off like that.'

'Where did he go, do you know?'

'No, and I doubt that he does either. He is quite beside himself. His whole body is singing, Hester. I feel it whenever he is near me.'

Hester could smell the apples cooking on the bottom shelf. She was ashamed that she should be preoccupied with food at such a time. Then, standing there smelling the apples, words came into her mind as they sometimes did when she had lost the thread of a story. The words were often seemingly unconnected, referring her back to an earlier incident which she had failed to give its full value. She said, 'You implied earlier that you had not been a very satisfactory wife to Michael. I think you are not wholly fair to yourself in that.' Up to this moment she had thought the criticism entirely fair. 'You didn't know my sister Sylvia. She was one of those generous women who seem to have so much room in their hearts that they can accommodate the demands of all those who have need of them. She died of kidney failure before any of us could afford to lose her.'

'I am quite aware that she died of kidney failure. As for her astonishing goodness – if that is meant as some kind of rebuke, I am in no need of such comparisons.'

'I am saying this because it may be something you need to know. Her loss inflicted a great wound on her family which has never properly healed.' That was a fact, though it wasn't given an airing very often. 'Michael was only seventeen at the time and he was emotionally dependent on her. His father was one of those men who resent sharing his wife's affections with a child and he always distanced himself from Michael. This disappointment of which you are so conscious in Michael may not be attributable to a failure in you so much as to the fact that he couldn't come to terms with the loss of his mother. He has probably always asked rather too much of you.'

Valentine shook her head and put her fingers to her temples, the first really theatrical gesture she had made. 'I'm sure that is very well-intentioned, but it is all too Freudian for me to take in.'

'Does he often speak to you of Sylvia?' Hester persisted, aware of some need to pursue this matter which was not entirely altruistic.

'You know he doesn't. Neither do you. It is something from which I have always been excluded. No, no, I am not making this up on the spur of the moment, Hester. It happens. I can remember incidents – one in particular – coming into a room at dusk and seeing you and Michael sitting silent in front of the fire. I had the feeling that a third person was present whom I could not see.'

For a moment neither of them spoke. Fat sizzled in the oven. Valentine said, 'But I fail to see how this is supposed to be of any help to me.'

Hester, who had been upset by what Valentine had said, lost her patience. 'Very well, then. Blame yourself. It is a convenient way out and goodness knows you have taken it often enough.'

'What do you mean "convenient way out"?' Valentine was startled and angry.

'One simply says – "I am as I am and so there is no point in trying". One . . .'

'Could you put this in your own words instead of talking like the Queen?'

'All right. You accept the idea of some kind of lack in yourself because it absolves you from making any further effort.'

'Thank you very much.' Valentine got to her feet in time to see Charles Venables and Shirley Treglowan coming in at Hester's garden gate. 'I must say I have gained little comfort from this morning's talk.'

'I'm sorry. I apologize . . .'

'And as I perceive you have visitors, I will take my leave.'

'Visitors?' Hester swung round towards the window. 'Really, this is too much!'

'I can see you are having a very trying Sunday morning.' Valentine swept into the hall and opened the front door. 'Do come in. I am just on my way.' She walked down the path, ignoring their protests and leaving her handbag behind.

'Is this urgent?' Hester disposed of good manners.

'Yes.' Charles could do the same when it suited his purpose.

Hester offered brandy in the interests of dulling her temper and they both accepted. They sat side by side on the sofa, Charles natty in dark blue shirt and pale blue slacks, Shirley in a bright green tentlike structure the hem of which billowed across Charles's knees. The sun had caught her cheekbones and two livid crescents glowed fierce as war paint on her plump face. She was sweating pungently.

'Desmond has gone missing,' Charles explained. 'Shirley wondered if either of us had seen him.' Hester detected a rather surprising intimacy in the way he spoke for Shirley. 'Or if he mentioned anything when last he did our gardens.'

'I was out when last he did our gardens.'

Shirley said, 'I had the most bizarre dream.' She looked at Charles, asking permission to repeat the story. He smiled indulgently into his glass. 'There was a man on TV talking about the Church and Aids; he said the Archbishop of Canterbury should nail his colours to the mast. And I went to bed and dreamt of the Archbishop on this boat, with a handkerchief knotted on his head and a black patch over one eye, singing "Once aboard the lugger and the girl is mine". There was something obscene about it. I woke up shouting "Desmond, what have you done?"'

Charles smiled covertly at Hester.

'He has taken himself off once or twice before, hasn't he?' Hester was neither impressed nor amused. 'Did he leave a note?'

'Yes. He said it was something important. What does that mean? I'm afraid of what Desmond may think important.'

'Whatever it may be, I don't suppose it is abducting girls and taking them to sea,' Charles said comfortably, revolving brandy in his glass.

'It was just the Archbishop being like that that made it seem . . . well . . . you could interpret it that the moral universe has gone awry.'

'I think it undoubtedly has,' Hester said crisply. 'But I doubt if Desmond is materially involved.'

'He probably thinks he is going to land a job,' Charles said. 'I expect he didn't want to raise your hopes until he knew the outcome.' This seemed eminently sensible as well as being reassuring and Hester wondered why he had not said it in the first place and packed Shirley off home.

'My hopes aren't raised that easily,' Shirley said wanly.

Charles said, 'Oh, come!'

He is enjoying this, Hester thought, but he has no idea how to bring it to an end. 'Would you like to stay for lunch?' she asked. There seemed no alternative if she herself was to eat. Shirley said she must get back to Tracy, but Charles, who was quite shameless about scrounging meals, accepted. 'I shall be seeing Hoaths tomorrow about Desmond's obsession with anthropology, so I can take Valentine's handbag,' he said, as though the handbag and Hester's lunch were inextricably connected.

Charles had expected to talk to Michael on his own, but Valentine was on this occasion behaving like a vicar's wife. Charles had always thought it so admirable in her that she distanced herself from the affairs of her husband and his parish work, her manner conveying that she had matters of greater moment to occupy her. It was a surprise, therefore, to find her presiding over the tea not in the least distantly but as if she expected not only to be privy to whatever disclosures might be made, but an active participant in any subsequent discussion.

Earlier she had surprised Michael when he said that Charles might wish to talk to him privately. 'Charles cannot have anything to say to you privately,' she had retorted. 'He is not a Christian.'

'I expect atheists have private problems.'

'But not ones that can't be discussed with man and wife. We *are* man and wife and Charles should not expect to come here and be served tea by me as if I were the housekeeper who would meekly withdraw after setting out the contents of the laden tray.'

There had been a faint flush on her face and neck. Although he chose to put her evident distress down to incipient 'flu, Michael nevertheless felt obscurely guilty. He therefore addressed Charles. 'You mentioned a problem. We have been quite at a loss to imagine what kind of problem it is on which you could possibly find it of help to turn to the vicarage.' The awful facetiousness was as foreign to him as the use of the connubial 'we'. It was very, very seldom that the Hoaths thought or spoke of themselves as first person plural.

It occurred to Charles that at some time or other he must have said something which had given grave offence. He acknowledged that there might have been occasions when he had spoken unwisely to Hoath on matters religious, or to Valentine on the question of her portrayal of Hedda Gabler. But he could not imagine what subject was peculiarly sensitive to them both. He decided that it was Michael Hoath whom he had upset. Of the two, Hoath seemed to him the more stable and if he was behaving oddly then there must be a reason for it. In Charles's view, unbalanced behaviour was to be expected in women.

He decided to reply to Hoath in the same vein and succeeded in sounding rather coy. 'I hope nothing I have said has ever given the impression that I would not value your advice on . . . er . . . indeed on any subject.'

Michael Hoath gazed about him. Charles had noted him doing this several times, his eyes resting on objects which must surely be quite familiar to him yet which seemed to occasion him something which Charles could only describe as astonishment. Had Valentine rearranged the furniture? It seemed unlikely and even more unlikely that Hoath should be disorientated by a change in the relationship of tables and chairs.

During this pause Valentine decided that the two men were waiting for her to leave them alone. She turned angry eyes on Charles. 'Are we to know this problem?'

Charles, who was by this time feeling extremely foolish, said, 'I think perhaps I may have made too much of this on the phone. It isn't really my problem at all.'

Far from clearing the atmosphere, this appeared to make matters worse. Valentine became still as a statue of a particularly breakable kind and Hoath seemed to be holding his breath as he looked into the dregs of his cup.

Charles hurried on, 'It's about Desmond Treglowan.'

The Hoaths spoke simultaneously. Michael said, 'Oh, Desmond!' and Valentine said, 'Charles, your cup is empty.' There was a pause while she replenished all the cups and was as fussy with milk and sugar as if Charles were playing Gwendolen to her Cecily. Eventually, Michael Hoath said, 'Now, Charles, what is this about Desmond? The lad returned home, I gather.'

Charles settled back in his chair, confident in the knowledge that he had a good tale to tell. 'It seems he went to Exeter in the hope of meeting Sir Arnold Bassett, of all people, who was attending a conference there. Not a realistic aim, one would have thought. But as it transpired, as well as the main conference there was a meeting meant to awaken the interest of what I suppose was once the-man-in-the-street but which has become the-man-in-front-of-the-television-screen. Old Bassett was wheeled forward to do his bit.'

'Who is this Bassett?' Valentine's expression was one of quite inappropriate betrayal, as though a late suspect had been introduced by Hercule Poirot of whose existence she could not possibly have been aware.

'An anthropologist of some repute – but not so well thought-of nowadays.' Charles was fussed at being interrupted when he thought he was doing his best to lighten the atmosphere. He went on, 'Desmond managed to get into this meeting which was rather poorly attended, I gather from a report in *The Times*. It seems that when questions were invited, Desmond took the opportunity to inform Bassett that he had made one or two mistakes regarding Darwin.' Charles thought this very funny but neither of the Hoaths did. 'And he hung on pertinaciously throughout question time, thus earning himself a couple of witty lines in the *Guardian* and no doubt the undying hatred of the great man.'

Charles chuckled. The other two were silent. Valentine sat with bowed head – the better, thought Charles, who was beginning to get rather cross, to look superb when she finally raised her chin. 'And that is all?'

'By no means. The chairman was a younger man who probably hated old Bassett's guts. It seems that after the meeting he came across Desmond who was hanging about in the hope of further exhilarating exchanges with Bassett. The outcome was that this fellow offered Desmond the chance to go on a dig in Turkey early next year. At his own expense. As he doesn't go to university until the autumn it would be a possibility provided he can raise the money.'

'And I suppose it is a matter of getting a grant?' Valentine said crisply. 'Really, Charles, I can't see why you have come to us. As a schoolmaster you must know more than we do about such things. And why, by the way, aren't you in school now?'

'This is the games afternoon.' Charles felt as if he were

explaining his absence to the head master. 'And it's not the money which disturbs Desmond's mother.' Somehow he could not bring himself to say Shirley. 'She is afraid the grandparents will fund him on the principle that "it was coming to you anyway so you might as well have it now". What worries her is that the expedition may compound Desmond's problem, not solve it; that he will just go to pieces in some lonely place with no one noticing what is happening.'

Valentine said, 'Perhaps he just knows what he wants. It was enterprising to go off to Exeter like that.'

'But unrealistic to imagine he could impress old Bassett by a display of adolescent cleverness.'

Michael Hoath said, 'A display of adolescent cleverness is not peculiar to Desmond. And he does seem to have impressed the other fellow.'

'But why anthropology? Anthropologists don't exactly grow on trees. Personally, I think it's some kind of therapy and she should be glad it isn't psychology he's taken up. But she is afraid this is the call of the wild; that he will go off into a desert place and become a recluse. That sort of thing.'

'And what am I supposed to do about it?' Hoath asked.

'She seemed to think you had an alternative life on offer – the loving Christian community.'

Michael Hoath looked as if he had been stung and Charles regretted the flippancy of his tone. Hoath said, 'The desert has always been an alternative way.'

There was another dreadful silence. The idea recurred to Charles that at some time he must have offended Hoath. Certainly a great air of offence hung over the sitting-room. He said, 'Anyway, perhaps you might care to have a word with Desmond. I leave it to you. But before I go – and I have taken up far too much of your time as it is.' Things were so bad he almost said, 'and that of your good lady.' He pulled himself together and tried to inject genuine feeling into his voice, which was always a mistake as it made him sound odiously insincere. 'Before I go may I say how much I, as an outsider, have appreciated the masterly way in which you have transformed the church services?' He hoped this was not going at it a bit too strongly, but Hoath's reaction was to look at him so tragically that he thought, dear me, perhaps the man is losing heart? Silence threatened again and Charles found himself forced to drum up more praise. 'Speaking as one who has never been able to take what your predecessor was pleased to call "the leap of faith" I nevertheless need the enrichment of the language and the ritual . . .' He went on to praise the music, the art of which the Church had been both inspiration and custodian, and even acknowledged his own debt to the Christian culture in which he had been reared.

The words "leap of faith" sounded like a cry in Michael Hoath's ears, a cry which he had heard all his adult life and about which he had been able to do nothing. Many unbelievers seemed to him like lapsed fundamentalists, people for whom every statement, doctrine, miracle must be examined in detail and proved irrefutably. Once doubt entered in they were finished because above all else they needed absolute certainty. And he could not answer them. They had cried out and he had been dumb, unable to deal with their arguments or adequately to explain his own belief. The great mysteries were not for him a matter for argument, they were jewels cast about his life's landscape, some of which he seemed to hold in the palm of his hand, others which his fingers would never touch; he watched and meditated on their richness and radiance and felt them sometimes closer than hand to face, at others remote as a star. Now, at a time when his emotions were so charged, he felt the agony of the tension between himself and Charles to be quite unbearable.

Charles had the feeling that Hoath was listening to very little of what he said, When finally praise petered out, Hoath got abruptly to his feet, muttered, 'Well, thank you for telling me about Desmond. I will speak to him,' and left the room.

'I do hope he believed me,' Charles said weakly.

'You were very patronizing,' Valentine said.

A faint colour tipped Charles's cheeks; it was not a description he liked. 'I trust not.'

'Surely you can't be so unaware when you mock.'

'No, no,' he protested. 'It means a great deal to me, I do assure you . . .'

'The music and the fan-vaulting and the language of the prayer book, but not, of course, the unambiguity of the crucifix which you probably think is in rather bad taste and which my poor benighted husband has tormented himself trying to preach, to live . . .'

Involuntarily Charles's lips moved in the slightest pucker of distaste. She said acidly, 'Exactly.'

She was angry that he had patronized Michael and even more angry that she herself had been included in his patronage. She saw herself as the outsider in all matters including her religion.

Charles was enchanted that anger so became her, a phenomenon much noted in fiction but rare in his experience. He would pay no heed to her words, but would treasure the memory of the impeccable line of the jaw, the icy fire in the eyes.

'You are most handsome,' he said.

'Are you never concerned with the guts of the matter?' Valentine surprised herself by the use of the word guts which was not a word she would normally have applied to religion let alone to anything pertaining to herself.

Charles raised his eyebrows, distressed by the realization that she meant him to take her anger seriously. Did he sense a whiff of feminism here? he wondered.

'You are so civilized you have become quite unrooted.'

Nothing he had said justified the way in which she was behaving and she was aware of this. She was angry with him because she saw something of herself in him. She, too, had a revulsion for the guts of life. But she was not a natural aesthete. He at least genuinely cared about the music of Bach. In a sense perhaps he did know where his roots were buried and searched for them in the hidden streams beside which Langland's peasants had ploughed their half-acre.

Charles left soon after this exchange. He was less at ease in his attitude to feminism than to Christianity, which he regarded as a spent force. Feminism was a force to be reckoned with. The liberation of women seemed to Charles something akin to the release of one of those deadly germs said to be immobilized in the frozen waters of the Arctic. On his way home he called at the florist's and ordered flowers for Valentine, writing a brief note of apology to accompany them. It was not a gesture which would normally have occurred to him, but he had heard that men sometimes did this at the end of an affair. For some reason, this seemed appropriate.

'To think I prided myself on being the one who introduced them,' Lois Drury said to Hester. She was looking through the sitting-room window on to the lawn where Hesketh was engaged in maniacal struggle to dismantle a maypole-like device for drying clothes. Her husband Jack was in the front drive changing a tyre. It seemed not to have occurred to either man to co-ordinate their labours. Lois said, 'It's going to be a very bad-tempered lunch.'

Lois was a dark, angular woman, comfortably lacking in charm. Hester thought that she could be relied on not to make matters worse by a flow of idle chatter. She looked at her wrist watch and said, 'And a late one.' She sipped her drink. The glass bore the floured imprints of Norah's fingers. 'Do you think we should offer to help in the kitchen? I was left in little doubt that that was why I was invited.'

Lois shook her head decidedly. 'She's not doing at all badly and we should only fluster her – or, worse still, she would opt out and we should have to prepare the meal. Norah can't work in tandem. Once someone starts to help, she sits back, as you must know.'

A young woman attired in a G-string strolled past the window. They watched as Hesketh desisted from his battle with the maypole and turned in slow motion to watch his daughter's progress across the lawn. She threw down a bathing towel and stretched out on it, her body smooth as marzipan save for two little eminences topped by glacé cherries. Hesketh came and stood over her, looking as if he might take a bite at any minute.

'Do you propose to join us at lunch in that condition?'

Her voice was not as resonant as his and the reply was inaudible. Hesketh conveyed its substance to them. 'Of course we are having lunch, that is why we have guests.' And after another inaudible remark, 'I don't want to hear you speak like that about your stepmother.'

'How has Norah taken her arrival?' Hester asked Lois.

'I have only had a few minutes with her, but she seemed in a surprisingly buoyant mood. Perhaps that is how people respond when something they dread actually happens.' Lois did not sound convinced of this.

Hester was doubtful, too. 'I can't see Samantha's arrival being a relief to Norah in any sense.'

'I wouldn't have said it was relief. She just seemed dissociated – as if she had been swigging the cooking sherry.'

At this point Hesketh broke away from Samantha and strode over to the maypole which he grasped by the stem and shook as if to throttle it. One of the wire spokes came adrift and hit him on the side of the head. He gave a roar of fury and rushing to the bank hurled the contraption into the river. Samantha got up, folded the towel and walked into the sitting-room.

'Do you mind about this?' she asked, presenting a honey-brown torso for Hester's inspection. 'My father thinks you will be affronted.'

'I'm not all that keen, since you ask.' Hester refused to be shamed into acceptance.

'You're shocked,' Samantha said disdainfully.

'Being shockproof isn't high on my list of priorities.'

'No?'

'Now you are shocked.'

'You're quite formidable, aren't you?' Samantha drew the towel around her shoulders. 'You make me feel self-conscious.'

Hester doubted that she ever felt anything else. Then she became guilty. The young often made her feel guilty – her own youth was so far away. Perhaps Samantha had really hoped that she might regain lost Eden in the secluded garden. Many pitfalls opened up when one tried to identify with the young, sentimentality not least among them.

Lois said practically, 'Anyway, what really matters is that your father is shocked.'

'My father is like all men, he sees women as dolls for him to dress up.' Samantha went out of the room and returned shortly in a tangerine shift which subtly outlined erogenous zones.

Hester, who had only met her once before, studied her with a writer's eye. She had coppery hair shaped to an elfin face, a tip-tilted nose and slanting eyes which never seemed to look straight at anything. She poured herself a glass of Perrier water and stood looking into the garden where her father, anger now a little abated, was trying to rescue the maypole without getting his trousers wet.

'What has come over him?' There was genuine dismay in her voice. 'He never used to be clumsy.' She turned to look at Lois and Hester noted a slight cast in one of the blue eyes which gave a permanently bad-tempered look to the face and reminded one that not all elfin mischief is harmless. 'Do you think he's got Parkinson's or something? He doesn't seem to co-ordinate properly. You saw how he was with that clothes thing. It's the same with door handles. You'd think he'd no idea of how they operate – he goes to work on them as if they were a new version of the Rubik cube and he couldn't get the combination.'

Hesketh came past the window, trousers clinging to his legs, the maypole trailing behind him. One felt he would have liked it to be a bull so that he could have been awarded its ears. He went into the kitchen and they could hear him shouting 'that infernal thing fell in the river.' The kitchen door slammed.

It did seem that Samantha had a point, Hester thought. Surely stairs must be unfamiliar to him, why else would he make such a foundation-shaking business of ascending them? A few minutes later, however, he had recovered himself. Urbane and in his right mind, he came into the sitting-room and immediately took control. 'I'm sorry you find us in such disarray,' he said, replenishing glasses and, in Hester's case, deflouring the glass itself.

Samantha walked out on to the lawn. Hesketh shrugged his shoulders in huge bewilderment and looked at Lois. She patted the seat beside her. He took her hand and lowered himself slowly as if his limbs were stiff. 'I'm making a pretty poor fist of this, old dear.'

Hester said, 'I think perhaps, if you don't mind . . .' and contrived to leave the room without drawing undue attention to her departure.

She sat on the stairs for a few minutes, watching Jack putting his tools away very slowly and methodically. Something about that narrow, impatient face suggested he was not usually so careful. He noticed her and came to the window. 'How are things in there?'

'I think your wife is exerting a soothing influence on Hesketh at this moment.'

'God, but it's needed! We arrived before you. It was terrible. I've never been so grateful for a puncture. He and Samantha were having the most almighty row because he had decided he must have a study on the ground floor and the only room which suited him – light and sunny – was the one which leads into the conservatory. So no one would be able to use the conservatory without disturbing him which, as Samantha pointed out, would mean asking his permission to come within a mile of it.'

'Does that mean that Samantha was trying to support Norah?'

'No. It meant she wanted it for her bedroom because it is light and sunny.' He wiped his fingers on a rag. 'I wouldn't believe it could happen. When I first knew Hesketh he always seemed to be on top of things. Never a hint of strain or effort. He used to ridicule people who "make a meal of life". As far as he was concerned it was a banquet and he was the guest of honour.' He squinted through the window at the half-open door of the dining-room. 'Look, I don't want to interrupt what good work Lois may be doing, but I am in great need of alcohol of any kind.'

'I'll make enquiries.' Hester disappeared into the kitchen and after some delay Norah came out.

'I think there's whisky in the dining-room. Will that do?'

'It will indeed.'

She was unfamiliar with spirits and poured as if it were vermouth. He looked at the glass reverently when she handed it to him. 'I'll sit out here for a while if no one minds.'

Hester followed Norah into the kitchen. She had stipulated that she could not leave her work until one o'clock and Norah had said, 'Come at one-fifteen, then. We'll eat about one-thirty and you can help with final preparations when everything comes to the boil at the same time.' It was now two-fifteen. Hester was glad to note that order had been restored since she last glimpsed the kitchen and encouraging smells were coming from all the right utensils.

'Gravy?' she suggested.

'Bless you.' Norah, who was sitting on a stool, made no move. Hester thought she looked very tired but not so strained as might have been expected. 'It's the first time I have ever cooked for so many.' She sounded satisfied, as though now that Hester had arrived her part was concluded.

Hester said, 'Shall I make the gravy?'

While she did this Norah sat on the stool, head bent over the kitchen table, tracing some design of her fancy with a finger. From time to time an involuntary smile lit up her face and Hester, looking at her, experienced a sudden fugitive joy, a shaft lodged long ago within her own being whose sharpness she had not felt for many years.

She had meant to suggest that Norah should take the opportunity to tidy herself before lunch. Her face was flushed from the heat of the stove and her hair was more wispy than ever. The apron had not entirely protected the tailored navy dress during pastry-making. Hester had wanted this occasion to be a success for Norah, but this no longer seemed important.

At lunch Hesketh sat at the head of the table looking like one of the more dissolute Roman emperors. Lois said to Hester afterwards that she was never quite sure whether he would pour more wine or hurl a glass against the wall. At first, he talked easily and wittily, mostly to Jack and Lois, but making occasional attempts to draw Hester into discussion. 'Now, as a writer this will interest you.' As this was high on Hester's list of boring remarks to address to a writer, she took little part in the conversation. Once, when pressed, she made her standard response. 'It has obviously roused your imagination. You write it.'

She was soon to regret having given him this opening.

'Oh, I mean to,' he assured her. 'When I have more time I mean to get down to some writing.' In a minute, she thought, he will ask me whether my characters take control. But she underestimated his self-concern. 'That is why I want to make plans for the study.' He deferred to her with hypnotic charm. 'You, of course, will understand the importance of having the right room in which to work.'

'Any room will do for me so long as there is plenty of paper and somewhere to put a typewriter.'

'Ah well, for your sort of writing perhaps.' She could almost feel the withdrawal of warmth. 'I don't suppose you do much research. I shall need a lot of reference books. But what about a word-processor? You would have to find room for that.'

'God defend me from word-processors.'

'Really? You do surprise me.'

Hester made no attempt to defend her attitude. She was resigned to the fact that nowadays people were not interested in the substance of books, only in the technicalities. Hesketh pursued the matter. 'Of course, I know some people find it hard to come to terms with technology, but I would have expected that you would be able to master a word-processor.'

Norah made her first contribution to the discussion. 'Hester is a creative writer.'

Samantha looked delighted to discover that her stepmother possessed that innate ability of wives to say in all innocence the one thing most likely to infuriate their husbands.

Hesketh said, 'Creative? Mmh, I see. Creative.' He rolled it around on his tongue like a wine-taster suspicious of a particular vintage. 'We are saying, are we, that Jane Austen is creative, Boswell not? We would admit Mrs Gaskell on to the lower slopes of Olympus but Pepys must not set foot on the sacred mountain. Is that what we are saying?'

'Some people, I suppose, would argue that there *are* no steps on Olympus.' Jack deftly diverted the main thrust of discussion. Hester wished him well in his chosen profession. If she had anything to do with it, he would be made an Appeal Court judge without more delay. 'They would say that you are either on the heights with Shakespeare and Homer or down on the plain with the Gaskells and Trollopes, Pepys and Boswell.'

Hesketh debated this with a lot of skill and a cavalier disrespect of literature until the cheese was brought in.

'That was a most satisfying meal,' Hester said to Norah.

'I'm a good plain cook,' Norah acknowledged.

Jack, who had been relieved to find that the meal when eventually served was indeed satisfying, said, 'Learnt at your mother's knee. What could be better?'

'A clip on the ear was all I learnt there,' Norah said in an aside to Hester. She looked amused and continued to seem amused when Samantha brought the discussion down from Olympus by saying, 'If you're going to write your memoirs you'll have John Mortimer to contend with.'

'John Mortimer? I don't fancy I would be greatly concerned about the result of any contention between myself and the repetitious Rumpole.'

'You have to admit he's very witty.'

'And you, my dear, need to beware of this tendency to begin sentences with the phrase "you have to . . ." As far as I am aware no law has yet been passed, no doctrine has been promulgated which compels . . .'

'Oh, fuck you! It's like arguing with Bernard Levin.'

Samantha and Hesketh rose from the table simultaneously. His command of invective relied less on the four-letter word and his voice was the more powerful organ. Samantha saw no choice but to have recourse to hysterics. Lois, whom Hester thought the more admirable the more she saw of her, took her by the shoulders and propelled her from the room. Hesketh said to Norah, 'She is your responsibility now. It would have been nice to have had a word from you.'

Jack said, 'Oh come, that's hardly fair.'

Norah looked steadily at the beam of light falling across the silver on the sideboard. Hester, visited by one of those flashes of intuition which are both inspiration and agony, thought: she is thinking of Michael. How else could it be that at this moment this troubled woman could look as if Olympus was for the climbing. After a few moments' contemplation, Norah said quietly, 'Yes, of course, you are right. What would you like me to do?'

Hesketh was completely taken aback. If she had deliberately set out to shame him she could not have succeeded more completely. But there was nothing pious in her humility and as she collected the plates she might have been meditating some matter in which Hesketh had no part. The current between them had been switched off at her end of the table.

Samantha was sitting on the stairs crying dismally when Hester and Norah went into the hall. Lois was crouched beside her, a comforting arm around her shoulders. Samantha looked like any other unhappy child.

Norah said, 'Come into the kitchen and help us wash up.'

Lois and Hester did the washing up while Norah talked to Samantha and Samantha alternately cried and dredged up fresh epithets to describe her father. When inspiration finally failed she said without much spirit, 'Things were all right before you married him.'

'What does that mean? Do you want me to go away so that you can look after him?' Norah made the suggestion as though it were a reasonable proposition.

'You think you're bloody clever, don't you?'

'Do you really think it was cleverness got me into this?' The good humour was holding out longer than Hester would have believed possible.

'You just wanted a man, marriage, home – all the things most of your generation are beginning to find they can do without. It's pathetic. Can't you see how pathetic you are?'

Lois paused by the table, a saucepan in her hand. She turned it over, seeming to wonder whether she should use it or not.

Norah said sharply, '*You* don't look any too good from where I'm sitting.' She turned her head away and screwed up her eyes. The impression was not of a person suppressing anger, rather, she seemed to be trying to bring some relevant image to mind. One could almost see light penetrating the eyelids. Her face was composed when she spoke again. 'I don't think we can come to terms, do you? I'm prepared to try, but I don't think we can do it. In a little while, perhaps, if we don't get too much on top of each other in the meantime, but not now.'

Samantha got up. 'If you think I'm going to come to terms with seeing my father getting more senile every day, you're even more stupid than I thought.'

'He wasn't in the least senile when you failed to come to terms with him just now,' Norah retorted. 'He was on top form.'

Samantha said shrilly, 'I'm getting out of here even if I have to sleep in a ditch.'

'There's no need for that,' Lois said cheerfully. 'Jack will be going back to London on Tuesday, so if you can hold out until then, you can come to stay with me for a few days.'

Samantha was patently torn between the desire to make as much trouble as possible and a healthy sense of her own well-being. Eventually she said grudgingly, 'How do I get to you? I haven't got a car.'

'Neither have I. I can't drive. But there are buses, three, in fact . . .'

'Three buses!'

Hester, foreseeing the imminent breakdown of this sensible scheme, said, 'If all else fails, I will take you.'

'What about your work?' Norah said when Samantha had departed, swearing defiantly to cover her retreat.

'You may well ask.'

'You're a good woman.'

'Just weak-minded.'

The kitchen door opened and Hesketh appeared, looking apologetic. 'Coffee?' he said. 'Should I . . . perhaps?'

They left him to make coffee and strolled out on to the lawn where Lois joined Jack who was pretending to admire the river.

'You have managed very well today,' Hester said to Norah. She was suspicious rather than congratulatory, like the member of the audience who is not entirely convinced by a conjuring trick.

Norah said vaguely, 'Yes, I suppose I have.' She sounded as if her recall of what had actually taken place was fragmented.

'It is all a matter of caring,' Lois said when Hester came down to the river bank. 'Sometimes the less you care, the better you cope.' They watched Norah poking about idly among the roses. 'And for some reason she wasn't really caring at lunch, was she? Once or twice, I felt she wasn't with us at all.'

Hester said unhappily, 'Oh, I don't know about that.'

'I hope she's not ill.'

Hesketh came out to announce that coffee was served. He had put a napkin over one arm and was making quite a performance of it. They all indulged him, Jack even going so far as to mention Jeeves.

8

Alone in the kitchen when all her guests had departed, Norah said aloud, 'There is no happiness for you in this.' Her expression suggested that her spirit denied this sober statement.

In his study, Michael reflected on the unwisdom of seeing Norah Kendall again. It was nearly dusk, yet the world seemed flooded with light.

Norah said, wringing out the washing-up cloth, 'I can make do with a little, a very little, if only I don't have to give this up.'

Michael told himself, I have had so little opportunity to love, I can't turn away from this.

Three days later he went again to the country park where the log cabin was being constructed. 'I'll take sandwiches and have a walk on the moors in the afternoon,' he said to Valentine. It was his one free afternoon and walking was his great pleasure.

As a rule, the Hoaths ate their main meal in the evening when there was less chance of interruption, so a sandwich lunch would normally have presented no problem. But Valentine was now attending so many rehearsals prior to the opening of *Hedda Gabler* that lunch, with attendant irritations, had become the main meal. 'Alcoholism is supposed to be a problem with clergy wives,' she had said only yesterday. 'I would have expected chronic indigestion to be more prevalent.' Now she said, 'I shall probably be out late tonight. It's our first dress rehearsal.'

'I could finish off that pie we had last night.'

He was usually punctilious about consulting her as to how they should spend his free afternoon and they would often go to an art exhibition, see a foreign film, work together in the garden. It was a bright day and she could not complain that this once he should make his own choice. She noted, however, that he did not suggest she should join him. It was a constant irritation to her that he could not accept that she did not like walking and hated moorland and must always persist whenever the occasion arose in putting her in the position of having to refuse him. How many times had she said, 'Why don't you just go?' She was dismayed when she handed him the sandwiches that this was what he proposed to do today.

'Will you be back for tea?'

'Don't wait for me. I know you hate breaking off from gardening.'

This was true, but had never before prevented his returning for tea. He had a sentimental love of tea in the garden and would sit there long after she had become restive. He could not understand that the one occasion she lost all thought of time, was unaware of herself, was when she was gardening.

She watched him walk away and then sat at the kitchen table, unmoving, her expression remote as that of a chess player contemplating a difficult move. In fact, she was not thinking at all, her mind was empty as a wind tunnel on a still day.

Once out in the garden, however, she was tormented by thoughts of what he might be doing. This spoilt her pleasure and in the afternoon she occupied her mind by going over Hedda's lines, aware as she did so of a widening gulf between herself and this woman.

Laura Addison had been weeding the paths in the graveyard, a task which she insisted on doing on her own, 'because I get so muddled if people try to help, I'm better when I can do things at my own pace.' This did not prevent her from telling people that 'the graveyard seems to get bigger and bigger as I get older.' As she rested from her labours to reflect on the burden laid upon her, she heard Valentine's voice. After a minute or two she got up and walked round to the back gate of the vicarage.

'Oh, it's you,' she said, rather as though Valentine might not have realized this. 'I thought you would be out as it is your free afternoon and such a lovely day.'

'No.' Valentine walked slowly towards her. 'Michael had a meeting this morning. But this afternoon he is going for a walk and I shall be joining him later.' She made this explanation as though it had been explicitly requested and Laura Addison flushed.

'I hope you didn't think I was interfering. It's just that I like to keep an eye on the vicarage when you are both out.'

'You are most kind.'

Valentine went back to work. She did not allow her mind to reflect on what had just happened, nor did she consider what she would do later in the afternoon. She was getting into a habit of not thinking. As she worked in the garden she felt much as she did when she was waiting off-stage. The cue would be given, she would make her entrance, with any luck she would come out with the right words.

Norah and Michael had chosen for their chance meeting-place the banks of a rock-strewn, peaty stream seldom visited by trippers warned away from this part of the moor because of a dangerous bog.

'No one will come upon us here,' Norah assured Michael as they ate their sandwiches. 'The locals won't go near the bog and the tors draw the tourists like a magnet. They have to go back with a trophy of some kind, poor things. "We got right to the top." Occasionally one of them breaks an ankle or a neck.' For some reason which he could not fully understand she seemed impelled to show him the less appealing side of herself. Now she was regarding him with a look which said, 'You didn't know I could be like this, did you?'

He said quietly, 'I don't like competitive people, either.'

'But you don't wish them dead. You've never had a spiteful thought.' She turned on him a face in which humour and asperity seemed constantly in contention.

It occurred to him that she was nervous. 'You're sure about this bog?' He affected mock anxiety as he looked towards the bobbing heads of cotton grass and the more beguiling bog asphodel. 'I remember a ghastly film *The Night has a Thousand Eyes* where the villains were swallowed up in quagmire.'

'You're quite safe. Not for nothing did I dwell beside the untrodden ways.'

'A maid whom there were none to praise and very few to love?'

'Yes, indeed. But not, I'm afraid, the sweetest thing that ever grew beside a human door. At least he didn't say "cottage door", you have to give him that.'

'You don't like Wordsworth?'

'I once had a boy friend who tried to convert me. It's a good job it was Wordsworth he was preaching and not God, otherwise I'd be an atheist now.'

'You have missed a lot.'

'I'm sure I have. And not only Wordsworth. I'm tone-deaf to most poetry. But then God doesn't whisper in my ear. I have always had to do things by the book. Dear old Laura Addison says she has an immediate awareness of "something received" at the Eucharist which is so precious that she can hardly bear to encounter people socially afterwards when we have coffee.' There was a hint of superiority in the way she spoke of Laura which was not quite masked by the amused good humour. 'But I don't have any feeling at all.'

'As a nurse, though, you wouldn't expect a patient to have an immediate feeling of being healed after an injection, would you?'

'It's exactly what I'd expect of some patients,' she retorted tartly. She flipped her feet up and down in the water, sending up little spurts of spray. 'As you must realize, I am rather a poor sort of Christian. After all these years, I can't control tongue or temper, and I have very little idea of how to come before God. I am always edgy and without peace of mind when I pray – without composure.' She looked at him, eyebrows raised. He was not sure what was expected of him. Reassurance? Or was it that the need to challenge had become a necessity to her, a way of survival?

He said gravely, 'Yet I have seen you with people who are ill when I have visited them and you have seemed composed then.'

She was as uneasy with praise as she was sensitive to criticism. 'Even that I have to work at.' She rested her bare feet on a boulder and sat, hunched forward, watching the brown froth of water swirling beneath her.

He noted that she did not feel any need to work at her appearance. Her clothes, plain blue skirt and blouse, looked as if they might date back to the days of her student nursing. She wore no make-up and her pale skin was painfully inflamed by the sun. She was as unself-conscious about her looks as she was spikily aware of her personality. He thought how arresting she must have been in her youth when her red hair was thick and glossy. She would not have needed to try to command attention. Valentine said she was one of those women to whom youth gives a fleeting attraction and the lasting expectation that they can achieve the same effect throughout life with the minimum of effort. Valentine thought Norah dowdy, but he was fascinated and moved to see the habits of youth still lingering in the woman. Although the hair was switched back in a meagre pony tail, she carried her head confidently as if it was crowned with fire.

'Tell me about your childhood,' he said, eager to add more strokes to the portrait. 'It can't have been bad all the time because you have a real capacity for enjoyment.'

She put one hand into the stream, letting the water cool her wrist while she thought about this. 'You don't think the capacity for enjoyment can be acquired?'

'I would like to think so. But my observations tell me that it is a gift of childhood.'

Above them the sky was cloudless and the larks were singing. 'What can I add to what they are saying?' she asked.

'I want to hear your song.'

'A simple song. When I was a child I was as excited by high moorland as some folk are by their first glimpse of the sea, the taste of salt on their lips and all that. As I climbed towards it and saw the light changing, I could smell freedom. The moors don't make big statements or issue challenges like mountains. They just wipe out all constrictions. This is the only place where I can breathe deeply. I suppose the sea does the same thing for some people, but it is alien territory and you can't walk on it – at least, most of us can't. But you can lie flat on your tummy and feel yourself a living part of moorland. When things were going well with us – which meant we had our chins above the pig swill – I had an old pony. And when he had to go, there were kind people who let me exercise their ponies. Those were the best times – the only times I have ever been pure in heart were on a pony's back with miles of moorland around me.'

They were both silent. She listened to the larks while he, looking with narrowed eyes to where ponies grazed near an outcrop of rock, tried to conjure up a figure riding with young, mutinous face and hair streaming like a Valkyrie.

'Did you know my mother?' he asked, excited by the image. 'She often came to stay with Hester.' He thought of his mother as a contemporary of Norah's because she had died when she was only forty.

Norah, visualizing a person of Hester's age, shook her head. 'I didn't come to town much until I joined the choir. That was when I met Hester. I've heard her speak of her sister but I don't ever remember meeting her.' She turned to look at him over one hunched shoulder. 'But you? You must have come often, too?'

'No. Hester only had the one spare room which my father found cramped enough without the added discomfort of a bed made up for me in the sitting-room. We only came the once, he and I.'

There was a pause while each played with the notion of a youthful meeting and wondered how it might have changed their lives.

When eventually they started to walk, Norah said, 'Tell me about your childhood.'

He had lived on the Ashdown Forest. The day had started with a walk across the forest to school and had drawn to a close with the walk home. At weekends he and his parents walked the dog in the afternoon. He had loved and grown to need that sense of space and freedom which the forest gave and the slow pattern which the walks made of his life. In the evenings in summer his parents had worked in the garden and he had gone to play in the forest with friends or, later, to sit in his bedroom doing his homework as the sun went down in a blaze which seemed to set the trees alight. In winter they had sat round the log fire, often in the dark.

'It seems now that those were the most precious moments of my life,' he said, 'those walks, those drowsy firelit evenings.'

'They seemed to go on and on for ever – the good things in childhood,' she responded. 'My pony whirled me off into eternity. Don't you still have fires, though? I always light a fire in the evenings.'

Valentine did not like the dust which fires caused or the subsequent clearing out of the grate which he so often failed to attend to. Fires were a thing of the past in their household. He was disturbed to find himself making comparisons; but not sufficiently disturbed to prevent his being aware, as he walked beside Norah, of many lost joys coming back to him. 'And at the end of walks there would be piled toast and hot strong tea.'

'Not at my homecoming.' The response was sharp this time. 'Bread and dripping if I was on time, and the switch taken from behind the door if I was late.'

He was silent. 'There I go again,' she said. 'You thought I was a contrary piece, didn't you, when we got onto the subject of women priests at that meeting? Admit it!'

'I expect I was a bit contrary, too. It's a subject I am uneasy about.'

'Can you tell me why?'

'I'm not sure of the theology yet.' Now that she was reassured of his feeling for her she was beginning to relax and as he bent his mind to the subject, she watched, tenderly amused, seeing the child in the man as she listened. 'But that's not entirely the answer. It's more personal. I feel as though a part of myself is threatened when women want to take over.'

'Not many men would admit that,' she laughed.

'I don't mean it in quite the way you probably imagine.' He shepherded them both back to the point at issue. 'It sometimes seems to me that in late middle life men have spent themselves – they seem puzzled, disappointed.'

'Women get tired by the years, believe me!'

'But I think they understand better what has happened to

them. Women know themselves. Or so it seems to me. And their goals are more often within themselves.' Beneath their feet the heathland bluebells smelt honey sweet; she breathed in the scent gratefully but he walked on unheeding. 'Whereas men are so often strangers to themselves all their lives. They, more than women, are expected to conform to group expectations, whether sporting or drinking – and to professional and business images.' She watched a golden plover wheel above and, eager to show it to him, touched his shoulder. He went on, his eyes on the ground, as though he must wrestle thought free of the tangled bracken. 'Women don't let their work take over their personalities, they seem to be better at keeping something of their own self untouched.' His voice vibrated, rusty with emotions not often released. 'It seems – I don't know how to put this – that this is something they have to do for all mankind, important that it isn't lost to the species. The feminists frighten me because I see them using men's weapons . . .'

'Adopting the worst characteristics of their oppressors?' she said lightly.

'If you wish to put it like that,' he said huffily.

They walked in silence for a little while, then she touched his cheek lightly with her hand. 'I didn't mean to mock.'

'There is some quietness in women. Theirs isn't a confrontation with life so much as an assent – for good or ill, they allow it to happen.'

She said sadly, 'This is what *you* learnt at your mother's knee.'

'We are all afraid of ourselves today. So afraid!' he cried out passionately. 'We have become so careful, so bland with one another. I want people to tell me what they make of this world of ours – not just repeat what the scientists and sociologists tell them. I want to know what questions they ask when they look up at the stars when they can't sleep at night, when they sit by the dying. I want to know what people are really concerned with, deep in their hearts and at the back of their minds – not what they are programmed to care about.' He had the wild look of the old-time actor who believes that the whole man should be used to convey strong emotion – why else was he given eyes, nostrils and mouth, shoulders and hands? 'But we are afraid.

There are so many destroyers. It is a very brave person who will any longer state a simple belief, reveal a dearly cherished love. It sometimes seems it is easier to die for the things that mean most to us than to speak of them. It's safe to speak of the ugly things – aggression, greed, lust – but to reveal the things one treasures, or to admit one's fears, doubts, disappointments, longings, would be to walk naked into a wasps' nest.'

He looked down and saw that her face was twisted in misery. His own face became gaunt with suffering. 'I'm so sorry. I have upset you.'

'I don't know how to answer. That's what upsets me. I don't know what to say to you when you speak like that. Things come out so jaggedly when I try to speak of my feelings.'

Only a short time ago he had tried to recreate the Norah of her youth. Now, he scorned the sentimentality of his imaginings. How could that plastic marvel have compared with this face before him now, the dry skin scored by as many lines of laughter as of tiredness and anxiety, the hurt eyes still undulled by disappointment?

'The fault is in me,' he said gently. It was on the tip of his tongue to say that Valentine had this difficulty with him, but he knew that were he to say it he would be led to make an unfavourable comparison. He kissed Norah on the cheek and tasted the salt of her tears. 'Oh, my dear, my dear, I need you so much!'

For a time they stood silent, presenting an odd spectacle on this bright, still day, holding each other stiff as a pair of scarecrows blown together by a strong wind.

When eventually they walked on, hands clasped, they seemed at peace. 'I think the part of my childhood I miss the most is those firelit evenings,' he said. 'Nothing can replace the intimacy of people sitting together over a fire, not feeling the need to speak. And the talk when it comes seems to well up from some deeper level; things can be said – ideas, reflections, questions answered or not answered – by firelight that don't get said at any other time.'

Norah's tears had long since dried by the time Valentine came in sight.

*

143

'I don't often see you on the bus, Mrs Hoath.' Mrs Pettifer made a rebuke of the statement.

'My husband has the car.'

Mrs Pettifer interpreted this as the opening of hostilities. 'If I hadn't come up before Jimmy Lander the week after my husband refused him a loan, I should never have had my licence suspended.'

'I didn't know you had had your licence suspended.'

'It was in the local paper on the front page.' Mrs Pettifer was incensed by Valentine's indifference. '"Bank manager's wife has close encounter with market stall."'

Valentine looked out of the window, entertaining a fantasy of Mrs Pettifer at the wheel of a vehicle bedecked with lace and silver-framed photographs and other bric-à-brac reminiscent of an old canal barge. The idea of Mrs Pettifer gypsying through life might well have served a modern Cervantes.

'Everyone knows all about his merchandise,' Mrs Pettifer was saying. It was apparent that it was the contents of the stall which she considered to be a matter for the law rather than the quality of her driving. 'I kept telling them the whole lot wasn't worth five pounds and anyway it probably fell off the back of a lorry.' And therefore fit to be trampled over, Valentine noted – she must have sounded like a latter-day Marie Antoinette. Valentine made a mental resolution to read the local paper in future, or better still, study the courts' lists for the coming attractions.

The bus was climbing now, the stops more infrequent as the houses thinned out. Surely Mrs Pettifer wasn't proposing to walk on the moors? Perhaps some such thought had occurred to Mrs Pettifer. The two women looked at each other speculatively. Mrs Pettifer said, with the air of one who has no reason to be afraid of laying down her cards, 'I am going to my bone man. That wretched stall played havoc with my back.'

'You would think he'd have a place in town.'

'He is *very* good.' Mrs Pettifer's tone made it clear that nothing so mundane as a town could accommodate such a man.

Valentine was beginning to experience some difficulty in breathing. 'It's stifling in this bus, isn't it?' She feared the clamminess of her skin might be noticeable.

'Going visiting, are you?' There were only a few houses up here and Mrs Pettifer knew the occupants of each one.

'I am going for a walk.' In fact, Valentine felt it much more likely she would faint.

'The moor is no place to walk on your own, even on a clear day,' Mrs Pettifer said, her motives not entirely solicitous.

Valentine bent her little finger back, a method of curing faintness which had proved efficacious on similar occasions. She knew that Mrs Pettifer was probing and detested having to respond. But since the purpose of this trip was to offer satisfaction rather than gratification to the Mrs Pettifers of the town, she must needs reply, 'I am meeting Michael. He likes long walks and I don't. So we compromise.'

'Oh, I see.' Mrs Pettifer had lost interest. She levered herself into a crouching position. 'You'll have to give me a little push, if you don't mind. All this jolting about has made my poor back worse.' Valentine responded with alacrity and Mrs Pettifer shot to the roof like a Jack-in-the-box.

The irritation caused by the woman's presence had been nearly as effective as the finger-bending. Now that she had gone Valentine was tempted to get off the bus. Only the thought of the last uphill stretch prevented her. It was difficult enough to see it happen, this gradual dissolution of the world, without having to force her body towards the void.

The bus stopped a little short of the plateau; the final haul she must do on her own. The knowledge of what lay ahead weighed like lead pieces strapped to her thighs. At each step her whole body seemed to pull her back as if rearing from a precipice. People, laughing and talking, passed on light feet, springing upwards like mountain goats. Above her head she knew that the sky was blue but she dared not look up and see it growing into dizzying immensity. The song of the larks was terrifying in its meaningless ecstasy, its soaring release from all things human.

The moment the ground levelled out she jerked her head up, knowing that one second's delay would lead to another and she would end up – as she had on previous occasions – lying face down on the turf. Once, long before she met Michael, she had refused to move from such a spot and had been carried away to a car by some chance hikers who thought she was insane. The elderly couple who had been her companions had thought she was petulantly intent on spoiling their pleasure.

Now, slowly, she began to walk down the track which led across the spine of the moor. She had extreme difficulty in keeping her balance. This, no doubt, was how people felt who were made to walk the plank by pirates. Only her fate was worse because her plank appeared to go on into eternity. At least she was facing the tors, only thumb prints on the sky, but something on which to nail her eyes.

She did not know which way Michael had gone, so she must not walk too far. Ahead there was the moorland equivalent of spaghetti junction. She sat in the middle of it, keeping her eyes on the tors and repeating the one mantra which had ever proved very effective for her, 'I am the jewel in the lotus.'

After an age, aeons, a century, or fifteen minutes, whichever way you were experiencing time, two dots appeared and evolved into people recognizable as Michael Hoath and Norah Kendall.

'I thought it would be nice,' she said when they were within hearing distance, 'if we all three returned to town together. If it's all the same to you, I'd rather we didn't make conversation.'

'I'm sorry about this,' Michael said later when they were alone at the vicarage. He was looking into the garden where the last sunlight fell on a gnarled tree worthy of William Blake, its writhing limbs displaying Jehovah in one of his arboreal manifestations. He spoke not in the tone of a penitent but as one viewing some act of Nature over which he has no control.

'At least be discreet in future,' she said.

This had the effect of turning him from the garden towards her. She was rearranging flowers in the bowl on the table, not idly but as if fully absorbed in the business of extricating wilting foliage and snapping off dead heads.

'You are very surprising,' he said.

'Yes. I surprise myself.'

He watched as she worked, ruthlessly creating a simpler arrangement.

'It's rather like that joke about God,' she said conversationally. 'Not dead – alive and well and working on a less ambitious project.' She stepped back to view her handiwork. 'Well, it will last a few more days.'

Behind her, she heard him walk out of the room. She went on staring steadily at the flowers, wondering why she was not upstairs packing her bags. Her mind seemed quite unable to answer this question; it was much too busy posing others, as if this affair had merely served to highlight issues which had long needed attention, such as the need to work out another kind of life for herself.

9

There was a particularly violent thunderstorm on the first night of *Hedda Gabler*. Backstage, in the old part of the building, buckets and bowls were put out and the stage manager warned the cast, 'Just watch where you are walking when you get your call.' His words did not go unheeded. On a similar occasion three years ago, Leontes had fallen over a bucket and broken his leg, thus bringing the run of *A Winter's Tale* to a premature end. It had been almost impossible to explain to the Director of the theatre that there were occasions when the show could not go on.

In the newer part of the building which comprised the foyer, cloakroom and bar, windows had steamed over and there was an unpleasant smell, as if a lot of old, wet dogs had been let loose.

Hester was in charge of front-of-house for this performance, a duty she tended to take over-seriously.

'How you find the time, Hester, is a mystery to me.'

'You're hardly the one to talk about time,' Hester replied. Her friend, Annie Cleaver, had recently been entertained at Her Majesty's expense for a week.

'Oh well, I know you need your little recreation.'

Hester, stung by the implication that her pleasures were superficial, the more so since there was some truth in the

148

accusation, retorted, 'You were known to enjoy yourself before you became so heavy with purpose.'

'If you knew what I have been through – and, of course, my experiences are nothing in comparison . . .' But here Annie was swept into the foyer before she could give details of her harrowing. 'If you can tear yourself away from your scribbling, you must come to supper one day next week,' she called over her shoulder before her voice was drowned by a roll of thunder.

Age! Hester thought, glaring around her; why do our lighter notes no longer sound? She walked towards the lobby, aware that she herself was not approaching her task with notable lightness of heart.

The main entrance to the building opened into the small lobby; to the left a few steps led down to the foyer and to the right stairs tunnelled up to the gallery. Anyone standing in the lobby commanded a good view of the people in the foyer. From this vantage post Hester was aware of a regrettable affinity with Captain Bligh on the look-out for mutineers on the lower deck. Obviously she was the kind of person who should not be entrusted with too much authority. Behind her the telephone rang. She approached it in nervous anticipation. The one question which hung heavy over anyone doing front-of-house was the identity of the stage manager.

'Who is that?' The voice at the other end of the line betrayed equal apprehension.

'Hester Pascoe.'

'Ah, my favourite front-of-house lady.'

'Flattery will get you a long way, George,' Hester said, unconvinced but pleased nonetheless. 'Are there any particular problems?'

'Apart from the fact that we shall soon be wading knee-deep back here, you mean? Well, yes. The producer wants a prompt start and a quick interval – so wheel them in pronto, there's a love, otherwise I'll have him crying all over me.'

'We're likely to have latecomers on a night like this. What about them?'

'Hold them back and give me a ring. I'd like a minute for things to settle. You're going to ring the bell at five to, aren't you?'

Hester enjoyed ringing the bell and was quite sorry it had to be tolled only the once. The foyer cleared quickly and there were no strays in the toilets. As she approached the stairs up to the bar she encountered the producer who said, 'All clear up there.'

Hester phoned the stage manager, noting with pride that the time was a minute to eight. She turned away from the phone to find herself confronted by a large man with a broken nose and an angry expression. Obviously he had anticipated making a quick get-away because he had no raincoat. He stood before her, steam rising menacingly from his large frame. Hester recognized that bane of the front-of-house person, the policeman going off-duty whose car is trapped in the car park.

'The curtain has only just gone up,' she said, sorry to note an ingratiating intonation in her delivery.

He regarded her with dislike, his wrath tempered by the knowledge that he had no authority to use the theatre's car park during performances.

'You can't expect me to wait until the interval.'

They both knew that this was exactly what the theatre management did expect, but Hester felt there were people better equipped than herself to remind him of the fact. She went up to the bar. The bar staff showed little inclination to quit their entrenched position and immediately busied themselves polishing glasses. Fortunately by the time she returned to the foyer one of the refreshment ladies had admitted responsibility.

Another problem was waiting in the presence of Charles Venables.

'You are very late,' she told him severely.

'Yes.' He shifted from one wet foot to the other, looking like a schoolboy who has been caught out of bounds – if there were any bounds nowadays for schoolboys.

Hester went to the phone and he said, 'Er, perhaps you had better wait a moment' and made an awkward movement of one hand in the general direction of the ladies' toilets. Hester raised an eyebrow. Charles turned away, muttering about programmes, his ears red. The door to the toilets opened and Shirley Treglowan emerged, remarkably refreshed by the rain, looking flushed, triumphant and guilty – a young person capable of almost Mozartian diversity, Hester thought as she obtained the resigned approval of the stage manager to let them into the auditorium. 'The bloody door knob has come off already, so what does another diversion matter?'

As she opened the inner doors to the auditorium, Hester was aware of that scuffling and throat-clearing which indicate that an audience has not settled down. Rain drummed on the corrugated iron roof. Then Valentine's voice rang out with a confident expectation of attention. Notice was given that from now on the audience would be expected to bend their minds to what was happening on stage. Not a head turned as Charles and Shirley slunk like thieves in the night towards their places.

Hester closed the doors softly. This was the time when she usually read a book. This evening she sat quietly, reflecting on the humbling discovery that Valentine appeared better able to handle authority than Hester Pascoe.

Charles looked forward to talking to Shirley during the interval about the producer's interpretation, which he felt was at variance with Valentine's playing of Hedda. It was apparent that Valentine had taken a strong dislike to Hedda. This was a ruthless portrayal of a woman with too little to occupy her time and no constructive idea as to how her situation might be remedied. Hers was the desperation of the woman who knows that she is being destroyed but cannot summon either the will or the courage to break out of the system which holds her. Eventually, when she has closed every door on herself, there will be only one course left to her.

From the performance of the rest of the cast, Charles guessed that the producer looked upon Hedda as the true sister of Nora and all other gallant women who refuse to be confined in a doll's house. The pistol shot was a declaration of independence. Valentine had told Charles she thought that by this stage neither Hedda nor her creator had the faintest idea what was to become of her. 'I don't believe in that pistol shot any more than Desdemona's handkerchief.'

Charles had overlooked the fact that Shirley often worked backstage at the theatre. As they made their way into the foyer during the interval he was surprised to find that she had definite ideas of her own about production if not interpretation.

'I can't think what he was doing allowing Tesman to mask Hedda like that,' she said.

'Like what?' Charles asked, mystified.

'And then, setting the chairs in a straight line so that poor old Brack had either to say all his lines out front as though Hedda wasn't there, or let us see the back of his head most of the time.'

'Would you like coffee?' Charles asked austerely.

'Please.'

When he returned she was talking to a haggard blonde who had played Blanche Dubois in *A Streetcar Named Desire* and had the distracted air of having become detached from reality ever since.

'Oh yes,' the blonde said wearily, 'they are all quite mad about her. Definitely the flavour of the month.' She turned to the Director of the theatre who was standing alone staring glassily at a damp patch over the kitchen door. 'I must say Tesman rose to the occasion when the door knob came off – just as if knobs came off doors all the time in his house.'

An alarming crimson tide suffused the Director's face. 'Well, they don't come off doors all the time in this theatre.'

'He'll have someone's head on a charger before the night is out,' Shirley told Charles.

'Really?'

She sipped her coffee, looking around for more people with whom to gossip and failing to find a likely candidate returned her attention to Charles. 'What did you think of that book I lent you?'

'It was amusing enough. I noted from the jacket that someone had suggested it might be a masterpiece. Personally, I found it rather like a packet of Rice Krispies – a lot of snap and crackle but little in the way of sustenance.'

'That's just what I felt only I could never have put it like that.' She gazed at him admiringly.

He began to talk to her about the producer's interpretation of the play and she listened with avid attention while her coffee grew cold.

*

The box office manager, who had left the theatre ten minutes ago, returned to tell Hester that the car park was awash. 'Better warn them when they leave that they'll have to wade to their cars.'

'Oh goodness!' Hester had worn her only respectable pair of shoes in honour of this occasion.

'It's not so bad if you go out of the dressing-room exit; but we can't have the audience tramping around back-stage.'

'No, of course not,' she said cheerfully. 'They their worldly task hast done so home must go and take their chance.'

She clanged the bell vigorously and watched her charges in the foyer troop back to the theatre. Then she checked that both toilets were empty before going up to the bar. Only three people remained there. She stood at the head of the stairs looking at them. A lurid flash of lightning heralded her arrival. The effect was remarkable. She could see herself in their eyes, hunched in her puce velvet jacket, like one of those small, malevolent creatures that decorate the fringes of medieval pictures of the gateway to the underworld. The woman cringed and lowered her eyes; the pop-eyed old man drained his drink. They went past her with averted eyes. 'I hope you enjoy the rest of the show,' she said, feeling they deserved a reward for good behaviour. Neither had the spirit to respond. One man remained. He looked at her brazenly and she bared her teeth at him in a basilisk smile. He poured a good half glass of whisky down his throat and headed for the stairs. She stood to one side so that she could follow close on his heels. He went at a good pace across the foyer and then darted into the Gents. Hester stood outside, snapping with frustration. He was there so long she began to think he was afraid to come out.

'Is there anyone else there?' she asked when he eventually emerged.

He shook his head and looked around furtively as if seeking another avenue of escape, then resigned himself to the second half of *Hedda*. She closed the pen doors behind him. One minute behind time, damn and blast him! Undoubtedly in a sheep dog trial she would be disqualified for taking a nip here and there.

'Sorry,' she said to the stage manager, 'One stray sheep.'

Her shepherding duties over, Hester went to the broom cupboard and then began to sweep the foyer floor. When her cleaning duties were finished, she counted the refreshment money. She was on her third recount when the auditorium door opened and closed behind Norah Kendall.

'Are you all right?' Hester asked, seeing that she looked very pale.

'I keep falling asleep and it is maddening Hesketh.'

'One way and another, I would hardly have thought it was a time to sleep. Shall I get you a coffee, or I expect that the bar could provide something more stimulating.'

'No, I'll just sit here with you if I'm not in the way. I've got a bit of a headache, I expect it's the storm.'

'I hope it's going to blow over. Veronica is staying with me and we planned to do a long walk tomorrow.'

'You'll be able to go for a swim instead.'

Norah wore the emerald green sheath which Hester remembered as her going-away dress. It hung more loosely on her now; she had lost weight since her wedding. In spite of this, and her evident tiredness, she seemed in good heart.

'The vengeful creature was burning a manuscript when I took my leave. Does that chill your blood?'

'I always keep a second copy to meet just such an emergency. And when I go away I take it with me in case the house catches fire.'

'Do you really expect the house to catch fire?'

'The part of me that decides how much insurance to pay doesn't.'

'What a lot of different people you are, my old Hester.'

'I encounter more than one Norah Kendall.'

Norah flushed and there was an awkward silence. Hester realized that now, if ever, she should say something and knew that there was nothing to say. She put the refreshment money in the paper bag provided and scribbled a note for the treasurer to the effect that her maths was not up to standard – a fact of which he was already aware.

'We had a letter from Samantha this morning,' Norah said.

'She is going to Spain to stay with a friend who has a villa there.'

'I would have thought that was a bit like slumming for Samantha.'

'I don't think she's fussy so long as the sun shines.'

'The last time we talked about Samantha your voice reached high C every time her name was mentioned, now you sound most equable.'

'I seem to have discovered an unexpected strain of sweetness in myself. Don't laugh at me.'

'I am far from laughing at you.'

'Hester, I would like . . .' Whatever it was that she would have liked to say to Hester was interrupted by the refreshment ladies who had finished in the kitchen. 'Don't forget to put the milk order out, will you?' one of them said to Hester as she bustled past.

'That's Millie Perkins, isn't it?' Norah said. 'Bossy little piece.'

'I'd better go and do it now. It is the one thing I tend to forget.'

The refreshment ladies opened the side door and rain surged in. Hester had to lean against it to close it after them. When she returned to the foyer Norah said, 'Are you joining us on the pilgrimage to Walsingham?'

'Yes, I thought the opportunity of observing the behaviour of pilgrims at first hand shouldn't be passed over.'

'That's not quite the right spirit. Does it mean you are going to put us in a book?'

'A short story is all you'll get from me.'

'I am told we may have to double up. Will you share a room with me?'

'If it has to be anyone, I'd as soon it was you.'

'Thank you for that grudging acceptance, my lover.'

'Unless, of course, you can persuade Hesketh to join you.'

'Hesketh? On a pilgrimage! That would be material for a volume of short stories.'

'Yes.' Hester wrinkled her nose, wondering if she could do it anyway without the material involvement of Hesketh. It certainly opened up a lot of interesting possibilities – a guide to the Retreat Houses of England written by a character very much resembling Hesketh would be really quite wicked.

'The worst part of it all,' Norah was saying, 'will be the long coach journey with young Alan Judge being the life and soul of the party.'

'And frequent stops for people who are travel-sick. There must be somewhere nearer than Walsingham where one can be a pilgrim.'

'It has to be Walsingham because Laura once had an "experience" there. Why Laura should expect to have two revelations when St Paul only had one, I can't imagine.' She sighed and said without undue remorse, 'How I do lack charity to that woman.'

'And what about Shirley Treglowan?' Hester asked. 'Is she coming?'

Norah was surprised. 'I shouldn't imagine so for one moment.'

'I was just thinking that she might bring Charles. Charles on a pilgrimage would be even better value than Hesketh.'

'Charles Venables, do you mean? Why ever would Shirley bring him?'

'They are here together this evening, she hanging on his every word.'

'I have always thought of Charles Venables as neuter.'

'So have I. But when I looked at him this evening I began to wonder. He had those rather protruding eyes which I associate with sexually aroused males.'

'Thyroid, more like, in his case.'

'Maybe, but I never cease to wonder at the capacity of ordinary people to surprise.'

Norah smiled to herself.

Smile if you will, Hester thought, but don't imagine you have any secrets from me. I know just where you are at this stage of the affair – suspended somewhere out of time in a place where you fondly imagine you cannot be hurt or yourself hurt any other person. And a hard coming to earth you'll have of it, my dear.

Their silence lasted until the gun shot rang out distantly. 'Well, that's that,' Hester said. When she opened the outer auditorium doors the applause had started; after a few moments there was a great crescendo in which thunder joined wholeheartedly. Someone in the gallery shouted 'Bravo!' A triumph for Valentine.

The storm continued during the night. Michael, who had come to meet Valentine, found the fire brigade pumping out water from the car park. When it was possible to reach his car, the engine would not start. Hesketh responded to the situation with an unexpected display of histrionic virtuosity, insisting on carrying Norah to his two-seater while declaiming 'Lord Ullin's Daughter'.

'The Bar's gain is the theatre's loss,' Valentine said to him as she and Michael waded towards the street.

By way of an encore he called after them, ' "There's a power of deep rivers with floods in them where you do have to be lepping the stones and you going to the south, so I'm thinking the two of them will be drowned together in a short while surely".'

'It seems to have been worse in other parts of the country,' Michael said to Valentine at breakfast the next morning. 'Serious flooding in Norfolk. A month too early.' The pilgrimage had been arranged before he came to the parish and he would have welcomed an opportunity to cancel it. 'At least it's not like a retreat. As far as I can gather I don't have to do much except be there.'

'And be jolly. I am assured it is very jolly. We all go to the pub in the evening and the locals are so surprised that vicars can be jolly – although this has been going on for so many years one would think the locals would have ceased to be surprised by anything.'

'You are coming, then?'

A place had been booked for the new vicar and his wife, but when Valentine heard of this she had made it quite clear that she had no intention of taking part. Now, she said, 'Why not? I, too, have a soul. Don't you want me to come?'

'Of course I want you to come.'

How easily you have learnt to lie in this far country which you now inhabit, she thought.

'I have to go to the Diocesan meeting,' he said. 'And this afternoon I thought I would call on Hester. She has Veronica staying with her.'

'I thought they spent all their time out walking.'

He looked out of the window. The rain had stopped but the lawn had become a lake. 'I don't think even Aunt Hester would walk in this weather.'

The opportunity to challenge him had passed, as had many others. Valentine told herself that it was no use issuing challenges while he was out of her reach. This sense of leading a charmed existence would not last and she would be wise to wait until, one way or another, the spell was broken. The last thing she wished to do was to risk letting loose a lot of violent emotion in the house; were this to happen she feared that when all the barriers were down what would be laid bare would be her own emptiness.

Michael's attachment to Norah Kendall had concentrated Valentine's mind on herself. Her unwillingness to blame him for what had happened interested her, and as she reviewed her attitude she had come to realize that the disdain and fastidious contempt which had for so long distanced her from other people was in reality nothing more than self-dislike. In any confrontation with Michael she must be the loser unless she could find a person within herself with whom she could be reconciled.

She thought about this as she washed up the breakfast dishes and fed the cat. The image of womanhood which she most constantly derided was that of the good and loving woman, sustaining and supporting her husband, nourishing her children and sending them out in due season to make their own way in the world. She had mocked this image most of her adult life – ever since, in fact, the time when she discovered she would not be put to the test of motherhood. Perhaps she would not have made a good mother, but not being given the opportunity to surprise oneself was rather like not being allowed to sit an examination. One did not like to think of oneself as being such a waste of an examiner's time. And it was no use behaving as though this was of little importance to her. The image of womanhood remained strong and undiminished by ridicule.

There was a distinct possibility that she believed in it, and that being so, having been rejected as a mother, she could not afford to be ruled out as a candidate for good wife. Or, if good was setting one's sights too high, then proper – a proper wife. If she did not make measurable progress towards that goal during this crisis in her life she would always despise herself. 'Proper,' she said, testing the word and finding it less daunting than good.

It was at the very moment when she repeated the word proper that she became aware of the smell. The torrential rain had ceased and most of the yard outside the kitchen had been dried by the wind. The few dark patches which remained looked something more than damp; had it been autumn she would have thought decaying vegetation had been blown into the yard. A closer inspection seemed advisable if not desirable. Valentine walked slowly into the yard, one hand over nose and mouth. The drain had overflowed but it was only too apparent that it was not the proper contents of the drain which confronted her.

Her first impulse was to retire to her bed with a bottle of eau-de-Cologne until Michael returned. Or she could phone Hester and leave a message for him. She had a vivid picture of how Hester would react; the situation might well form the basis of a short story. Valentine straightened her back and raised her head; then, aware that her posture owed more to Joan of Arc approaching the stake than a housewife dealing with an unpleasantness in the back yard, she consulted the yellow pages. In a few moments she was assured that help would be on its way very soon. In spite of the damage caused by the storm, it seemed that an overflow from the main sewer rated priority treatment.

She went into the kitchen and made sure that all the food had been put away. Within half an hour a taciturn man arrived and lifted the manhole cover in the yard. Valentine, watching from a distance, was aware that it would be years before she would be able to contemplate the contents of a stewpot with equanimity. He put down the rod and immediately, with a subterranean gluck-gluck, the whole evil boiling disappeared. Valentine paid him what seemed a very large sum of money for so little effort.

She had hoped he might be persuaded to clean up the mess but he merely said, 'Little bit of Dettol will soon get rid of that.'

Whatever else Dettol might do, it would not sweep the yard clean. Michael would not be home until after tea. Valentine meditated on whether a proper wife would reserve this task for her husband. Then it occurred to her that whatever the proper might do, Mrs Pettifer would certainly be out in the yard with broom and Dettol.

She went up to her bedroom, found a stocking and pulled it over her head, carefully cutting slits for the eyes. Then she went into the yard armed with a bucket of water and a bottle of Dettol. As she swept, the yard broom held at a fastidious distance, she reflected on the never-failing ability of life to make a bawdy joke of lofty pretension.

After seven applications of water and Dettol, she was satisfied that there was no danger of typhoid. She was left with the problem of the yard broom. It was inconceivable that it could retain a place in her household; equally inconceivable that it could be taken anywhere in the car, which would undoubtedly be Michael's solution if she left its disposal to him. She removed the stocking mask, ran a comb through her hair and left the vicarage carrying the broom. Proud and haughty, offering no explanation to anyone whom she met, Valentine made her way to the Council's tip, holding the broom at a disdainful distance like a deranged Britannia descended from her throne.

Only when she had cast the broom into one of the skips did she relax, standing in the deserted yard, weeping at her weakness.

'It's so nice not to have to hurry,' Veronica called down the stairs to Hester, who was waiting to put toast in the rack.

In Hester's opinion much misery – breakdown of marriage, disaffection of children, loss of friendship, to say nothing of many minor irritations and discomforts – could be avoided if people would only refrain from breaking their fast together. Some might rise from their beds light of spirit and kind of heart, but these were the few. The majority, of whom Hester was one, come leadenfoot to the table, the night still like grit in the deep crevices and crannies of their personality.

She had offered Veronica breakfast in bed, or the opportunity to 'have a lie in as it is raining and get your own breakfast when you feel like it'. What had not been on offer was breakfast together combined with no need to hurry.

'I grow more intolerant with the years, Tabitha,' she said to the cat who was agitating to be fed. 'And you are no better.'

By lunchtime all this had changed. As they had their pre-lunch drink and Veronica brought her friend up to date on matters in which Hester was not very interested, such as the old aunt's health, Hester reflected on the propensity of modern writers to approach old age as if they were reporters, medical dictionary tucked under one arm to make sure they had all the symptoms at their finger-tips. But in reality, she thought, old people don't look at each other making mental notes of brown splodges on wrinkled arms, arthritic finger joints, hiccups in articulacy and quirks of memory. Amazingly, when they say 'You haven't changed!' they really mean it. They actually look at each other, as I am looking at dear Veronica now, and see the person they have always seen. Perhaps it is different with men – there are two ages for men, one with and one without hair. But Veronica sitting there resolutely disposing of strong gin is recognizably the Veronica who mapped our walk along the Pennine Way with such fine disregard for contours that we twice failed to reach our overnight stop; the Veronica of the perpetu-ally broken heart who believed that one should never say no to love, the Veronica of the good beginnings who has furnished me with much factual material on matters as diverse as psychical research, pig breeding, hotel management and Russian Ortho-doxy at which she has at last arrived via Coptic art and transcendental meditation.

'You have had quite a journey through life,' Hester said enviously.

'But I have ended up where I started from.'

'You didn't start within a thousand miles of Orthodoxy.'

Veronica, who always maintained that her present affiliation was the constant of her whole life, smiled mysteriously and said, 'Ah, the Spirit, you see. Only the Orthodox understand the Spirit.'

'I don't know about that.' Hester could be mettlesome too. 'The Orthodox Church hasn't changed much in a thousand years. Some might say that is hardly allowing the Holy Spirit to work within it.'

They argued about this all through lunch, so that Hester was in a good mood when Norah Kendall arrived, saying she had not seen Veronica for so long she felt she must call and hoped it was not inconvenient. Even when Michael arrived saying much the same thing, Hester remained tolerantly amused. Veronica, of course, was delighted and only too willing to see herself as the focus of interest. The attentions of those younger than oneself become increasingly precious over the years, Hester thought indulgently. One must not begrudge Veronica her little triumph, delusory though it might be.

She sat back and let Michael and Veronica debate the attitude of their respective churches to the Holy Spirit while Norah tickled Tabitha behind the ears.

Veronica's grasp of theology was tenuous and she soon tired of listening to Michael expounding the one vital difference between the two Creeds. 'This must be very boring for you,' she said kindly to Norah. She screwed up her eyes, gazing back an infinitely long way to her own period of unenlightenment. 'I can understand how bewildered you must feel.'

Norah, usually well able to note condescension and put it down smartly, smiled as if indeed no thought of any consequence had ever troubled her mind.

'Do you remember when we were young, Hester,' Veronica hastened on before Michael could set himself to giving Norah an exposition on the Creeds, 'how we used to gather round the piano and sing? Every Christmas guests arrived with music,' she explained to Norah. 'People made their own pleasures when we were young, you see. We would sing pieces like "We'm come up from Somerset". I don't suppose you have ever heard of that.'

'Indeed, I have.' And Norah surprised Veronica by singing 'We'm come up from Zummerset where the Zoider apples grow . . .'

'Yes, well,' Veronica said. 'There was "The Gentle Maiden", too.'

Norah said to Hester, 'Do play for us.'

Hester, who had enjoyed those far off days, was not unwilling. Sunlight wavered on the window sill as if uncertain of a welcome after its long absence and sent an exploratory ray across the hearth, demure and unassertive. What more seemly activity to match this meek, nostalgic mood than the making of music? Hester played 'The Gentle Maiden' and Michael sang in his deep, grave voice, while on the hearth Tabitha switched her tail, stroking the rug gently as a feather duster. They all sang 'Cockles and Mussels' and 'Early one Morning'. Norah's voice was high and sweet and Veronica regarded her without favour. She was much taken by Michael and suggested a number of songs well-suited to his strong baritone, such as 'Drake is going West' and 'The Fishermen of England'. Tabitha kneaded the rug and purred, dribbling a bit because she was very old.

The sun, filtering through the leaves of the trees, sent little green flames darting across the keyboard. The feeling of shared pleasure grew stronger and a convivial warmth spread through the group around the piano. Michael and Norah smiled into each other's eyes as they sang. There was a subtle change in the vibration of their voices. The flames danced up and down the scale and in and out of the notes and behind the eyes of Michael and Norah a banked fire silently established its hold. Hester, feeling the itch of old scars, thought, enough is enough, and struck up the 'Song of the Western Men'.

> 'A good sword and a trusty hand
> A merry heart and true,
> King James's men shall understand
> What Cornish lads can do . . .'

Michael sang as if the words had been written yesterday for men with hearts afire. Veronica, carried away, joined croakingly in the chorus while Norah, flushed with febrile excitement, head held high, looked to Hester's jaundiced eye ridiculously like one of those damaged pagan figures whose disfigured heads still bear blazing torches.

'And have they fixed the where and when
And shall Trelawny die
Here's twenty thousand Cornishmen
Will know the reason why.'

As he sang the last chorus Michael let loose the full power of his voice; magnificent, triumphant, it seemed to Hester to ring out a message telling the whole of the West Country what was afoot in this small terraced house. She slammed down the lid of the piano.

'I want no part in this,' she said, looking at them with angry eyes. 'It was wrong of you to come here. Very wrong.'

She got up and went into the kitchen. In a few minutes Veronica came and joined her. 'Now what was all that about? They have gone without waiting for tea.' Her tone implied that if her party had to be broken up in this way, then the least Hester could do was to make a good story out of it. Hester, shaken beyond discretion, complied.

When she had finished, Veronica said, 'You very nearly wrecked your cousin Harry's marriage before you decided not to go through with the affair.'

'I can't even claim that much credit. He it was who broke away and made a dash for home and that dull little woman.'

'You never told me.'

'I can't think why I have told you now.'

Hester inspected the geraniums on the window sill, prodding the earth although she could see at a glance that it was parched.

'Since you have told me, perhaps you can say why if you thought it was right for you . . .'

'I didn't think it was right.' Hester ran water into the sink. 'There is no right and wrong at such times, as you well know, Veronica. It is a kind of madness.'

'Then let them have their madness.' Veronica spread out her arms in the manner of a conductor asking a choir to raise the roof with jubilation.

'It doesn't last,' Hester said flatly, beginning to submerge the pots in the sink. 'We aren't mad all our lives. And Michael believes in the absolutes – however far short he may fall and however often he falls, he believes. That will not have changed when the madness passes. Desire is totally selfish,' she said sternly to the gaudy geraniums. 'I remember how it was to love, but the man himself has become nothing more than a stimulant to sensation. That is all Norah is to Michael. His marriage to Valentine is much more important than this affair, an intrinsic part of all that he is.'

'I don't know how you can possibly say that.' Veronica's eyes travelled round the room as if seeking a clear image of lost loves.

'It has just come to me in one of those revelatory flashes which give one so little comfort.' Hester watched the water bubbling round the pots. 'It may well have been true for Harry and the anaemic Gwynneth.'

'And Norah?'

'I have received no such revelation as to Norah's condition.'

'She is probably one of those women who will be able to roll up the memory of her one true love in cotton wool and store it away snugly inside her,' Veronica said contemptuously. She looked at Hester and saw that her face was bleak.

'If you feel so badly about it, you shouldn't have been so melodramatic, slamming down the piano lid and practically telling them never to darken your doors again. What would you have done if I had behaved like that when you and Harry made use of my house?'

The smell of the geraniums was hot and as strong and unsubtle as the traces Tabitha sprayed about the garden. Hester said, 'Envy. I envy them, Veronica; even at my age I envy them their madness and all the pain it will bring them.'

Mrs Flack was cleaning the brass when the Vicar came into the church. The door to the graveyard was open and the church seemed full of the smell of rain-wet earth and the singing of birds. Mrs Flack had the sensation of being young again, a state of which she had little recall. Her life had been sliced in two when her husband died and the severed part in which she lived her widowhood had drifted away like an ice-floe. But now she saw a little girl dressed as a fairy sitting on the steps to the chancel while older children enacted a scene from a play.

Suddenly the little fairy burst into tears and cried out, 'Mummy, Mummy, I've wet myself,' and a young woman ran from the body of the church and, gathering the fairy into her arms, carried her out into the graveyard where raindrops hung from branch and leaf, glistening like the tiny beads sewn round the neck of her fairy frock. Mrs Flack blinked her eyes in a beam of sunlight. She saw that the Vicar was standing transfixed at the door leading into the graveyard and was surprised because he hadn't been at St Hilary's long enough for light and sound and smell to play tricks with his memory. Suddenly, he reached out and closed the door; then he locked it and, walking across to the main door, locked that, too. Laura Addison would have objected to the church being shut an hour early, but it was not the way of Mrs Flack to object. She went on cleaning the brass and minding her own business. When the Vicar came out of the vestry he did not acknowledge her, but strode, stern as an Old Testament prophet, towards the sanctuary where he seemed to lose his sense of purpose and stood, shoulders hunched, looking down at the worn floorboards. As she was not a person who expected to be noticed, and certainly not to be thanked for her efforts, Mrs Flack was content to remain invisible.

When she had finished polishing she went into the vestry and put away the cloths and Brasso. It should have been obvious that, having locked both the outer church doors, the Vicar was intending to leave by the vestry door. Mrs Flack's mind, however, was on other things. She bolted the door into the church and, smiling rather foolishly, went out of the vestry door into the sunlight.

Michael Hoath's mind was also on other things, and he had hung the key to the graveyard door on the appropriate hook in the vestry and absently put the key to the main door on the table. So it was that when he had read the Office he found himself locked in the church.

At first he refused to believe what had happened and walked from door to door, tugging and knocking. The graveyard door had glass panels covered by wire mesh and alone offered a view of the outside world. He stood by it while the sounds of early evening came to him, children shouting on their way home from the playing field, the fluting of a blackbird, the continuous hum of outgoing traffic inching across the bridge over the river. He saw moisture hung on the roses atop the garden wall, the refracted light glittering yellow, indigo, violet. He watched a large thrush pecking for worms in the ground beneath the tree where he had knelt with Norah. For him, as for Mrs Flack, this glistening garden had the quality of fairyland; a world new-made, full of magical delights awaiting those brave enough to turn their backs on the wearying world of here and now. He was desperate to step out into this secret place where Hester's anger could not follow him. Never before had a rain-cleansed garden seemed so lovely in its innocent refreshment. He wanted to be part of this joyous celebration of earth and tree and flower, to tunnel into this green enchantment until his mind was drugged by sensual delight, his body exhausted. He put his fist to the door and leant his head against it, crying out, 'I will not be trapped here.'

He had never before felt such desperation at being thwarted. For some time he stood by the door, looking out because he dared not turn inwards. He took hold of the handle and shook it. He had a vision of his own face, hideously distorted, eyes protruding, lips bared, like a gargoyle spewing out venom. He looked up at the stained glass windows which contained figures of saints, imperviously benign, each with one hand uplifted in blessing. Rage and panic were so strong that he turned and blundered down the aisle towards the chancel steps where there was a heavy stool. He found himself facing the crucifix. It stopped him, but he did not fall to his knees; instead he turned into the lady chapel and sat down, trying to compose himself to wait. His heart thumped and he found it difficult to draw breath; his hands were sweating. This was ridiculous. In an hour and a half the choir would arrive for practice. There was no reason to believe that they would discover their vicar dead of suffocation. He thought of the longest poem he had ever learnt, which was 'The Battle of Lepanto', and began to recite. It imposed its own strong rhythm on his mind and kept the panic at bay. He was repeating – in word and heartbeat – 'strong gongs groaning and the guns boom far' for the eleventh time when the organist arrived early for choir practice.

'I got shut in the market cross once,' he said sympathetically, noting that the Vicar seemed in a pretty poor state. 'Gives one an awful feeling of claustrophobia, doesn't it? And the worst of it was that I could smell the food cooking in the Indian restaurant. You could have knocked on one of the windows on the north wall, someone in the street might have heard.'

'I was afraid of breaking the glass,' Michael said hoarsely.

He walked slowly back to the vicarage, breathless and shaking. He wondered how he was to explain his condition to Valentine, but as it turned out she had some story about sewage to relate.

'You'll miss John Cleese,' she said when they had finished their meal.

'Will I?'

'You've got Desmond Treglowan coming in ten minutes.' She poured coffee. 'Do you remember when we had that woman staying with us at Oxford who was going through a crisis of belief and she came across us convulsed over the attempts to dispose of the dead body at Fawlty Towers?'

He stirred his coffee. 'I had forgotten about Desmond. I haven't thought what I am going to say to him.'

'Better ask questions and let him do the talking in that case.'

As he sat opposite the youth in his study, Michael experienced the listlessness he had felt many years ago at college when he had been expected to discuss any difficulties he might have with his spiritual adviser, and had been unable to think of a thing to say. And it hadn't been the case that he did not have any difficulties. He had realized then that once one can articulate a problem it is half-way to being solved – the other person is merely a sounding-board for one's own ideas.

He recalled that Charles had reported Desmond's mother as saying that he had an alternative life on offer – the loving Christian community. He could not remember a time when he had felt less able to measure up to that challenge.

Desmond, who did not mind himself being responsible for long silences but did not much like them to be caused by other people, said, 'I've read these books' and shoved them into Michael's hands. Michael, unprepared, dropped both books.

After a confusing scuffle which just avoided head-butting farce, they righted themselves and Michael flipped through the pages of *The Star Thrower* to give himself time to recover his equanimity.

'A man of some passion, Eiseley,' he said, 'filled with an awe in the face of Nature and its mysteries which most of us Christians have lost.' He looked out of the window. 'I suppose our landscape is wrong, so small and domesticated . . .'

'Yes, that is precisely how I feel about him,' Desmond said eagerly. Michael was taken aback: the purpose of this meeting was not that they should agree with each other but rather explore their differences.

Desmond, elaborating the theme, was already some way from the small and domesticated, speaking of Eiseley's acceptance of the unpredictability of the universe as though he was the only man to have made this discovery.

Michael said, seeking to get the discussion back on the rails, 'All scientists would accept some such description.'

'But most of them don't apply it to life as ordinary people live it.' As Desmond talked he raised his eyebrows so high they seemed in danger of disappearing in the brush of tow-coloured hair, a feat which plainly startled the wide, colourless eyes. 'Most scientists seem unaware of the weather in the streets, holed up in their laboratories. The people who have really let the darkness in in this century have been artists and writers. You don't get protestors starting riots and hurling bricks when the Royal Society meets, and daubing walls. The censor doesn't get busy.' Desmond's Adam's apple bobbed about and he looked as agitated as a boy soprano who finds his voice breaking in the middle of a crucial aria.

'And this darkness – it appeals to you?'

'It's there, isn't it, whether it appeals to me or not. It seems a good place to start – with the darkness, I mean.'

Michael looked at the book again. This was not quite how he had expected this talk to go. For him, it was the pain in Eiseley which communicated itself; he liked the man because he believed in the pain which drew him to life's failures. He had thought that perhaps they would talk about Eiseley's deaf-mute mother, the isolated prairie artist, and that this would then lead to a delicate exploration of Desmond's own feelings about his father's desertion. He perceived it was not going to be as simple as that.

He turned the pages of the book. 'Certain coasts', someone, not Eiseley, had pronounced of Costabel, 'are set aside for shipwreck.' Eiseley had said, 'with increasing persistence I had made my way thither.' And then, 'Perhaps all men are destined to arrive there as I did.' The idea that shipwreck is inevitable at some time in one's life released in Michael a sudden gush of warm, unfocused anger. He said, 'This sort of thing is all very well, but in life one must be positive and buoyant. Too much concentration on our wounds can lead to psychological sickness. It is impossible for people to go through life avoiding acts of betrayal and even cruelty.' His blood was pounding.

Desmond said, 'Yes, I see that.' It was apparent he thought Michael's anger both surprising and inappropriate.

Michael put down the book. 'Let's forget about Eiseley, shall we?' He made an effort to compose himself. 'It seems to me that it is the day-to-day patterns of life with which most of us need to be concerned. Ideas which a brain like Eiseley's can encompass are too vast for most of us, our minds can't accommodate them. We have to concentrate on the here and now of life.'

'I don't seem able to see any day-to-day patterns,' Desmond said. 'It's all too close and muddled.'

So this is what it all boils down to, Michael thought impatiently. Eiseley's main attraction for Desmond is that the man was a solitary and what intimations of immortality he had came from encounters with animals rather than human beings – a man most at ease at some distance from his own species. He said, 'You can't escape, Desmond. Even the remotest tribe in Africa will have a pattern to its life. There is a pattern to life.'

Desmond said, 'Nature is a pattern.' He drew the back of his hand across his mouth, tugging down the lower lip as though seeking to slow down the torrent of words. His voice was sharp and staccato when he continued. 'You talk as if studying the patterns of Nature is some kind of retreat, a running away from life. But it's not. The awareness of animal life, a knowledge of rock and stone and desert places, is genesis.'

Michael was aware of being involved in a struggle for authority. He said, 'To live outside the human pattern is to be mad, Desmond.'

'But anthropology is a study of patterns, isn't it?'

'If you are prepared to accept it as a discipline, yes. But if what you are after is a kind of emotional satisfaction, if you entertain some idea of examining ancient skulls in the hope they may eventually reconcile you to what goes on in the human heart, then you will be disappointed.'

Desmond stared at him, looking as unemotional as a camel.

'Have you considered that it may be here, in the place with which you are familiar and of which you have some understanding, that you have to begin your search for a meaning in life?'

'I'll tell you what I really think.' Desmond spoke brusquely; but it was no longer the awkward brusqueness of the adolescent, it was the voice of a man who feels that enough of his time has been taken up. 'I think that if God created the universe, he should blow a whistle at half-time and then we would be expected to find our way back to our beginnings, bearing with us the knowledge gained during the first half. That's about the only idea which really excites me.'

Valentine must have left the sitting-room door open; Michael could hear her laughing at John Cleese, genuine delight in the sound. Here in the library it was getting dark, which was apt enough, he thought grimly, since he found he was unable to speak of the ideal of the loving Christian community to this young man. He said wearily, 'You are not alone in that view. Others have been haunted by the need to find a way through ancient tracks. It's not an idea which is new to me, Desmond, although I suppose I would express it differently, seeing it as man's eventual return to God at the end of his long journey of discovery, bringing with him all the fruits of human consciousness. But whatever words we use, religious or otherwise, the quest is a perfectly honourable one; though I fear it may present greater perils . . .'.

And yet, was it really more perilous, the lonely Odyssey, than the rooted life within the human stockade? He was still thinking of this after Desmond had gone and Valentine had left camomile tea and biscuits on his desk and departed upstairs.

Desmond slept well that night but Michael not at all. The boy is too sensitive, he thought, flinching from the direction in which his thoughts constantly led him. True, his father had abandoned him and his mother might now be contemplating another unpromising relationship; but the daughter had survived relatively unharmed. The boy's reaction was abnormal – a flaw somewhere. But why had he felt so uncomfortable during this talk about the patterns in life? The path to the desert had never been a source of fear because he knew that it was not for him. Something else had disturbed him. Here, that was what he had said; it was here in the place with which Desmond was familiar that he should try to find his pattern in life. We have to concentrate on the here and now of our lives.

Here. Here for Michael Hoath was this bed in which he lay beside his wife. He looked at the patterns of light and shadow made by the moonlight in the room. They always slept with the curtains drawn back because he felt suffocated in dark enclosed spaces. Valentine preferred a dark room. The nightingale was singing in the graveyard. It was many years since a nightingale had nested there and now people often came at night to listen to it. Valentine was upset by this invasion of the graveyard because she was afraid that louts would destroy the nest. The darkest, deepest place in the wood was where she would have the nightingale make its nest. The forces of destruction seemed to her stronger than beauty. He had raised himself on one elbow as he listened to the nightingale, and now he looked down at his wife. It was not Valentine's cares which slept but the will and the facade which the will held in place during the day had peeled away. The nose thrust up like a beak between the sightless eyes, the lips parted in a silent cry, and anguish loosed the jaw. In the moonlight the face seemed ravaged by strain and stress and long unrest.

When he lay back he felt as if a leaden weight had been laid over his heart. He tried to bring his mind to the aid of his labouring lungs, setting his own will to work, attempting to conjure up a self-justifying picture of the Valentine who was so deeply hurtful; he reviewed all that she had neglected to do, the small rejections, the many refusals to respond, the lack of spontaneous warmth. But in spite of all his efforts, it was the good things which crept out of the shadows as he looked at the moon-washed face. He remembered the daily acts of service which he took for granted because hers was the kind of giving which disdains display and brushes gratitude aside; her moments of light gaiety, her tenderness. Yes, tenderness. When they made love he wanted flame to consume them and then she always failed him; but sometimes when he was tired and felt defeated she surprised him with a brief, radiant tenderness, fading fickle as a dawn dream when he tried to capture it. Now, when he least wanted it, this fitful tenderness was an added torment to bear.

The nightingale sang on and he was dizzied by the thought of all the energy thrilling through that tiny cage of bone, hour after merciless hour. In the morning he had an appalling headache.

10

A new day, Hester thought, as she stepped out of the house carrying her small case; even at my age a new day is exciting. She was glad she had decided to walk to the coach. A paper boy went up the path to Charles's house whistling; his bicycle was propped against the gate and in the sunlight the spokes of the wheel shone like a great flower. At the bottom of the hill a young man waited for the bus, leaning relaxed against a lamp-post, no pressures on him yet, life unfolding ahead of him, the vistas ever widening.

As she watered the garden earlier she had been quite overwhelmed by irrational happiness. Crustacea, soil, trees, sun and water, she had chanted as she sprayed the roses, a whole world went to the making of me. This was going to be a good day – not one of her 'as flies to wanton boys' days.

She still felt good about life even when she got into the coach and saw that the seat beside Laura Addison was empty. As Hester approached her, Laura said gratefully, 'I was saving this place for you, of course,' and Hester knew that she had been watching people pass her by. There had been a party game when Hester was a child – 'Come and sit on my chair,' people had chanted when you were allowed into the room; if you sat on the wrong chair, you were tipped off it. She could remember the hurt as she went from chair to chair, dreading that none of her friends had chosen her, that the chair reserved for her was in the hands of a kindly adult who had probably said, 'Well, if no one else is having Hester Pascoe, I'll have her.' On such despised kindness Laura Addison had had to depend all her life. One must remember, Hester told herself, that a whole world went to the making of Laura as well.

'Now, you are the expert on this,' she said. 'So I shall look to you to keep me in good order.'

Laura tittered happily. 'I'm afraid some of us are going to be more difficult to keep in good order.' She tilted her head towards the front of the coach where Andy Possett was sitting beside Norah Kendall.

Michael called them to attention and they composed themselves as he began the prayers for the journey. He had reached the final prayer when Laura began a fierce scrabbling in her handbag.

'"... within you to keep you, before you to lead you, behind you to guard you ..."' Laura was becoming frantic. Hester whispered, 'Turn it out in your lap.' Laura did this and two biros, a frozen cologne stick, sun-glasses and a rosary fell on the floor of the coach. '"And may the blessing of Almighty God, the Father and the Son and the Holy Spirit come upon you and remain with you for ever."'

There was a murmur of Amen and Laura said tearfully, clutching the rosary, 'I have forgotten my Kwells.'

'Perhaps we could stop near the chemist in Station Street,' Hester suggested to Michael.

'We're not going that way.'

'I can run to Boots,' Alan Judge, a perpetually eager young man, volunteered. 'It won't take long.'

'Go easily,' Norah called out to him. 'It's very hot already.'

But he was much too excited to heed her and shot off down the street, a short, pudgy creature pounding legs not designed for speed.

'How that boy does love to show off,' Laura said to Hester.

In ten minutes he came into sight again, face glowing like a beacon. Everyone cheered and clapped as he arrived at the coach in a state which suggested one of the casualties in a

175

marathon staggering into the nearest ambulance, rather than the image he had hoped to present of one whose fingers touch the tape.

The driver started the engine and the coach moved off. Alan gasped and wheezed alarmingly and a tin of Refreshers was passed down to him from a well-wisher at the back of the coach. Laura swallowed two Kwells and wiped her watering eyes. Mr Pettifer explained to the deputy organist, Ewan Hughes, that Mrs Pettifer had had to stay behind to look after the house. He spoke as though this was the very first time this had happened, although everyone knew that Mrs Pettifer had not left the house for a single night since she returned to it from their honeymoon in Bere Regis. The divorcee, who had surprised everyone by her decision to come, took out a copy of John Robinson's *The Human Face of God*. Michael edged down the aisle handing out a leaflet he had prepared giving details of the programme on arrival at Walsingham.

Andy Possett took off his jacket and began to unbutton his shirt. Laura hissed at the old churchwarden, Walter Ellery, who was sitting across the aisle, 'I'm not sure we should have let him come.'

The old man smiled. 'Of such are the Kingdom.'

Norah said, 'There's a strong through draught, Andy; I think I should keep my shirt on if I were you.' She took a bottle of barley water from her basket. 'What about a drink? And you promised Mrs Hardacre to take this tablet as soon as we set off, didn't you? I've got one of the dratted things to take, too.' She produced a bottle of Vitamin C tablets. Andy accepted the cup of barley water and, after watching Norah swallow her vitamin tablet, solemnly consented to swallow his rather different tablet.

Valentine took out a copy of *Casanova's Chinese Restaurant* and began to read. Alan, who was sitting across the aisle from her, had recovered sufficient breath to announce that personally he did not care for birds' nest kind of food.

They had lunch and were well on their way to the convent which was to be their overnight stop before Alan started to entertain them on his guitar.

'"Wherever you travel, I'll be there, And the creed and the colour and the name won't matter, I'll be there,"' they roared as the coach went through the convent gates.

Hester had wondered how Norah would behave towards her after their last encounter. She was ashamed of her outburst and hoped it could be forgotten. To her relief, Norah behaved as if nothing had happened. It was only when they returned from Compline and were bedding down for the night that she said, as if continuing a briefly interrupted conversation, 'I can settle for very little, Hester.'

'But for how long?' Hester replied, caught unawares and not best pleased.

'We have walked and talked and held hands . . .' Hester could see it was going to be one of those conversations when responses are not relevant to the questions posed. 'And kissed, that, too. Kissed and embraced. Nothing more. So little. Why should we be held to account for so little?'

'Who is holding you to account?'

'I just want to see him, to be with him occasionally, to share thoughts and feelings. That's not much to ask, is it? Some people have had relationships like that which have lasted years and years. It couldn't possibly hurt Hesketh.'

'And Michael's relationship with Valentine? That is to remain stagnant, I take it.'

Norah was silent. Whatever she might think of Valentine she kept to herself. Hester, who had said hard things about Harry's wife, felt herself reproached, and the fact that Norah could not have done this knowingly in no way mitigated the offence.

Norah said, 'To live with nothing – it's not possible; it couldn't be borne . . .'

This is no justification, this is the end, Hester realized, knowing only too well the dying fall of hope. Finished – and so late begun!

'I'm sorry,' she said to Norah. 'Believe me, I am truly sorry.'

In the dim light Norah's blanched face looked like that of a much older person. 'All this freedom we hear so much about,' she said. 'All this freedom, and yet . . .'

There are no words for the pain you feel, Hester thought. Sex has been set free and the freedom can be exercised in pornographic detail. The thing not much mentioned is love, that slow, benign growth. Perhaps the deep will always keep its secrets from the market place.

To Hester's surprise Norah slept heavily and Hester had some difficulty in waking her for the early start the following morning.

They had an uneventful journey and arrived at Walsingham early enough to visit the Roman Catholic Slipper Chapel before driving on to the village.

'It is a walk of about a mile,' Michael said. 'Pilgrims used to walk from here to the Shrine, some without slippers, but I don't think anyone need feel they have to do likewise. So when we have looked at the chapel the coach will be here for those of us who decide not to walk.' Valentine had counselled him that he should take the coach if he wanted to deter the elderly from attempting more than was wise and he had reluctantly accepted this advice.

After they had visited the Slipper Chapel and been pleasantly surprised by its simplicity, Michael and Valentine and the older members of the party, with the exception of Hester, climbed into the coach. 'You have done this before,' Hester said to Laura, 'so you have earned your rest.'

'I know you like walking.' Laura's reply was merited since it was the need for exercise rather than piety which motivated Hester.

The walk to the village along what was still a country lane proceeded enjoyably until Alan Judge, who had elected to walk barefoot, trod on a sharp stone. For the rest of the way, wound wrapped in bloody handkerchief, he hopped, arms around the shoulders of Mr Pettifer and Ewan Hughes, neither of whom was built for the supporting role. They arrived too late to refresh themselves before joining the coach party who had already peeped into the Shrine Church and been unpleasantly surprised by its extravagance.

The party from St Hilary's stood in the nave looking about them, bewildered by the many altars and chapels – chapels of the Resurrection, of All Souls, of Our Lady of Sorrows and above, on a balcony, the Orthodox Chapel where they could see several icons and had a general impression of brilliance and richness, foreign to the pale primrose image of God's light engendered by the English climate. As they went from chapel to chapel, the divorcee whispered to Hester that she was reminded of a visit to the Alhambra where groups of tourists of various nationalities vied for admission to the bathing rooms, the room where the Sultan's women perfumed themselves, the room where the Sultan's women slept . . .

Special times had been set aside for each party to pray on arrival in the Holy House at the feet of Our Lady of Walsingham and they had been led to expect that this would be a very moving moment. In fact, the party ahead of them over-stayed their allotted period, behaviour lamentably unChristian and particularly unacceptable in English Christians. Michael said, 'Of course, we mustn't behave selfishly and keep the people following us waiting,' and they virtuously agreed to renounce the precious minutes lost. But when they eventually entered the Holy House many were unable to resist the temptation to glare balefully at the departing culprits in the hope of shaming them. Pulses pounding, angry thoughts bubbling just below the surface of their minds, hungry and travel sick, they bowed their heads and tried to compose themselves to the act of veneration to which they had so looked forward. 'Oh Blessed Mary, Mother of God, Our Lady of Walsingham, intercede for us,' they chanted, chastened and confused.

At the first Mass it was little better. Here all the groups of pilgrims gathered together, filling the church. Most had travelled long distances and people were weary, agitated and fractious. Fretful children cried and stamped their feet, wrestling to free themselves from restraining hands, prayer books were dropped, dry throats required constant clearing, chairs scraped; old people whispered loud complaints that they could not hear and hardly anyone could follow the unfamiliar service. Those who had not lost their place early on, repeated hopefully on behalf of them all '. . . and happy the pilgrim inspired by you with courage to make the ascents . . .'

Hester, as disturbed as anyone, reminded herself that this was pilgrimage, not retreat, and that no doubt all this unrest went with pilgrimage.

179

She and Norah had a room in a house near the hospice. When they returned there after Mass, Norah took a tablet which Hester suspected was not Vitamin C. She saw Hester looking at her and made a wry face. 'It can only get better, can't it?'

Hester, whose spirit responded more readily to candour than any amount of spiritual uplift, said, 'It's a way of looking at things. We are being altogether too serious about what is a festive occasion.'

Festivity was not hard to come by. When they went out they found the street lined with people, all looking excitedly in the direction of the Slipper Chapel.

'What is it?' Hester asked. From the expression on their faces, one might have thought them Roman Catholics awaiting the Holy Father.

'It's the West Indians,' a man told her. 'They are coming with a steel band.'

Children hopped up and down impatiently while adults assured them 'They are marching all the way from the Slipper Chapel.' Hester was so swept up in this excitement that she understood how Jessie Brown must have felt when she heard the pipes of Havelock sound at the relief of Lucknow. But the West Indians marched without their band. They sang, however, loudly and joyously and the watchers clapped hands and wriggled unaccustomed joints to the rhythm.

At supper there was considerable discussion on the extent of the veneration of Mary – 'Rose of Jericho' and 'Star of Bethlehem'; the Chapel of All Souls where prayers were said for the departed; the relic of the True Cross; and the attitude to be adopted by the non-Orthodox to the icons. It was apparent to Michael as he listened that most people were unsure what they personally believed and he did not think this was a bad thing – certainty closed an awful lot of doors. What was unfortunate was that there was even greater uncertainty as to what the Anglican Church believed. Surprise and bewilderment might well have given place to consternation by the time they had experienced the gamut of what was on offer here. He could see that some kind of course might need to be devised on their return.

He was glad when a diversion was created by the arrival of Alan Judge who had had to have a tetanus injection, thereby missing Mass. He had consoled himself by piling his plate with chipolatas and beans. 'I thought you were trying to lose weight, Alan,' Laura said reprovingly. The conversation turned to matters of diet. Valentine picked fastidiously at a cheese salad. Michael could see that she was not going to come to terms with pilgrimage in whatever guise it was served up to her. Unexpectedly, however, she was making a genuine effort to be amiable and to look after those of the party who were least at ease. In this respect, her performance compared favourably with that of other vicars' wives present.

It was a rather sultry evening and the party from St Hilary's sat on benches outside one of the pubs, drinking beer with a feeling of well-being and righteous in the knowledge that this was all part of being a pilgrim. Travellers' tales were exchanged, the more elaborately embellished the better received. Ewan Hughes was particularly amusing, shrewdly judging what this audience would find acceptably outrageous. The divorcee contributed a quite restrained account of an adventure in the Kasbah.

Michael Hoath was not good at this sort of conviviality, and he could not pretend. He sat among them looking rather bewildered, like a serious, intelligent Viking with a limited knowledge of the language who finds that the natives speak too fast. Every now and then he got the drift of a story but always missed the crucial point. After a time, he gave up and studied the low wall of stone and brick in whose sheltering arm they sat as if it might hold some clue he had failed to find in the conversation of his companions.

Norah, pretending to shield her eyes against the slanting evening sunlight, watched his face, intent and strained as a look-out tracing the line of a distant shore.

Hester, sitting beside Norah, felt longing overwhelm her like a tide. She saw its deep blue waters and the creamy froth on the ridges of the waves and if she bent forward she would see her own broken reflection and that of Harry. Three days they had snatched in County Galway, he on a course in Dublin and she on her way to meet Veronica in Sligo. And each of those days they had looked across the bay to the low green hills of Clare which seemed to belong to an Irish fairy story, a place that beckoned yet remained always out of reach; for the only bus which went to Clare arrived, for some peculiarly Irish reason, ten minutes after the departure of the only bus which would bring them back. Each day their longing for the hills of Clare had increased. Yet we could have gone, she thought. It was only that we couldn't get back. She looked at Michael and then at Norah and saw that for them also the distance was now too great, infinitely greater than the troubled waters of Galway Bay.

'Hester is looking like a despondent garden gnome,' Ewan Hughes said affectionately. Hester thought that she must hold their attention lest it occur to them that she was not the source of desolation; but then she saw that they were not in the least aware of desolation and wanted little in the way of explanation.

'I was contemplating matters of great moment,' she said. 'Like whether I wanted another beer.' She stood up and insisted on buying the next round.

Mr Pettifer came with her to help with porterage, and when they returned Ewan Hughes and Michael were talking about the art of dry stone walling and Norah was advising Alan Judge that he should rest his foot. Valentine was engaged in disjointed conversation with Andy Possett and Laura Addison.

Later Hester and Valentine walked round the village in the grey of evening and Valentine marvelled that a place so much frequented could have retained such simplicity, the straight-faced stone houses showing little evidence of the signs of improvement which turned so many villages into mirrors of suburban life. 'If they could just take away that awful extravagance I could live here,' she said.

'You'd find it a cultural desert.'

'My life is a desert anyway, so that would be nothing new.' She turned to Hester and said sharply, 'It's all right for you. Somehow or other you will do something with all this, even if it is only turning the wine back into water.'

Hester was unprepared for the savagery of this attack – Valentine's more severe criticisms were usually reserved for herself. She walked slowly back to her lodging house, meditating the rebuke which on the whole she thought justified. By the time she arrived she had resolved to leave her notebook behind tomorrow. Norah was already fast asleep.

The next day began with a pilgrimage Mass. At breakfast they were given information as to the various ways in which they might occupy themselves during the morning – Stations of the Cross, a healing service, attendance at the Orthodox liturgy in the converted railway station, or, for those already glutted with unaccustomed rich fare, matins at the parish church. Hester decided to attend the Orthodox liturgy, after being assured by Michael that she would not be expected to stay the entire length of the course. 'It won't worry them if you go out, they are used to that,' he said. 'They don't expect us to have the same stamina.' Norah decided to go to the Stations of the Cross.

The only other members of the party to opt for the Orthodox liturgy were Alan Judge and Andy Possett. Alan, leaning heavily on a stick, talked all the way up the hill to the church.

'This is very important to me. I started off as a Baptist; but it's all so cut and dried with them. You feel there will be nothing more to find out for the rest of your life. I haven't quite made up my mind where I belong. I mean, I don't think I could go over to Rome, it would kill my mother. But I don't think she'd mind so much about Orthodoxy. I mean, people don't know enough about it to mind, do they?'

'What about staying where you are?' Hester asked.

'It's awfully hard to know where that is, isn't it? I mean, there's Don Cupitt on the one hand and All Saints' Margaret Street on the other and nothing much going on in between. I want to belong to a church that cares, not one where some of the people have decided that God doesn't exist and some are just "don't knows".'

'What about the Quakers? I'm not sure where they stand vis-à-vis God, but they do seem to care.'

'I tried that. But I wasn't keen on so much silence and when they did talk it was like hearing someone give a report to a Committee at the U.N.'

Andy Possett said, 'God will tell you where to go.'

This effectively silenced Alan.

The liturgy was already in progress when they arrived. In contrast to the chapel in the Shrine, the church was quite homely, rather like a suburban sitting-room containing furniture both Orthodox and unorthodox, sacred and secular. A few other visitors were present, some sitting on chairs, others on the carpet. Alan lowered himself carefully, stretching one leg straight and laying the stick beside it. Andy Possett stood above him, erect as if on sentry guard. Hester sat back on her heels. She could not make much of the liturgy but was fascinated by the participants who included a very tall man in a red kilt; an ancient woman dressed from head to foot in a grey robe which might have covered the body of woman in any century since Abraham and his family migrated from Ur of the Chaldeans; and a small, ebony boy in an embroidered tunic, his glistening face brimming with mischief. As those communicating approached what Hester assumed to be the altar, the boy put a hand flat on his woolly head and measured his height against what was obviously a fixed point on the kilt of the tall man in front of him.

After three-quarters of an hour Hester decided to leave. She touched Alan on the shoulder and was amused when he gave a convulsive start. Ashamed, he indicated that he intended to stay. Andy took no notice of her.

It was warm and sunny in the street and she decided not to go to another service. She walked slowly round the village, meeting several other pilgrims also slothfully unoccupied. The notes which Michael had provided had said that pilgrimage was the coming with some difficulty and cost to a holy place and the odd thing was that Hester did feel that it was costing her, though exactly what she could not have said. She had expected to remain outside the experience, not from any belief in her own separateness but simply because this was usually what happened to her; but, in fact, whatever else she might feel about it, there was no doubt that she was a part of this experience.

Large assemblies in places like the Central Hall and, worse still, the Albert Hall, had the effect of putting her out of sympathy with her own species. Even the more modest comings together in her own town gave her a feeling of exclusion. But here, where a village and its surrounding fields were the meeting place, where one could walk about on one's own or join a group in a pub as the whim took one, she was surprised by the realisation that she was actually a part of this community. She had that same sense of taking for granted which family life at its best can give, the knowledge that you have all started from the same place. There was a certain kind of acceptance which was a combination of freedom and shared experience. She decided that, although it was all a dreadful mishmash, pilgrimage had beneficial side effects.

It became apparent during lunch that she had missed the main events of the morning. Andy Possett had begun to undress during the service at the Orthodox church. His hosts had at first thought that he was over-hot and had politely ignored what was happening until Andy got to the point of no recall. 'It was dreadful.' Alan Judge became scarlet at the memory. 'He went quite rigid and there was nothing anyone could do about it. Someone put a sheet around him.' Hester had a picture of Andy looking like one of the more inflexible prophets standing in tableau with the man in the red kilt and the delighted ebony boy. Michael had gone up to the church to explain – which was hardly necessary – and to see what could be done, apart from waiting.

Norah, who might have been helpful on such an occasion, had fallen during the Stations of the Cross.

'If you can call it falling,' Valentine said contemptuously to Hester. 'She didn't trip. She went neatly backwards and created a lot of attention without putting herself to much risk.'

'Norah wouldn't do that,' Hester protested. 'And even supposing, she wouldn't do it during a service.'

'She has done it before. At the first Mass of Easter, in the graveyard. She is that sort of woman.'

Laura Addison said, 'And though I don't like to say it, she does tend to have a sick headache whenever she is faced with anything she doesn't want to do.'

Hester went back to their lodgings and found Norah lying on the bed. 'All those disbelieving faces staring down at me,' she said wanly. 'Even Michael felt I'd let him down, I could see that.'

'Perhaps you shouldn't have come at all if you didn't feel well.' Hester felt a necessity to be unsympathetic to both Valentine and Norah in some attempt to keep them in balance.

'I'm not unwell,' Norah said tetchily. 'When I'm upset this is the way it takes me.' She swung her legs over the side of the bed and sat for a moment looking down at her feet.

'I should stay here and rest if I were you,' Hester said. 'We've got a long journey ahead of us.'

But Norah insisted on coming to the ceremony of the sprinkling at the holy well. Hester said grudgingly, 'So long as you don't trip down the well.' She hoped Norah was not going to take part in the final service if there was any risk of her being 'upset' again.

They assembled as required in the nave of the Shrine Church where Michael reminded them that, almost a thousand years ago, a spring of water was the sign given to mark the place where the Holy House should be built. At the time of Cromwell, Walsingham was so devastated that the site of the Holy House was lost. The well had been discovered when the work of restoring the Shrine began in 1922 and when it was unblocked water had sprung forth again.

They went in twos to the well, were sprinkled and received the sign of the cross on their foreheads, then made a cup with their hands into which water was poured. Hester found the ceremony surprising, exotic, comic and, as she stretched out cupped hands to receive the water, inexplicably familiar, the return of the traveller to a place long lost. Later, as they packed their cases in their lodgings, she said to Norah, 'I was unprepared for that little ceremony.' She looked down at her hands which felt cool as if water still ran between the fingers.

Norah said, sounding really troubled, 'How could we ask for a miracle of healing for ourselves when we look at someone like Andy Possett?'

Hester, having no ailment other than the years, thought this too hypothetical a question to demand a reply.

Their pilgrimage now drawing to a close, they assembled in the garden, all those who had shared this confused weekend. Each holding a lighted candle in a carton like an upturned lantern, they processed slowly towards the Shrine singing the pilgrim hymn which Norah had said made up in length what it lacked in musicality. She was singing now in a voice clear and sure, but she watched her movements, placing her feet with what Hester thought was rather exaggerated concern. There were so many of them that the long hymn had been sung twice by the time Hester reached the building. She paused on the threshold to look back at the garden, storing the moment in her mind, knowing that the jumble of experiences could only be assimilated later; that only in retrospect would the fragmentary images come together and be made into a whole. The voices sang calmly, releasing the words without effort or thought. The grass was dappled in shadow, the candles flickered among shrubs and roses, not glowing theatrically as they would have done at night, but taking their place among the living things around them. In the faces of the people moving towards her she saw nothing to suggest ecstasy or wonder, none of the drama of a great rally, instead – the reverse of such upheavals – a settling down seemed to have taken place. None of the singers looked as if they were entering a Pilgrim of the Year contest. Women with bags over arms consulted the words as they might a shopping list. Fathers held skipping children by the hand. A few walked with heads turned, looking their last, taking a gardener's pride and pleasure in the order of things in bed and border. And so, quietly, they came to the Shrine.

Here they knelt for Benediction, these people who had come together the day before, nerves jangling, fractious, unrested, who had junketed about in pubs and jostled one another in the refectory. They had spent their time in activities calculated to make this final service even more hectic than the first one had been. Yet now as they knelt together at the end of their pilgrimage there was complete stillness. Hester, sitting with bowed head, had no words of her own for this moment, no explanation of this random gift, only acceptance of a peace neither anticipated nor earned.

On their journey to the convent where they would again spend the night, Alan Judge entertained the party with songs. The divorcee told Valentine that she had been called to minister. Valentine thought she was the kind of woman to involve the maximum contention in any call she might have. But, no, this was to misjudge her, for it transpired it was the mission field to which she felt she had been called. Valentine had not the heart to tell her there was scarcely a corner of this particular field where a white face would now be welcome.

In their room at the convent guest house Michael and Valentine talked over this and other events of the day. The one subject which was not touched on was Norah's fall.

'Do you know what Andy Possett said when he came out of his trance? He said he wanted to be received into the Orthodox Church.'

As he said this Michael looked apologetically at Valentine, his eyes screwed up as if he winced at the pain he must be giving her. It was not so much Andy's defection which troubled him as his own attitude to religious belief. He believed with his whole heart that Christ was the Way, the Truth and the Life, but he was unable to be whole-hearted in claiming that the way was exclusively Christian. He saw the risen Christ as standing where all roads cross and whatever road the traveller came, He was the way. This had once led him to tell a parishioner, 'If you really feel that Buddhism is your way, then you must take it.' He thought it a poor exchange but that had not seemed relevant to the other man's condition. It was not in his nature, however, to be relaxed in belief or feeling and so he was tormented by the knowledge that tolerance can only too often be a form of indifference.

Valentine, who saw no necessity for soul-searching in this matter of Andy Possett's churchmanship, said, 'And how did members of the Orthodox Church there present receive that?'

'I'm afraid they thought he had been seized by the Holy Spirit.' She chuckled and he frowned. 'I don't know what to do. Should I warn them that these seizures occur rather frequently?'

'You mean that the frequency renders the intervention of the Holy Spirit inoperative?'

'Put like that . . .' He rested his fingers on the bridge of his nose, plucking at the scant flesh. 'But what should I do?'

'Do?' She twitched her shoulders irritably. 'Why must you do anything? Surely after all these years the Orthodox Church must have devised quite an adequate system for examining those who knock on its doors?'

'But suppose Andy is making a mistake?' He turned to her, his face grave.

'How can one tell?' She made a little throwaway gesture with her hands. 'It is difficult enough to identify one's own mistakes.'

'If I really believed in my own Church it would sear me, this defection . . .'

'Oh Michael! Tend the wounds you have, they are enough.'

She turned on one side, placing a hand between cheek and pillow. Now, even if she did not sleep, she would be lost to him. He wanted to cry out like a child afraid of silence and the dark, 'Don't leave me!'

They had not made love since that excursion to the moors, but at night he had begun to talk over the problems of the day with her, something which in the past he had not done and which she would probably not have permitted. It came to him, lying sleepless in this unfamiliar room, that without understanding what he was doing, he had been holding on to her. Hester's anger had shaken him and presented him with a moral dilemma; but this realization, this knowledge that he had not been true to either woman, pierced to the very heart.

What am I? he thought, what manner of man am I that I can long for the wild freedom of moors, for water gushing from hidden streams, while another part of me tries all the while to strengthen my hold on this imperfect, compromised relationship which frustrates and hinders me at every turn?

The party was not due to leave the convent until after lunch. Michael spent most of the morning in the chapel. Other pilgrims, perhaps feeling they had spent long enough on their knees, opted for a little pagan worship in the convent's rose garden.

He had stayed at this convent on previous occasions, on his way to London or to his home county of Sussex. The chapel was bare and simple, its harshness only redeemed by a certain warmth in the pinkish stone. On the windowless East wall, beyond the altar, hung the great crucifix. He knew of another, more homely chapel, where the empty cross hung, seeming to be part of the natural world of trees and passing birds. This symbolism he had found congenial. Here, in the gaunt chapel, he had tended to avoid looking straight at the crucifix; his eye had glanced around it, as though its dominance were a piece of bad taste on the part of the architect.

Now it stood before him, uncompromising in its very ambiguity. Here, too, birds sang and their shadows flickered briefly across the walls; beyond the long south windows, honeysuckle nodded in the breeze. But all that was outside, just as the resurrection was outside life. Here there was the polarity of the cross. The body, pulled by different forces, offered no immediate promise of release; this suspended figure was the true symbol of man's being, incomplete, not perfectible or homogenous, always in conflict, torn by the opposites in his nature, in a state of contradiction never on earth to be reconciled.

For hours he stared at the crucifix nailed to that implacable stone wall. Then, some minutes before the bell was rung for Sext, the sun shone through the long south window. The wall lit up with a rosy glow and blood ran in the cracks of the stone blocks and between the legs of the torn figure, across the ribs, down the outstretched arms and God said, 'This is my beloved Son.'

At last he understood that desire, pain and joy, the need for certainty and the insistence of doubt, cannot and will not be resolved; they can only be lived. He understood, too, at that moment, though he knew how fleeting would be his hold on it, that this tension within him which sometimes seemed unbearable was life. And the greatest paradox of all was that only by accepting this would he make some progress in his pilgrimage and find that peace which is not of this world.

When other pilgrims came in they found him kneeling with unbowed head. His face looked primitive, antique; no individuality in the slashed mouth and gaping eyes.

Valentine did not come to Sext, but Norah came. When the service was over she passed him on her way out without seeming to be aware of him. He watched the sunlight fall on her abstracted face as she crossed the threshold, his new-found understanding already threatened by a passionate longing for all that lay beyond his boundaries.

11

⁓✻⁓

'What's this all about, then?' Mrs Quince, arms akimbo, faced Charles across the broken bed. She was wearing a shapeless purple garment which seemed to Charles to be neither dress nor overall but a representational robe designed to suggest majesty and power. Androgynous, she might have been Boadicea or the Inquisitor.

He said, 'I was trying to fix a light bulb.' He had spent some time trying to think of an excuse and this was the best he had been able to contrive.

It did not serve. 'I'd 'ave said yer bin jumping on it.'

Charles felt his entrails turning to burning liquid; any moment he might confess. 'It's very old,' he croaked, leaning a hand on the brass head-rest.

'Putting it out for scrap, be yer? It might do for my Jennifer.'

'No, no. It can be mended, I am sure.' Whatever happened the bed should not go to Mrs Quince's Jennifer.

Mrs Quince walked round the bed, inspecting its injuries. Charles was still as a marionette hanging from a string, but his eyes darted nervously about, bulbous with terror lest some evidence of Shirley's occupation should be found. I should die, he thought, quite seriously. I should die on the spot. People laughed at bedroom farces, but this was a way of exorcising terror not presently open to him.

'I'll leave you to get on with it,' he said, when agreement had eventually been reached that Mrs Quince should not attempt to move the bed, but dust and vacuum around its fallen splendour.

He ran down the stairs, rubber-kneed, and fled to the security of Hester's house. Hester would not be back until the evening, so if necessary he could spend the whole morning there. Or he could go to the school. The caretaker would think it odd, since he was not a master who usually went near the building during the holidays; but the caretaker was no Mrs Quince, and Charles did not mind what he thought.

He stood in Hester's kitchen. In the garden he could see Tabby sitting on the wall, pretending to be unaware of him, tail switching lightly from side to side. 'A good job you can't speak, my girl,' he said. A real trouble-maker that, if ever there was one!

This morning when he woke after a troubled sleep on the broken bed he had wondered if he was making a mistake. Mrs Quince had put a stop to that line of thinking. He was in his late forties and he could not advance towards old age at the mercy of such as Mrs Quince.

Charles's aunt, who had little liking for him, had once told him he was a man much motivated by short-term needs. This being so – and he was not inclined to quarrel with the judgement – he should surely be doing better for himself in an age given to the gratification of needs both long- and short-term. In the past his sexual encounters had been brief and unsatisfactory. Since his physical needs were somewhat at variance with his intellectual requirements, the women of his choice had proved deplorably unable to share his day-to-day life.

He meditated on this while he prowled Hester's garden, playing the game essential to some need in Tabby which required the stimulus of hide-and-seek as a preliminary to both bed and board. 'Tabby, nice puss,' he chanted insincerely, circling the rose bushes and remembering how he and Shirley had chased each other round the house. 'The things one did not do in one's youth still wait to be done,' he told Tabby, to whom this scarcely applied. Charles felt that he and Shirley had played their games in the spirit of youth – innocent and exhilarated; but

193

he could see that this was not how it would have seemed to Hester, overhearing, as she must have done had she been at home, the noisier moments of their transport of delight.

'Good Tabby, nice fish!' he said, pouncing successfully and hauling her up to shoulder level. She looked at him, ears back, amber eyes wild with excitement. Her claws dug in his shirt, her tail lashed to and fro and she purred and dribbled copiously. 'Altogether beside yourself, madam.' He put her down on the kitchen floor in front of the fish and she leapt on to the window sill, upsetting a pot of primulas. Whenever Hester went away Tabby contrived to leave a trail of wreckage about the house although normally she was careful where her paws landed. Charles said, 'Naughty pussy' and she spat at him.

He went to the window, ignoring Tabby's attempts at rapprochement. How pleasant the two gardens were. He was dismayed at the thought that he must leave. Some kind of compromise – separate houses, perhaps? This was becoming quite acceptable, though not yet in the West Country. In any case, they could not get married until Tracy left home. Desmond did not present a problem, since he would be abroad in Turkey next spring and later at university. Tracy, however, had made it quite clear that she was not going to university 'just so as to get me out of the house'. There was no possibility that he could inhabit the house with Tracy in it. No doubt something would happen to sort out these complications. The immediate need was to find a place where they could pursue the excitements of recaptured youth uninterrupted. One of his fellow masters had a cottage on the edge of the moors which he was happy to let to friends at a peppercorn rent. The original idea had been to let it for profit to holiday-makers, but this had not proved a success because those who were prepared to overlook the lack of amenities – such as running water and cooking facilities – were not prepared to pay what the owner referred to as the 'going rate for country cottages'. Charles thought, I could hire it for a month or so. There could be no question of living there, of course; but we should have a few gypsy hours. He had an enjoyable picture of the games they might play on bright starlit nights, becoming one with Robin Goodfellow and his cohorts. He was astounded at his daring in actually living his fantasies.

It wasn't all fantasy, of course, he thought, stroking Tabby who bit his hand. That would be unhealthy. There was the other side.

She read the classics avidly, as though each book had been written yesterday and the air still quivered with the energy the author had expended. This is how writers must hope their books will be read, Charles thought, by people thirsty for what they offer, not dead meat to be cut up and analysed. This was what mattered. When all the excitement had passed, this would be the bedrock of their marriage. He might not have the stamina to romp into old age, but he could happily spend the rest of his life shaping her mind and arousing her sensibilities. He saw them both grown old, sitting on either side of a fire while he read *Piers Plowman* aloud.

He was preparing Tabby's evening meal when Hester arrived home. 'I hoped I might have Tabby here for you,' he said. 'But she is out in the garden.'

'She won't come in yet. She always has a sulk when I come back, bless her.' Hester looked at him, noting a contusion on his lip. 'I trust that wasn't Tabby?'

His face went scarlet. How silly of me, she thought, that is the kind of bite Tabby is not equipped to make. Oh dear, oh dear, has it come to this? He had been a good neighbour and she had reached an age when she disliked changes in her life.

The doctor, who was busy, was at first irritated that a nurse should come to him with the symptoms of middle-life tension. As he read her notes he tapped his fingers on the desk; at one point the rhythm faltered.

'Headaches, you say?'

'Yes, I'm very tense, I can feel that. Being a second wife is even more difficult than I had expected.' A light laugh. 'I can feel my spine becoming quite rigid and then, of course, I lose my balance . . .'

'How often?'

'How . . . ?'

'How often have you fallen?'

'Once, twice . . . I went down in the graveyard earlier in the year, tripped over a root, perhaps . . .'

'Did you feel anything afterwards – pain in the ankle, perhaps?'

'No. I bruised my seat.'

'Then you didn't trip, did you?' He scribbled on his pad and she watched him, looking from the moving hand to the impassive face.

'Second wife, eh?' He looked up, blandly cheerful now. 'Do you find yourself getting angry? A bit unreasonable?'

'Angry and unreasonable.'

'Well now . . .' He tapped the palms of his hands on the desk. She recognized the little mime – what shall we do about this, why not be sensible? He said, 'I think we might have a few tests. I'll arrange for you to see Dr Hamilton.'

Although she remained seated in front of him, her withdrawal was as unmistakable as if she had moved away; her eyes condemned him for betraying a confidence. 'But he's a neurosurgeon.'

'Just to eliminate the possibility.'

She gazed down at her hands, examining the tracery of veins while she thought this over and made a decision. She said, 'I fall asleep a lot, too.'

He looked with interest at the paperweight on his desk. 'Any particular time of day – in the afternoon, after lunch . . . ?'

She released a long breath and said quietly, 'Any time.' All the nerviness had left her. She might have been half-asleep now.

He said bracingly, 'It could be any number of things.' She gave a little crooked smile which said, 'Name them, brother!' He said reprovingly, 'Mustn't start doing our own diagnosing, must we?'

She raised a hand to her temple, fingers between the eyes. 'There's something wrong here.' Her face crumpled.

He had not expected this – after all, she was a nurse. 'There is no need for that,' he said briskly. 'The trouble with nurses is they tend to expect the worst. Doctors, too. A professional hazard.' He ushered her out as quickly as he decently could.

The sun shone brightly on the slate roofs of the houses and the green hills beyond. She said aloud, 'I should have noticed before I came to the surgery.'

'And it was such a lovely day,' she said over the phone to Lois.

'And there will be many more for you to enjoy.' Worry made the tone the more robust. 'Would you like to come here until you have the tests?'

'I've got Hesketh arriving in a few hours. He'll be here for several days. Don't worry about me, my lover. I'll be all right so long as I can pick up a phone and talk to a friend when I get panicky.'

'And even – just *supposing* – there is so much they can do nowadays.'

The voice was crisp at the other end of the phone. 'What they can do nowadays is to give people who might have died peacefully a year and more of pain and anxiety.'

'Norah . . .'

'*And* they are not going to nibble me away, either.'

Lois said, wretched, 'I don't blame you.'

'But it may well be all right.' Norah sounded suddenly bright as a child who sees the clouds lift and has no thought that they will soon gather again. 'Thanks, Lois. I feel much better now. I am going to make apple and red-currant pie for my lord's supper. That should ensure a convivial evening, don't you think?'

'So long as you serve it on time.'

'DON'T BE SO BLOODY SELF-RIGHTEOUS! I'm sorry. I'm sorry. I *am* sorry. Forget I said that.'

Ten days later Hester walked up the path to the Kendalls' house, fists clenched, trying to control her annoyance at being summoned so peremptorily. Norah was generous with her time; Hester miserly with hers. Hesketh opened the door to her. His face looked rather strange, as though someone had taken hold of the lower half and pulled hard, the fingers leaving dents in the fleshy cheeks. His eyes stared accusingly at Hester. He said, 'She's in the kitchen' and walked away to the sitting-room.

Norah was ironing a shirt. She looked up as Hester came in and said, 'I've got a brain tumour. Malignant.'

'It's not possible.' Hester was chilled, seeing death's shadow all across her own threshold.

'Two, in fact – secondaries. The main one is slumbering away in my chest. So there is nothing that can be done. You understand that?'

Hester came slowly into the room, choking back expressions of comfort which she recognized as being purely selfish. Unfortunately there seemed to be nothing to put in their place. She was shocked to realize that at this moment her mind was entirely occupied with her own reactions.

Norah said jokily, 'I had hoped to grow into old age pottering among my roses . . .' The tears came and she jerked her head away.

Hester, moved by the tears, whispered, 'Oh, my dear . . .'

'At least it probably won't be too hard.' Norah brushed her cheeks with the back of her hand. 'It seems I shall probably just sleep more and more. It's unlikely I shall go ga-ga.'

Hester wondered how true this was. It seemed to satisfy Norah for the moment, so that was all that mattered.

'How is Hesketh taking it?'

'He was angry. For himself.' Norah folded the shirt with a precision Hester envied. 'He covered it up quickly, blustering away about the hospital and asking why they hadn't kept me under observation. He didn't feel anything for me but dislike.'

'People react in strange ways to shock,' Hester murmured.

Norah was reacting strangely herself. Her own anger needed a focus and Hesketh presented himself irresistibly. 'He is totally selfish,' she said, her voice high and angry. 'Unfortunately it now seems his first wife was something of a saint and I am going to have to listen to quite a lot of comparisons.' She pressed her hands against her cheeks but could not stop the tears which now came in a bitter flood. 'I am so very far from being a saint.' The anger died down as quickly as it had flared up. She put the shirt to one side and Hesketh along with it.

Hester said, 'We shall all try to help. All your friends. You can phone me whenever you need to.'

Norah smiled weakly. 'Except in the mornings.'

'Any time of the day or night,' Hester said firmly. She did not mean it, but she recognized this as one of those occasions where an intention must be clearly stated and the actions made to suit the words. 'You have done this often enough for other people. You have a lot of credit in the bank.'

'But I'm a nurse.'

'All to the good. You will be able to tell me what to do and between us we'll muddle through.'

They stayed talking for a little while and then when Norah seemed calmer Hester left her to get on with the ironing. Before she departed she went into the sitting-room. It would not help Norah were no attention to be paid to Hesketh at this time.

He was standing looking out into the garden and did not turn round when she came into the room.

'I am sorry about this,' she said, unable to bring herself to be more direct in her sympathy.

It did not matter, he appropriated sympathy to himself. 'Twice,' he said; then, turning to look at her, repeated as if reproaching her for being deliberately obtuse, 'The second time.'

Hester said, 'Yes, that is hard.' She could see that it was indeed hard.

'There is Samantha, of course. But she and Norah don't hit it off. And I'm away so much . . .' He looked down, cracking his knuckles, waiting.

Hester said, 'You needn't worry about that. We shall all keep an eye on her.'

'You are very good.' He hated having to say it. He knew his feelings were lamentable but could not do anything about it. Unexpectedly, she felt sorry for him.

In the kitchen, Norah walked up and down, up and down, hands against her mouth, pressing back the tears. Every so often she stopped and looked about her in astonishment and then the weeping began again.

'The second time,' Hesketh said when Michael Hoath called that evening. 'This is the second time this has happened to me.' He looked as though some higher authority must answer for this.

'How does she seem to be taking it?'

'She's lying down.' No humour was intended. 'When I last looked in she was asleep.' He ran a hand across his forehead. Michael could see that his fingers were shaking. 'The second time. They told me that Carrie must have been feeling bad for some time but she never talked to anyone about it. Wanted to spare us the worry. So we never knew.' He looked fiercely at Michael. 'A saint.'

'Did they say how long?'

'They told her at the hospital that they could control it for probably a couple of years. But she doesn't believe that. So she asked the GP and he said he didn't think she'd see Christmas. Of all the things to say to a patient! Can you understand that? Should be crossed off the medical register. But she seems quite satisfied. I said to her the hospital knows more about it than the GP. She said hospitals are always unrealistic about life expectancy. I don't know where I am between them all.'

The door opened and Norah came in. Hesketh said, 'You are supposed to be sleeping.'

She said quite lightly, as if he were the patient to whom she must explain the illness, 'Sleep isn't going to be a problem. Keeping awake is the difficult part.' She had not yet looked at Michael.

Hesketh said to Michael, 'Perhaps you can have a word with her,' rather as if he thought she might be talked out of the whole business. He went out through the French windows into the garden.

They waited until he was out of sight. Even then there did not seem much to say.

'You will help me, won't you?' Norah said, still without looking at Michael. 'I am going to need help from all my friends.'

He was wounded by the generic description and mortified that he should be wounded at such a time. He drew her on to the sofa and sat beside her, holding her hand. This had happened so quickly; it was like a road accident, the actual experience of which has to be reconstructed in retrospect. At such times his emotions seemed to take themselves off, like panic-stricken survivors fleeing the wreckage. In this case he was not even sure of the physical presence left at the scene – whether lover, friend or spiritual adviser.

'I will come whenever you need me,' he said.

She looked at him then, a look in which longing and renunciation were so inextricably interwoven that he felt himself become a symbol rather than a person. He said hoarsely, 'You are not to think like this!'

Suddenly she jumped up, her eyes on the mantelpiece. 'Nine o'clock. I have to telephone my aunt. She's at Guy's and they said I would be able to catch her if I rang at nine.'

She went into the hall and after a few minutes he heard her telling her aunt, 'It has caught up with me at last.'

Hesketh came in from the garden. 'She spends a lot of time on the phone,' he said.

After she had spoken to her aunt, Norah telephoned someone else. They heard her say, laughing, 'Just testing that the support system is working.'

'It will take time for her to compose herself,' Michael said to Hesketh. It was as if another person said this while he himself stood by thinking 'pompous idiot'.

Norah returned looking quite elated. The three of them talked aimlessly for a few minutes and then Michael left.

Later, in the room where she now slept alone, Norah walked up and down, up and down, trying to gather up the pieces of her personality so that she might confront her death.

Hester went to see Norah regularly during the following weeks. Sometimes she found her remarkably in command of herself, at others irritable and fault-finding. Hesketh, when present, was irascible, liable to outbursts of childish anger if his clumsy attempts to be helpful were not well received. All this Hester bore with apparent good humour and no little compassion, but she often emerged from these visits with fretted nerves and immediately sought the company of some unfortunate good listener. Proximity made Charles particularly fitted for this role. He, in turn, looked for someone to whom he could unburden himself; and so the shock of grief and anger was passed from one person to another like so many collisions in a shunting yard.

Shirley Treglowan had recruited a friend on whom she planned to off-load her woe. The friend, who had been lured with promises of lunch and a bottle of plonk, sat huddled on a park bench while Shirley bowled up and down the gravel path, keeping an eye on her small charges who showed a preference for the shrubbery rather than the open expanse of lawn where their activities could be closely monitored. In her multi-coloured play suit Shirley resembled a Russian doll. The friend amused herself by imagining the dismantling of the dolls and the emergence of ever smaller, yet equally rotund, Shirleys.

Shirley took this play group each morning during the holidays. In the past Desmond had helped her, but now he had withdrawn his services. 'Get your fellow to help,' he had said. 'He's a teacher, isn't he?'

'I am a schoolmaster, not a social worker,' Charles had said.

'You've got to be a bit of both as things are today,' Shirley had told him and he had retorted that people today had things better than they ever had in the past. She had replied that this was all relative and they had had their first quarrel.

It was a windy day with chaotic cloud mottling the sky. The air smelt of rain. Unemployed young men sat in a circle on the grass, eating chips and playing bowls with beer cans.

'No wonder the place looks like a tip,' Shirley's friend said.

'Perhaps they feel they are part of the tip.' Shirley always felt she must stand up for anyone subject to criticism. Only yesterday Charles had told her – rather shortly – that there was no virtue in being undiscriminating.

There was one mentally-retarded child in the play group and the other children would not admit him to their games because it frustrated them to go at his slow pace. Shirley's expert eye selected the child most vulnerable to guilt. 'You look after Tammy, Hazel,' she said. 'Your mummy and daddy play with you when you go home, but this is the only chance poor Tammy has to have a bit of fun.'

It was evident that this was not the first appeal of its kind to come Hazel's way. She said, 'I *hate* Tammy' and went into the shrubbery after the other children.

Shirley knew that the shrubbery was forbidden territory – an exciting, dangerous place where the moral writ did not run. Desmond had inhabited it as a child and had occasionally allowed his father to cross the threshold, his mother never. She suspected that all this business of studying anthropology was nothing more than a return to the shrubbery. I should have had them out of there, Shirley thought, still holding back. It bewitched them both.

It had begun to rain and the friend was getting restive. The young men got up, leaving their litter behind them. They looked at Shirley and her friend as they passed by just to make sure they had noticed.

'It's one of the few gestures they can make,' Shirley said. The friend said she could think of a gesture or two.

Hazel emerged from the shrubbery looking shamefaced. 'I'm sorry about Tammy,' she said to Shirley. 'I'm luckier than him.' Shirley watched her trotting purposefully across the lawn towards Tammy – another martyr to the moral order and no looking back from now on to love and hate instinctively given.

She said to her friend when eventually they walked home from the park, 'You know, yesterday, when I was reading the Scottish play with Charles, the most weird thing happened. It was that bit when The Lady is waiting at the foot of the stairs before going up to Duncan's room and she is psyching herself up to the deed – it suddenly came to me, as if I wasn't me but another person, how exciting it must be to have murder in mind. Not the doing so much as that moment when you know you are going to take that tremendous leap and find yourself outside all the nagging questions. Do you know what I mean?'

'Not really,' the friend said, trudging drearily with bent wet head. She thought Shirley would do well to think about the men who had brought her bad luck instead of indulging in this talk of the Scottish play' and 'The Lady'. 'But then I can't see why you have this thing about Charles. It's just the Clifford story repeating itself, isn't it? Another man who's no good to a woman.'

They walked in silence until they came to the high street, then Shirley said, thinking of Charles, 'It's really unsettled me, this business of Norah Kendall. She was the person who saw me through that time after Clifford left. It wasn't that she took charge or anything like that, but I could always phone her or go round to her place in the evenings. She was there when I needed someone. Since then I've always felt that if anything bad happened to me she would be there again. It's been a great comfort.' She felt like a trapeze artist who finds that the safety net has been whisked away just as she is preparing for a double somersault.

It was raining steadily by the time they reached Shirley's house. The friend went into the bathroom to rub her hair dry while Shirley got busy in the kitchen. 'Pancakes?' she called out. 'Tuna fish pancakes, all right?'

'And you know what happened?' The friend related this to some imaginary companions as she watched Shirley gather the odds and ends which needed using up. 'Of all things, what does she do? She uses margarine instead of butter, topping up the milk in an old carton (how old is not revealed) with water and a drop of evaporated milk which has been hanging around waiting just such an emergency. To her intense surprise the mixture sticks to the pan. After several unsuccessful attempts, she abandons margarine and uses cooking oil (and three different frying pans). By the time the mixture has run out she has wasted half a packet of margarine, the remains of her cooking oil and two large eggs to say nothing of milk and flour. And then, going to the larder to see what else she can make with the tuna fish, she naively admits that in fact she doesn't have any tuna fish – only sardines.'

At this point the friend asked, 'Are you going to offer me sardines on toast?'

'I can see you are angry,' Shirley answered. 'Would sweet and sour from the take-away placate you?'

She allowed the friend more than her share of the plonk by way of making amends. It only made the friend morose. She told Shirley she wasted too much time taking short cuts which didn't work out. 'I like experimenting,' Shirley said. 'If you aren't prepared for a failure here and there you get set like concrete by the time you are forty.'

When the friend had gone in a state of middle dudgeon, Shirley set herself to clean the house from top to bottom, wondering as she did so where she and Charles would eventually settle down and whether it really was a good idea for them to be married.

Later that evening, waiting for Tracy to come home from the disco, she sat by the window watching the rain drowning the last of the day. Across the roof tops a light came on in a dormer window. The light had a shade which reminded Shirley of a Christmas lantern and it hung there, over the roof tops, like the light that lifts the hearts of lost travellers in the nicer fairy stories.

Valentine had never been one of those good troupers who are prepared to take their turn at playing small, unrewarding parts. Dramatic societies tended to tolerate prima donnas, so she had got away with it. Now, when she seemed constantly to be looking back over her life, she recognized that it might have been to her advantage to have had a little preliminary practice in self-effacement so that she did not come totally unprepared to its real-life enactment. For enactment it must be. No miracle transformation had been wrought in her, and she realized that what changes were needed she herself must effect at much cost and with many failures.

'I have been special so much of my life,' she told Hester. Someone must act as her confessor and it was hardly a role she could expect Michael to play. He had burdens enough. 'My mother was one of those gentlewomen who regard with tolerant amusement other people's way of living – their houses, pictures, furniture.' She herself looked very patrician as she related this, sitting straight-backed as a ballerina, ignoring the advances of Tabby. 'It was quietly understood that our circumstances, our possessions, our attitudes, were in all ways superior. We were people apart. Belonging – in a town, a village, a community of any kind – was for those who needed it. The Adlams did not need it.'

Hester, squatting on the fireside stool, felt like a frog at the feet of a princess. 'I'm not very good at belonging myself,' she said.

'That is different.' Valentine tilted her chin austerely. She did not want Hester muscling in with confessions of her own. 'You have worked out your place in society. I was brought up on a myth. It is not strength which holds me back from involvement. My persona is very fragile.'

Hester thought there was something rather comic about the

tragic way Valentine delivered herself of this statement; but a darkening of the big violet-grey eyes betrayed the fact that the acknowledgement of weakness, however portentously phrased, was genuine.

'You are not the only one to believe in that myth,' she said. 'Being self-sufficient and successful is a very acceptable image nowadays; but don't you find that the people who really touch you deeply are often those the most wounded by life?'

'I don't think you are understanding me.' Valentine began to see the case for the confessional; priests didn't answer you back or try to rephrase your confession for you, they just listened and asked 'How many times?'

At home in the vicarage it was Valentine who listened. She did not know how Michael seemed to others at this time, but to her his movements had the erratic desperation of a lost animal, snuffling false trails, bounding towards chance strangers only to halt at the last minute, dumbly bewildered. His conduct of the church services was unsure and his sermons echoed the confusions in his own mind. To add to his troubles, dissension had broken out among members of the P.C.C. and one of the parishioners had offended the organist. Valentine was as intelligent as Michael and more perceptive. In the past she had been impatient when he seemed obtuse. Now, as he talked of his problems with the P.C.C. she realized with dry satisfaction that it was possible for her to sharpen his vision without being destructive. She was less sentimental and this, allied to a certain ruthlessness, had sometimes upset him; but when she addressed her mind constructively to issues instead of using them to score off him, he listened to her with respect. She was alarmed by the thought of the responsibilities which respect might lay upon her and, like a climber daunted by an arduous ascent, she was tempted to loosen her hold.

He, however, had gained confidence and one evening he spoke to her of the guilt which tormented him. 'This thing which has struck Norah down – it's like a judgement. I can't see it any other way.'

'Then it must be a judgement for something unconnected with you. She had been falling about the place for some time.

Don't you remember? She fell in the graveyard at the first Mass of Easter. Drawing attention to herself, I thought in my uncharitable heart.'

And what if it wasn't a judgement? What if their love was a gift, the last and most precious life would offer Norah? Suddenly Valentine was crying; crying for her own lack, for all the hurt and pain, the struggle which had passed her by. Michael was speaking to her, astonished and gentle, telling her how good she had been, how much he admired her. He thinks I am crying for Norah, she thought. Am I to accept approbation so unearned? Once, the proud disclaimer would have flashed out, but now the touch of his hand on her shoulder so awakened her physical need of him that she could only accept in the hope that in time other expressions of love, however constrained, might follow. Has it come to this? she thought; that I am to scrabble about like a pauper at a jumble sale, making use of anything available, every scrap of material, any remnant, however flawed and snagged.

Norah had made a practice of going to confession three times a year. Until recently her confessor had been an elderly priest whom she had first known in her days as a student nurse. He had been a stabilizing influence on her and it was to him she turned now and not to Michael.

'I'm very lucky,' she said to him. 'Either Lois or Hester come the nights when Hesketh is away. I get a lot of letters. There are plenty of people I can telephone.' There was a strand of hair which worried her and she was constantly stroking it aside as she talked. She blinked her eyes a lot as though cobweb threads hung in front of them.

Although the priest was old, his was still a bulky figure – a considerable force sitting opposite to her, waiting until the flow of words was exhausted.

'I used to think when I was on the maternity ward that there was nothing more terrifying than birth.' She was bringing herself closer to the brink now. 'The separation from the warm darkness, emerging naked and alone into an unknown environment, totally helpless. But death . . .' She screwed up her eyes to contemplate death as though it was a phenomenon for people set apart, not for ordinary run-of-the-mill people. 'It is so tremendous.'

'But the dying you must not think of as tremendous.' The old man was not of the school which believes that it is harmful to give advice. 'You must try to look upon it as being like spring-cleaning. If you think of the whole house, the task seems mountainous; but if you take it room by room it gets itself done. What have you been doing with your time?'

She gave up the strand of hair and ran both hands down her face in admission of defeat. 'Nothing very special, I can't seem to . . .'

'Don't worry about anything special.' If he was unfashionably didactic, he was also profoundly absorbed with this matter of her dying. She listened to him, head slightly on one side in the manner of a deaf person anxious to catch every word. A shaft of sunlight fell across her face and she raised a hand to shield her eyes. 'Take what comes day by day. And whatever you do, don't make changes in your pattern of worship and start doing silly exotic things or attending services you wouldn't normally attend. I have known you for a long time; all you need is already there – prayer, observance, discipline.'

He was too wise to speak of detachment; he knew that this would come anyway, an inevitable part of the process of which, perhaps, she herself would scarcely be aware.

'And go slowly, dear Norah,' he said, taking her hand when she left him. 'Walk, speak, think slowly.'

As she walked Norah frowned as the light sparked from slate and stone; she glanced into gardens bright with late summer's abundance, her expression fretful and angry. From a long habit of obedience, she went home slowly and slowly she went about her household tasks and in the late afternoon, unpegging clothes from the washing line, she said aloud, 'Just letting it happen. I suppose that is what we mean by playing it by ear.' The idea of playing her death by ear seemed momentarily to amuse her. She held one of the garments close to her face, savouring that special freshness of clothes which have dried in the sun.

As the days passed she did her daily tasks as thoroughly as

her fluctuating health would allow and she tried, no less successfully than usual, to keep to some kind of routine in the preparation of meals. She tended to the seasonal needs of the garden and she resisted the temptation to set aside prolonged periods either for meditation or self-pity but contented herself with those observances which were a normal part of her prayer life.

Michael came to see her regularly; sometimes he found her alone, at others with neighbours who thought it their duty to be with her as often as possible. As he listened to her talking, talking, talking, she seemed to him like a musician tuning an instrument, trying to find the right note. Then the day came when her ear was satisfied. All that remained was to be kind about the discordancies of others and this she achieved, bearing with courtesy the mistimed offers of assistance, the nervous attempts at reassurance which drained her strength.

'I have no feeling of God,' she told Michael one afternoon when they were alone together. 'None at all. But then I always had to live by the book.' She had become quite composed and others saw in her a quiet gaiety of spirit of which she herself was unaware.

Michael wanted to rejoice for her, he wanted so very much to rejoice; but with the calmness had come a distancing. She was like a person leaving for another continent, her bags already packed, listening politely to the talk of neighbours about matters in which she will have no further interest. The pain this caused him was so intense he could not hide it from her. She looked at him sadly, perhaps remembering how once she had delighted in that face which showed every claw mark, thinking hers the balm which would ease away the hurt. She said, 'Poor Michael.' And this, he knew, whatever might follow, was their parting. He was shaken by a gust of desolation like a blow in the breast which took his breath away and when he left her he headed towards the moors as if some great calamity had struck the whole neighbourhood and only space could nullify its impact.

Three days after this visit, Hesketh telephoned the vicarage. 'They have taken her into hospital,' he told Valentine. 'The headaches had become intolerable and they say they have some new treatment they want to try.' He was very agitated.

'That is good, surely?' Valentine asked cautiously.

'She was so distressed. She didn't want to go. She says they are just going to mess about with her.'

'They can't force anything on her, can they?'

'She was much worse. I don't think she's in a state to make any decisions for herself.'

'You mean, they asked you?'

'What could I do? I said they must do what they thought best. What else could I have done?'

Michael was out and Valentine decided to see Hesketh. She was interested in this man who, albeit unknowingly, shared her situation. He was grateful for company and insisted on pouring her a glass of sherry.

'I thought you were remarkably good as Hedda,' he said. They talked a little of the theatre; inevitably, he counted several well-known actors among his personal friends. As he talked Valentine glimpsed the man he must have been in the days when life went well, a sophisticated, amusing man, admired and well-respected. Now he had become an elderly child, feeling his way in an unfamiliar setting, seeking a hand to hold. She saw that he would never recover. They sent down no roots, he and his kind; dilettante, cultivated, uncommitted, they hovered like a little shadow over the surface of life. Whereas Michael, who risked so much of himself, would not lose his capacity for joy and pain, hope and disappointment. The more unsure she became of Michael, the more she appreciated him.

Hesketh was talking about the urgent engagements which necessitated his return to London, a tremor of anger in his voice which he could not control.

'She has never been a well woman,' he said. 'I didn't realize that when I married her.' He wanted Valentine to know that he had been cheated, but even as he said it his face flushed as much with guilt as anger. She looked past him to the French windows.

'What a lovely garden.'

'You haven't been in it? Then let me show you.'

Big, bold dahlias had taken over the borders and neither

Valentine nor Hesketh was disposed to take heart from this riotous display. If one was to learn anything from Nature, Valentine thought, it was that one was of little account. She and Hesketh walked down the lawn to the river, running fast after the rain of the last few weeks.

'Had it occurred to you,' Valentine asked, watching the exuberant race of water and wishing she had the control of it, 'that the doctors may feel, because you are a barrister, that you would be capable of making trouble if treatment of a kind were not to be meted out to Norah?'

'But what does that mean? I couldn't tell them not to treat her, could I? What would people think of me if I were to do that?'

'You said she was distressed. Perhaps she has cause. She is a nurse, so she knows something of what is involved. I don't see why you couldn't . . .'

'I am unpopular enough in this place as it is.' He shook his head as if he were trying to rid his mind of the whole wretched muddle. Valentine saw that his feelings were too ambivalent for him to contemplate any intervention. She felt sorry for Norah who had seemed to have made her peace and must now have the doing of it all over again.

At the top of the steps leading to the main entrance to the hospital Michael Hoath paused, scratching the inside of one leg, taking long, shuddering breaths. One might have supposed he had arrived here on foot after a taxing uphill walk. He stood for a few moments recovering himself. It was a soft September afternoon. A man was cutting the grass in the public gardens opposite the hospital while another man heaped fallen leaves and twigs ready for a bonfire.

Two young women in summer frocks came out of the hospital. They looked subdued but cheered up in the sun's gentle warmth. 'So long as she takes things easy for a bit she'll probably manage,' one said to the other as they ran lightly down the steps.

Michael Hoath straightened his shoulders and went through the doors to the reception desk. The receptionist, taking one look at the dog collar, directed him to the floor where Norah was in a small amenity room off the main ward.

'She is very ill,' the ward sister told him. 'We had intended taking her to the operating theatre yesterday, but she was so bad . . .' Her tone suggested that the patient had misbehaved.

'Was it necessary to operate?'

'Mr Hinch thought there was a good chance of relieving pressure.'

'And that would have given her . . . ?'

'Perhaps another year of reasonable life.'

'She may have felt it didn't seem worth going through so much for another year.'

She pleated her lips and he saw that she felt the system had been criticized, not only by him but by the patient.

Norah was lying quite still; her mouth was half-open and she was frowning as if a lifetime's problems had come together within her aching head. He sat beside her and took her hand and she gave a little whimpering sound. He stayed with her for an hour. Once she woke briefly and said, 'I must have slept through the afternoon,' as a person might comment on a winter evening, the dusk coming sooner than was expected, cutting off the day.

As Michael was leaving a relative arrived, one of her brothers. He had had a long, tiresome journey and was much put out. 'How is she?' he asked Michael. 'I mean, do you think she knows what's going on? Of course, if it means anything, I'll stay as long as necessary.'

'I always assume people are aware at some level,' Michael said, 'even if it is not apparent.'

The man said huffily, 'It's easy for you. You chaps have got the hang of it.' In fact, on these occasions Michael felt like a swimmer, thrashing about, unable to let the sea carry him, but sometimes aware beneath the nervous agitation, the trivial distractions, of something strong and steady, unwaveringly holding to its course.

He went again to see Norah the next afternoon, pausing on the hospital steps as though it had become a necessary ritual. There were flowers on the tulip tree in the public gardens and Michaelmas daisies, powder blue and mauve, cast long shadows across the lawn. People in the street moved at a leisured pace, grateful for this late summer blessing.

He climbed the stairs to Norah's ward slowly. The sister looked grave. 'We have tried to get her husband, but it seems he has had to go to London. Old Father Dewes has given her the last rites.' Michael felt himself an intruder.

The room was hot and the flowers smelt sickly sweet. The minutes ticked away and Norah lay unmoving. Her breathing was slow but not laboured and her face was composed, the fretful lines eased out. Michael held her hand and, since he had no prayer of his own to offer, repeated at intervals, 'Lord have mercy, Christ have mercy, Lord have mercy.' In the corridor the tea trolley rumbled by and a cheery voice said, 'Oh, doing very well, aren't we, Mrs Piper! But don't overdo it, dear. We don't want another little accident, do we?'

The flowers reminded Michael of the ante-room of a funeral parlour. He studied one or two of the cards in which people had written messages varying from 'Your roses are looking splendid and we hope you'll soon be back among them' to 'Underneath are the everlasting arms'.

He was aware of the faintest stirring from the bed and saw that Norah had moved her head on the pillow. Her eyes were open and she looked round in bewilderment, first at the curtains, then the walls, the bedpost, and finally at him. She smiled and he thought she looked like a sick child waking from a troubled sleep and realizing this was home and that all was well. She gave a small, contented sigh and was still. When the sister came into the room, he said wonderingly, 'She seems so young!'

The sister looked at him strangely and, even as she felt for a pulse, Michael realized that Norah was dead.

On the way home, he felt himself enfolded in a great calm. It would not last. He knew that in time he would seem to forget Norah – perhaps for days, weeks – and then suddenly when he was not on guard, in the garden or standing chatting at a bring and buy stall, sadness and longing would claim him. But now, at this moment, he was calm and grateful.

At the funeral service the church was full of roses on which Hesketh had spent a vast amount because he insisted they were Norah's favourite flowers. He fixed his eyes on one of the altar vases from the moment he entered the church and continued to stare at it, unblinking, throughout the service.

Valentine was in a frenzy of agitation for Michael. She heard him begin his address, his voice firm and steady, 'Many of you have known Norah Kendall for much longer than I have. Some of you remember her as a child, for she has spent her life among you. Others will remember her as a nurse who cared for their children. Whatever your memories, you will know . . .' It is going to be all right, Valentine thought; he will not dishonour Norah by allowing space to his personal grief on this occasion. He had a gift for communicating some profound urgency to his audience, for reaching out to each individual present as if, although silent, they were vital components in a circuit. The service became a celebration, the drawing together of the threads of a life courageously lived, a completion. Hester sat beside Valentine, clenching and unclenching her hands, a few thin tears trickling down her nose.

There was no burial space now in St Hilary's own graveyard and so it was to the municipal graveyard that the cortege made its way after the church service. It was a crisp autumn day – a return to sanity, Valentine thought; all over now, the summer's madness, only one last furious streak of red in the pale, lucid sky. She put her hand in Hester's. Hester was feeling this death deeply. Her face had a mauvish hue Valentine had not noticed before and her body seemed to have shrunk – or perhaps it was just that when she was at her least resilient one realized how small she was. Even so, as they stood side by side while the coffin was lowered into the earth, Valentine felt that the current established between them flowed more strongly through Hester's veins.

As they walked slowly towards the waiting cars, Hester said, 'Nothing came easily to Norah. How I do love people who have to struggle. They have so much more to teach us.'

'If you have dying in mind, let me assure you, you won't die, you will be consumed by your own energy!'

When eventually they returned to the vicarage, Valentine said to Michael, 'That was a very moving service.' She went into the kitchen to prepare tea, leaving him alone. When she returned to the sitting-room he was humped over the empty grate, his hands dangling between his knees. He looked as if he were made of sawdust.

Michael was thinking of the past, of evenings spent by the fireside and long walks through the Ashdown Forest. Life had seemed to dance in the flames of the fire and dart ahead of him through the trees. He had thought that sometime he would catch and embrace it. Norah had represented a last chance and now that she was dead he knew that this was not the way of things.

During the weeks immediately following the funeral Michael and Valentine became more at ease with each other, as if Norah had broken some deadlock between them. Indeed, it seemed to Valentine that, rather than taking her husband from her, Norah had lifted a load from her shoulders. For years Michael had made a symbol of his wife instead of accepting the living reality of her. What she had to give, he had not seemed to want. Now that he hoped for less, Valentine could delve into her neglected store, searching among the small treasures for appropriate offerings.

So it came about that one late October evening, as Valentine put down the tea tray, Michael looked up from his book and said to her, 'You have come well out of this. Better than I have.'

The cost to him in saying this was nothing to the cost to her of receiving it. The indifferent disavowal was there, ready waiting in Valentine's capricious mind. She gave a little spluttering cough as she choked it back. It was getting dark and she put out a hand to the lamp on the table but did not switch it on for fear that the light would demand words from her. In the dimness, there was still a chance she might feel her way. She had failed to answer the claims of her husband's love; how had it come about that she now found herself asked to accept the burden of his respect? She, whose successes must always seem to be inadvertent, spontaneous, arising from natural attributes, not earned, was now seen to have 'come well out of this' – as if she had worked at it and must be rewarded. Mere respect is not something I will ever settle for, she thought, beginning to tremble. It would be wiser to disabuse him now. For a moment her finger touched the switch, then her hand dropped to her side. Instinct told her that if ever they were to make something of their life together, this was where they must start from. So she held her peace and, while the room and everything in it suffered the dissociation of darkness, she waited for what it was that he had to say.